A FRIENDLY EMBRACE

Sir Frederick impulsively folded her into his arms. "My dear girl," he murmured. She raised her face, a look of surprise in her eyes. Sir Frederick laughed and bent his head to kiss her.

He meant it as nothing more than a fleeting touch. But she made a sound in her throat and melted against him. Her soft responsive lips pressed warmly against his. Sir Frederick's senses swam. His arms tightened about her.

Abruptly he realized what he was doing, and sprang back. He stared at her, appalled. "Miss Holland! I don't know what to say. I beg your pardon."

"Oh, pray don't! I didn't mind it in the least," exclaimed Guin, her deep blue eyes shining.

Sir Frederick shook his head. He was stunned alike by his actions and the feelings that had been roused inside him. "You don't understand. I have taken the worst advantage of you."

"Didn't you wish to kiss me?" asked Guin falteringly.

Sir Frederick hated the dejection he could see forming in her eyes and how it caused a perceptible wilting in her demeanor. "My dear girl! I should think that was obvious."

Cupid's Choice

Gayle Buck

A SIGNET BOOK

SIGNET
Published by New American Library, a division of
Penguin Putnam Inc., 375 Hudson Street,
New York, New York 10014, U.S.A.
Penguin Books Ltd, 80 Strand,
London WC2R 0RL, England
Penguin Books Australia Ltd, Ringwood,
Victoria, Australia
Penguin Books Canada Ltd, 10 Alcorn Avenue,
Toronto, Ontario, Canada M4V 3B2
Penguin Books (N.Z.) Ltd, 182–190 Wairau Road,
Auckland 10, New Zealand

Penguin Books Ltd, Registered Offices:
Harmondsworth, Middlesex, England

First published by Signet, an imprint of New American Library,
a division of Penguin Putnam Inc.

First Printing, September 2002
10 9 8 7 6 5 4 3 2 1

Chapter One

It was a gray, chilly day in February when the cumbersome traveling coach, accompanied by two outriders, rolled up before a respectable town house located in a quiet side street situated off Albemarle Street. A fine mist had turned to cold drizzle an hour before, and the slighter of the horsemen was huddled miserably inside his greatcoat.

Swinging down from the saddle, the broad-shouldered horseman glanced over at his companion. He laughed and in a cheerful, rallying way, said, "Come, Percy, this is fine weather compared to what I have seen in a Spanish bivouac."

"You are undoubtedly right, Uncle. However, that happy reflection does not bring warmth to my face and hands," said Lord Percival Holybrooke. Under the lowered brim of his hat, his face was imperfectly seen; but it was a handsome countenance, possessing a long straight nose, a mouth that was thin-lipped but well-shaped, and a firm chin.

The young earl stepped down from the creaking saddle, grimacing as his boots splashed into a hole of dirty water. "I no longer envy your soldiering experiences, sir!"

Colonel Caldar laughed again, the weathered lines at the corners of his eyes crinkling. Throwing the reins over his horse's head with a large gloved hand, he said, "Well, lad, let us see how your mother and sister have faired the last leg of the journey. We shall all be glad of a hot meal and dry bed, I'll wager."

One of the coachmen climbed down from the coach seat and took the reins for the horses so that the two gentlemen could go around to the side of the coach.

A footman had emerged from the opened door of the town house, and had run down the wet steps to unlatch the coach door. The iron step was let down, and the passengers were respectfully requested to descend to the streaming walkway.

Colonel Caldar and Lord Holybrooke were in time to take the footman's place and hand down Mrs. Holland and her daughter. As soon as Mrs. Holland was safely on the flagstones, she reached out with both kid-gloved hands to take hold of the broad-notched lapels of the earl's dampened greatcoat.

"Percy! I feared for you riding in the rain. You haven't taken a cold, have you, my dear?" asked Mrs. Holland anxiously, her dark eyes taking stock of her beloved son's face.

Shaded by his riding hat, Lord Holybrooke's black brows drew together over gray-blue eyes that held mild irritation. "Of course not, Mama," he said with admirable restraint. "I am not a child, you know."

"Leave him be, Aurelia. A little wet never hurt anyone," said Colonel Caldar mildly.

Mrs. Holland shot a glance at her brother. "I beg to differ, Arnold. I for one am quite susceptible to the damp, and dear Percy has always taken after me in that respect. I only hope that he may not come down with an inflammation of the lungs."

"Come, Mama! I am not so sickly," said Lord Holybrooke, the flicker of a smile touching his face. He gently pushed aside her clutching fingers.

"If you insist on arguing the point standing on the walkway in the rain, we shall all no doubt contract influenza," said Colonel Caldar acidly.

Mrs. Holland glared. She turned to her son with a regal toss of her head. "Pray escort me into the town house, Percy. I refuse to bandy words in such a vulgar fashion with your uncle."

"Of course, Mama," said Lord Holybrooke, taking his mother's arm. He glanced backward over his shoulder with a wink for his uncle and sister.

With a sigh, Colonel Caldar turned to his niece. "Well, Guin, we have been blessedly forgotten for the moment. Shall we go in, my dear?"

Miss Guineveve Holland had stood by patiently during the skirmish between her elders. Now she smiled affectionately up at her uncle, droplets of water dripping steadily from the brim of her bonnet. Colonel Caldar was not above medium height, but her own short inches made him seem large to her. She tucked one hand into his arm. "Oh, yes, Uncle, I should like to do so! My half boots must be quite soaked through, for I stepped into that puddle when I stepped down and now my feet are frozen."

Colonel Caldar glanced down at her with sudden concern, his thick sandy brows contracting. He covered her slight hand with his large square one. "My dear! You should have said something at once."

"It doesn't signify, dear sir. Mama wished to assure herself that Percy had taken no harm, you see," said Guin calmly. She stepped slightly aside as the footman carried some of the baggage past her toward the town house doorway.

Colonel Caldar's lips tightened as he continued to look at her, but he said only, "Aye, I do indeed see." He escorted his niece straight up the steps toward the front door, calling for the porter to see to the remainder of the baggage. "And send word to the kitchen to have a hot posset sent up to my niece in her room."

Guin anxiously scanned Colonel Caldar's grim expression. She thought her uncle did not precisely understand how it was. The servants should not be busied on her behalf when there were other, more important, claims on them. "No, really, there mustn't be any trouble taken over me, sir! It is Mama and Percy who are affected by

the cold and wet. They should have the services of the
staff first. I shall do very well once I have put off my
wet half boots, I promise you."

"You'll do as I say, young lady," said Colonel Caldar
in a tone of authority. "Percy is like whipcord. He'll do
in a pinch. As for your mother—" His firm lips tightened
again. There was a flash of anger deep in his blue eyes.
"Your mother is very capable of seeing to her own com-
forts. She is one of the most selfish creatures I have
ever known."

"No, no! How can you say so, Uncle?" exclaimed
Guin, astonished and distressed by the colonel's assess-
ment. She glanced quickly around the small entry hall,
fearing that her mother might overhear and take offense.
She was relieved to see that except for the back and
forth bustling of the footman and porter, the entry was
deserted, her mother and brother having apparently already gone upstairs.

"I can say it quite easily, my dear. She is my sister, so
I have known her all of her life. The only being Aurelia
has ever cared for as much as herself is Percy. And how
that can be when you were born twins, I cannot and
never will understand."

"Oh, no, no! You are being unjust, sir!" protested
Guin at once.

"Scarcely that, Guin! As you very well know, if you
could be brought to admit it," said Colonel Caldar in an
undertone, casting a glance at the passing footman to
assure himself that the servant man could not overhear.
"My sister is a monster of selfishness, and she treats you
scarcely better than an indigent relation! I wish you
would stand up to her, my dear!"

Guin found that she could not speak, for her voice
was suspended by the tight constriction in her throat. She
made a gesture of denial with her hand.

Colonel Caldar saw the startled tears in his niece's
large dark blue eyes and realized that he had gravely
upset her. His fierce expression softened. He put a stal-
wart arm around her shoulders and gave her a swift,

awkward hug. "Never mind, Guin. You are a good, sweet girl. Percy knows your true worth, as do I. Now, here is the maid ready to take you up to your room. Do as I say, and drink the posset! It will warm you inside."

Guin gave a small laugh. Shaking her head at him, she turned and obediently followed the somber-dressed maid up the broad carpeted staircase to the second landing. She was relieved that her uncle had not continued to speak so slightingly of her mother. It was distressing to her whenever her mother came under censor, for she always felt her emotions torn.

In this instance, loyalty toward her mother warred against the depressing conviction of the truth that Colonel Caldar had so unexpectedly tossed out. Guin unconsciously shook her head, denying it to herself. It wasn't true! Her mother didn't treat her badly, precisely. It was unfair of her uncle to say so. It was just that Percy was able to cajole their mother. And Percy was more deserving of attention because he had been heir to the old earl. She understood perfectly. She had always understood.

Guin could not reconcile her jumbled thoughts. Her uncle's words could not be easily shaken. Guin made a determined effort to thrust aside what her uncle had said. She would not think about it any longer, she thought resolutely.

The maid stopped before a heavy paneled door, and opened it. The tiring-woman showed Guin into a bedroom. "Here we are, miss."

The bedroom was bathed in the last rays of the gray day outside the window. The noise of the rain, now falling in earnest, and the occasional clip-clopping passage of a carriage sounded distinctly from below the narrow window. Obviously she had been given a front bedroom overlooking the cobbled street.

Guin entered hesitantly, glancing about her at the unaccustomed furnishings. The bedroom's proportions were small. A large four-poster bed commanded the room, its faded rose damask curtains neatly tied back at the rounded posts. An old-fashioned mahogany wardrobe took up nearly one wall. Next to it was a massive cheval glass. A chaise lounge was shoved into the shadows of the farthest corner. There was a washstand with a chipped bowl and pitcher. A single wing chair, with a small parquet occasional table beside it, had been arranged in front of the hearth. Someone more sophisticated would have unhesitatingly stigmatized the bedroom to be dowdy, as well as inconvenient, situated as it was above the street, but to Guin's eyes it looked quite comfortable.

A small fire burned on the hearth. Guin was drawn immediately to its welcoming glow. Unbuttoning her kid gloves, she peeled them off, laying them carefully on the high wood mantel before bending to spread her chilled hands to the flames. When she felt the warmth beginning to thaw her cold hands, she sighed contentedly. It had grown cold in the coach, and she had stifled a sneeze or two. In fact, now that she was in front of the fire, she realized she was chilled all the way through. Her brown pelisse was serviceable enough, but standing in the drizzle had gotten it damp enough that it no longer served to keep her warm.

Behind her, the maid bustled about opening and pushing aside Guin's few pieces of baggage until she opened a modest strapped trunk. Out of it, she began to pull out the few necessary articles for which she had been searching. "You'll be wishful to put off them damp clothes, miss. I've found a nice clean dress," said the maid. "If you'll remove your bonnet, I'll help you with the pelisse buttons. We'll have you changed in a trice."

Guin straightened from warming her hands to look around at the maid in surprise. "Why, I have always dressed myself. Surely you'll be wanted by my mother, Mrs. Holland."

The maid looked queerly at her. "No, miss. I am to be your maid. The mistress has her own dresser, who arrived two days past. And a nose-in-the-air piece she is, too!"

A knock sounded on the door. The maid went to open

it, the modest wool merino gown she had found still flung over her arm. There was a short murmured exchange, then the maid closed the door and came back with a tray, which she sat down on the occasional table. "Now, miss, here is your posset come and you not ready to drink it!"

Not saying another word, Guin untied the sober-colored ribbons of her plain velvet bonnet and removed it from her head. The maid twitched the damp headgear efficiently out of Guin's hands.

Guin blinked. She was still shocked by the notion of having her own maid to dress her. She had never been vouchsafed such a luxury in her life. Even at Holybrooke, where they had gone to live permanently after her brother had inherited the title, she had still dressed herself.

"Why don't you sit down, miss, and drink your posset while I remove your half boots," suggested the maid.

Guin started to object, embarrassed by the attention, but something in the maid's expression stopped her. Instead she mutely did as she was told. Things were certainly going to be different in London, she reflected, not at all certain she could readily adjust to the changes.

She picked up the porcelain cup containing the posset that had been brewed for her. Holding the hot cup between her hands and allowing the heat to pleasantly sear her palms, she took a cautious sip. The warm liquid soothed the tickle in the back of her throat and left a wonderful feeling of well-being as it went down into her. Guin closed her eyes, breathing in the warm aroma. It was so nice. She would have to thank her uncle for ordering the posset when she saw him later. She scarcely noticed while the half boots were pulled off of her feet.

"Miss, your half boots are soaked through!" exclaimed the maid. "Your stockings are that damp!" Efficiently she peeled off the woolen stockings and began to rub her new mistress's feet dry with a rough towel.

Guin's eyes flew open. She looked guiltily at the tiring-woman. "I-I stepped into a puddle, you see."

"Your half boots could be proper ruined," said the maid, turning her attention back to the footwear for a critical examination.

Guin was appalled. All feeling of well-being fled. The familiar panicked feeling settled in her stomach, tightening into an unpleasant knot. Involuntarily, she exclaimed, "Oh, no! They cannot be! Mama will be so angry with me if they are!"

The maid looked up quickly, an astonished expression in her pale blue eyes. "Miss?"

The hot color of embarrassment flooded Guin's face. She nervously turned the cup around and around in her hands. "My—my mother is very insistent that I am not wasteful or—or frivolous. I don't wish to be required to purchase another pair."

After meeting Guin's worried gaze for a long considering moment, the tiring-woman rose to her feet with the half boots still clutched in her hands. She said decisively, "Never you fret, miss. I'll see that they're dried proper and well greased so they'll not crack. Now, let's see about getting you changed."

Guin was relieved and grateful that the embarrassing moment had passed. The maid seemed confident that the soaked half boots could be salvaged. She had said no more about it while she undid the mother-of-pearl buttons down the front of Guin's pelisse.

Instead, the woman concentrated on dressing her young mistress and did so with a slightly chiding monologue that Guin found peculiarly soothing. Little was required of her except that she turn this way or that while the gown was twitched into place and fastened up the back, and that she hold up first one sleeve and then the other to be buttoned.

In fewer minutes than Guin thought possible, she was changed into the dull blue merino gown and a ribbon had been threaded through her freshly combed glistening black curls. The maid gave her a soft gray wool shawl to drape over her elbows, and Guin felt ready to brave the halls of her temporary home. She smiled at her tiring-woman, with whom she had established a perfect understanding. "Thank you, Morgan."

The maid nodded and gave a spare smile. "I will have your room straightened for you before you return from dinner, miss."

Chapter Two

Guin left the bedroom, closing the solid door behind her, and began to retrace her way back along the unfamiliar hallway toward the head of the stairs. Her maid had told her the general location of the front parlor on the ground floor, where the family would gather before dinner.

She didn't know which bedrooms had been given to the rest of her family, but for the moment it was a matter of little importance. Indeed, she had not the least desire to find out. Guin hurried her steps. She expected to meet Colonel Caldar and her brother downstairs once they had also changed for dinner.

Guiltily, Guin acknowledged to herself that she was going down early in order to escape any summons from her mother. Guin assuaged her conscience by telling herself that her mother would probably have laid down for her customary hour nap, leaving herself free to look for her brother and her uncle. Since she had not already received a message to come to her mother's room, she could only suppose that fortune smiled on her.

She hurried on, not wanting to linger and perhaps be found by her mother's dresser. Guin had already gathered the impression that this individual was rather awe-inspiring, and she preferred to put off meeting the woman as long as possible, especially considering the likelihood that the only reason the dresser would have for seeking her out would be to relay a message from

Mrs. Holland. Guin nodded to herself, as it occurred to her that the new dresser would undoubtedly be very capable of caring for any needs that Mrs. Holland might have.

Able at last to set aside her most overriding anxiety, Guin began to feel a bubble of anticipation. It would be interesting to explore some of the town house before dinner. She had never traveled to London before, nor ever set foot in a town house. Rather, she and her brother and mother had always lived in the country. So, therefore, she was curious about their new surroundings.

As Guin left the landing and started down the stairs, she was hailed by her brother. "Guin! Wait and I'll walk down with you," said Lord Holybrooke, loping along he paneled hallway toward her, the carpet muffling the sounds of his boots. He had changed into a tight-fitting bottle-green coat and fawn breeches. His unruly black hair had been ruthlessly brushed, and his crumpled cravat replaced with a fresh one. His dark gray-blue eyes gleamed with liveliness, while a wide grin flashed across his face. As she always did, Guin thought there could not be anyone who was more handsome than her own twin.

"Of course, Percy." She waited until he caught up with her, before saying with a mischievous smile, "Mama would frown to see you rushing through the house in such a reckless manner, Percy."

He shrugged nonchalantly. "Never you mind, Miss Anxious. Mama told me that she wished to rest an hour before coming downstairs. We have some time to ourselves. Let's take a quick tour of our fancy London abode." He took her arm in an innately polite gesture that was as much a part of him as breathing, and now he urged her on down the stairs.

Guin gladly accepted her brother's company. They had always been inseparable. She was never more happy than when she was with Percy. He was her confidante and her best, and only, friend.

Together brother and sister made a tour of the various rooms on the ground floor that opened off the entry hall.

The town house had been let to Lord Holybrooke sight unseen, his agent assuring his lordship that it, and the small staff engaged for the Season, would be found to be all that was proper.

However, Lord Holybrooke was now discovering, somewhat to his dismay, that all was not as sanguine as he had been told. The front parlor was found to be of a good size and tastefully arranged, though the furniture was in need of a good polish. The library was a small, irregularly shaped room with a rather gloomy atmosphere due, Lord Holybrooke insisted, to the number of cobwebs in the corners and empty hearth. "It looks like something out of one of those dashed silly romances that Mama is so fond of!" he exclaimed.

Guin pointed out that since Mrs. Holland had decided to set out for London almost a week ahead of their scheduled departure from Holybrooke, there had been very little time for the newly engaged staff to set the house in order before their arrival. "I am certain the housekeeper will order a good cleaning, and it will look ever so much better to you, Percy."

"So I should hope!" said Lord Holybrooke, backing out of the library with a last glance of revulsion.

The back sitting room and dining room were found to be barely adequate, which even Guin was forced to acknowledge. "They are not very large, are they?" she remarked doubtfully.

Lord Holybrooke agreed, adding bitterly, "Lord, won't Mama kick up a fuss."

The town house had been leased furnished, and Lord Holybrooke regarded each room with a darkening gaze and a sometimes critical word. Guin agreed with his disappointed assessments, though she thought the gilded mirror in the back sitting room was very fine and the front parlor was rather quaint.

"What does 'quaint' mean?" asked Lord Holybrooke, shaking his head and looking around again as they reentered the front parlor. It was by far the most pleasant room, having large windows that let in the last of the sunlight, and by mutual consent they had returned to it. Candles had been lit in candelabras that were set around the parlor, adding to its cheerful aspect.

"Well, I think it sounds better than old-fashioned," said Guin with the glimmer of a smile. "Indeed, perhaps we should describe the entire residence as quaint, for Mama will not care for us to call anything about it old-fashioned! Not when she is living here! It was her biggest complaint about Holybrooke, after all."

Lord Holybrooke grinned, the expression in his eyes affectionate. "You're a born diplomat, Guin. You're able to find a good word for everything."

Used to her brother's ways, Guin paid scant attention to his funning compliment. She looked around thoughtfully, speaking her conclusions out loud. "The town house is not nearly as grand as Holybrooke, is it? And the furnishings are very nearly as out of fashion."

Lord Holybrooke's smile faded as a frown once more descended on his face. "What else can one expect of a place only leased for the Season? My agent was fortunate to find even such a fashionable address as this one, you know. I am just as thankful he did, for Mama would have pitched a fit if we had not been able to come up to town for the Season." Lord Holybrooke threw his lean length into a wing chair in front of the crackling fire.

Guin sighed. She sat down on the cushions of the striped sofa opposite her brother. "Yes, I know. Poor Mama! It was difficult for her to be in black gloves and not able to go to any parties. She was very bored at Holybrooke, I fear."

"Well, I certainly wasn't! Every day I was up practically at dawn to go over the accounts or to tramp over the fields, all the while with old Grimsley droning on and on about estate business. The only thing that brightened my days was when I could persuade Mama to let me take you riding with me," said Lord Holybrooke on a long-suffering sigh.

"Those were the best times for me, too," said Guin with a quick smile.

"Well, then, you do understand," said Lord Holybrooke, responding with his own grin. "I was never more relieved in my life than to come up to London for the Season and leave old Grimsley behind."

"I know it was difficult for you, Percy. But Mr. Grimsley was pleased with your progress, surely?" asked Guin.

"Oh, as to that! He was well enough pleased, I suppose." Lord Holybrooke frowned for a moment over his thoughts. He looked up. "The only thing is, Guin, Grimsley expressed some reservations about what the estate resources could handle at this time. Our reprobate of a grandfather, whom I am glad we never met, ran everything into the ground so devilishly bad that it will take years for a profit to be turned again. I only wish Mama had not insisted on coming up to London as soon as we put off black gloves."

"As do I," said Guin quietly. Looking down, she clasped and unclasped her hands in her lap. "Mama had a long talk with me before we left Holybrooke. She has expressed her desire to see me wed, Percy." She looked up at her brother with a troubled expression. "I-I don't know that I wish to be wed just yet."

Better than anyone, Lord Holybrooke understood the depths of her concern and what she had not said. "You don't have to marry unless you want to, Guin. I shall see to it that you are not bullied into it," he said forcefully.

"Thank you, Percy. You are the best of brothers," said Guin, smiling tremulously. Her countenance bore a strong resemblance to her brother's, with the same straight nose and short upper lip. But her face was a more perfect oval and her chin was pointed rather than determined. Her eyes were also a darker and truer blue, being the shade of a midnight sky on a moonlit night.

"After all, I am the head of the family," said Lord Holybrooke with an exaggerated assumption of arrogance. He narrowed his eyes and flared his nostrils, looking down his nose at Guin. As he had hoped it would, his playacting made his twin sister laugh.

"What? Are you already becoming affected by the rarefied air of London and puffing yourself off, Percy?" asked Colonel Caldar, coming into the front parlor in time to overhear his nephew's declaration. He had put off his riding clothes in favor of a well-cut dark blue coat and breeches. His thick wavy hair had been brushed back from his broad brow and that, together with his unmistakably soldierly bearing, made him look almost leonine.

Lord Holybrooke and Guin laughed, their eyes automatically searching one another out as they shared their amusement. Their features and even their mannerisms were remarkably alike, although it could be observed by the discerning that Lord Holybrooke possessed a greater air of self-confidence than did his sister.

"I am an earl, after all," said Lord Holybrooke, still with a grin lingering on his lips.

"And a very fine one, too," agreed Colonel Caldar with a hearty laugh. "Now, my lord! I am come to discover if you would care to go about the town with me a little later this evening."

Lord Holybrooke bolted to his feet on the instant. His gray-blue eyes glowed with pleased surprise. "Would I, sir! I can think of nothing grander!" He suddenly bethought himself of his sister, and he turned toward her hastily, his expression at once falling. "But Guin—"

"No, Percy, you mustn't spoil your own evening, or indeed, our uncle's, upon my account. You know that Mama will wish me to wait on her," said Guin with a smile, putting on a brave front even though her heart had sunk.

Colonel Caldar muttered something under his breath. He turned away to kick a log farther into the fire, creating a shower of crimson and gold sparks.

Lord Holybrooke grimaced. "That's just it, Guin! How can I be so selfish when I know what a rotten time you will have of it?"

Guin stood up, her smile determinedly held in place. Not for anything would she have betrayed her true feelings. If she had ever been asked about it, she would have said that it was right that she was in the habit of putting her brother's interests above her own. "I don't mind very much, really! After all, I can't go with you to all those horrid haunts that our uncle is certain to take you."

"No, of course not," said Lord Holybrooke, still with a clouded brow. "But still—"

"I am rather tired, you know, after the journey. I had a tickle in my throat, too. I expect I shall go up to bed early," said Guin. Quickly she added, "And I expect Mama will, also. You know how pulled she gets after a long journey."

The earl's countenance cleared. "Truly, Guin? Then that's all right. I mean, if you really intend to retire early, it wouldn't be very amusing here anyway."

"No," agreed Guin, stifling a sigh. She turned to her uncle. "I want to thank you for your kindness in ordering the posset, sir. It was very warming and did my throat some good, as well."

"Guin, you're not sickening, are you?" asked Lord Holybrooke worriedly.

Guin laughed and shook her head. "Of course not! When have you ever known me to be ill? I only got a little chilled, but I am quite all right now."

A footman came into the room to announce dinner. The conversation was immediately abandoned as Lord Holybrooke pronounced himself to be starved. "Mama hasn't joined us, so she must not have come down yet. She will be waiting for me, I expect. I shall go up and charm her a trifle as I bring her down to the dining room, shall I?"

Lord Holybrooke exited the front parlor, leaving Colonel Caldar to escort Guin.

Before he led his niece out of the room, Colonel Caldar said gruffly, "I wasn't thinking, my dear. I should never have suggested an outing our first night in London. I shall tell Percy that I've thought better of it."

"Pray do not, for Percy would be horridly disappointed,"

said Guin quickly with an earnest glance upward at her uncle.

"But you, my dear! You cannot like the prospect of an evening spent solely with my sister," said Colonel Caldar with characteristic bluntness.

"Mama and I are very comfortable together," said Guin stoutly. "Besides, it wouldn't be fair to tie Percy to my apron strings."

"I wish your mother felt the same," said Colonel Caldar. His pleasantly featured face was troubled. "I apologize, Guin. I didn't think it out. She'll object to Percy's going out on the town with me, which means she'll make it deuced uncomfortable for us all, but especially for you."

"Oh, no. Mama always lets Percy have whatever he wishes," said Guin calmly.

He slid a glance down at his niece. "And what of your wishes, my dear?"

Guin looked up quickly. Under his sympathetic and knowing gaze, she flushed. With a constriction in her throat, she said quietly, "Percy takes very good care of me, Uncle."

"I wonder how you will fair without Percy," murmured Colonel Caldar, a shade grimly, as he finally escorted her out of the front parlor and toward the dining room.

Guin thought her uncle's comment odd, but she didn't give it more than a fleeting moment's reflection. When she entered the dining room on her uncle's arm, she saw that her mother and brother had already come in. At once Guin felt tension in the atmosphere and perceived that her mother was in an ill humor. Lord Holybrooke's face betrayed some strain underlying his polite expression.

Instinctively Guin tensed. Of all things, she disliked the unpleasant scenes that Mrs. Holland was capable of producing. Her stomach knotted again, and she wondered whether she would be able to make an adequate dinner.

Colonel Caldar politely seated Guin at the table, his

fingers lightly pressing her slender shoulder when she turned her head to thank him. "My pleasure, Guin."

Mrs. Holland was a striking woman. In her day she had been an accredited beauty, and the hours she spent pampering her skin with crushed strawberries and under the hands of skillful coiffures made her show to advantage. However, the still lovely features were ruined by a petulant expression.

Mrs. Holland's brown eyes flicked in her daughter's direction, but otherwise she didn't acknowledge Guin's entrance. She was far more interested in the cause of her displeasure. "I am by no means satisfied, Percy. This house is not at all what I envisioned. Why, only look at the size of this dining room!"

She made a sweeping gesture to encompass their surroundings, paying no attention at table to the butler and two footmen who were waiting at table. "I daresay we shan't be able to seat more than twenty couples! I dare not describe to you what I felt upon laying eyes on the ballroom upstairs. Such an insignificant room! I have not yet inspected the rest of the house, but I fear it must be quite beneath your consequence, my dear."

Though Lord Holybrooke was smiling, there was a hard glint in his eyes. "Oh, the house is well enough. Guin and I took a quick turn around the ground floor before dinner. I daresay with a little dusting and polish, it will be quite comfortable."

"Comfortable!" exclaimed Mrs. Holland. She gave a small tittering laugh. There was growing temper in her expressive eyes. "That is certainly not how I should wish the Earl of Holybrooke's town house to be described by the *ton*, Percy! It is quite unpardonable of your agent to have obtained such a paltry place for you. You must send for him in the morning, Percy, and demand that he find us another house!"

"Mama, it will be quite impossible to locate another address this late in the year," said Lord Holybrooke, beginning to look harassed. "We must simply make the best of it and—"

"Nonsense, Percy! You must simply tell your agent to find us another house or replace him with someone who is more attuned to your consequence," said Mrs. Holland. A footman offered the pea soup, but she waved it aside with an irritated expression. "No! I don't wish any soup!"

"Aurelia, let the boy alone. If you would but take a moment to reflect, you would know what Percy says is true. Any other residences still for lease this late in the year would scarcely recommend themselves to you. I daresay you would much rather remain situated in the fashionable quarter, no matter how paltry you believe this house to be, than to remove to a dowdy address!" said Colonel Caldar roundly.

Uneasy silence fell while Mrs. Holland stared at her brother with an arrested expression. Suddenly she bestowed a lovely smile on Colonel Caldar. It was like the sun coming out from behind a threatening storm cloud. "Why, Arnold! You have quite cleared the air. I was forgetting the main issue for just a moment. You are quite right. Forgive me, Percy. I shan't say another word against this very . . ." She glanced disparagingly around the dining room, totally disregarding that it was handsomely paneled and well lit. "What word am I looking for?"

"Guin has offered up 'quaint' as the proper term, Mama," said Lord Holybrooke, his expression lightening with his mother's change of mood. With a mischievous look in his eyes, he glanced across the table at his sister. "You know her droll way."

"Percy!" exclaimed Guin, at once fearing what her mother might make of such effrontery on her part. She knew it wasn't her place to voice an opinion.

However, on this occasion Mrs. Holland merely laughed and shook her head. "Indeed, quaint is quite apt. Now, we must simply make the best of things, despite all the drawbacks of our present circumstances. I shall speak to the domestic staff on the morrow so that all is arranged just as you would like it, Percy."

"Thank you, Mama," said Lord Holybrooke with easy confidence. "I am certain that I may rely upon you."

Mrs. Holland smiled fondly at her son. "My dearest, of course you may! And Guin shall help me. There will be invitations to address and all sorts of lists to be made and, I daresay, any number of errands."

Guin drew in a relieved breath. It had surprised her when Colonel Caldar had volunteered his opinion, for he usually did not. And he had hit on just the right thing to say, too! The storm had been averted and passed completely over their heads. She was so thankful that they had been spared a painful scene that she was eager to agree to do whatever her mother required of her. "Of course I shall help you, Mama. I will be only too happy to do so."

"Let's not forget that Guin is supposed to enjoy herself this Season," said Colonel Caldar, a sharp crease forming between his brows at what he had just heard.

Mrs. Holland's posture stiffened, and she turned a frosty glance on her brother. Lord Holybrooke intervened, saying quickly, "Oh, that goes without saying, Uncle! I shouldn't like to think of Guin stuck here at the town house while I am attending some *soirée* or other. It would quite cut up my own enjoyment."

"The very notion, Percy! When you know, as does Guin herself, that I intend to bring her out this Season," said Mrs. Holland, her expression easing. She smiled over at her daughter. "Guin will have a splendid time of it, you'll see."

Guin murmured the expression of agreement she knew was expected of her. "I am certain I shall, Mama." It would not do to voice her hesitant reservations.

Dinner was accomplished without further strife to mar it, Mrs. Holland going so far as to pronounce the two courses quite tolerable. "Naturally I shall speak to the cook, for we shall require much more elegant fare when we begin entertaining," she concluded.

"Naturally," said Colonel Caldar dryly, but in such a low tone that only his niece overheard him.

Guin choked on a swallow of wine. At her mother's disapproving glance, she apologized profusely. "I am sorry, Mama! A-a crumb caught in my throat, and I was trying to wash it down."

"Well, see that you do it more discreetly, Guin," said Mrs. Holland.

Chapter Three

Beginning with that first evening in London, Colonel Caldar did his duty by introducing his nephew into the elite membership of several clubs, to which he was himself admitted to by right of birth and profession. The colonel's return to London was hailed with friendly acceptance by many old acquaintances.

Lord Holybrooke was initially admitted into male circles because of his uncle's sponsorship. However, his lordship was modest and possessed an innate dignity despite his youth, and this engendered him swift acceptance on his own account.

The young earl was generally well received and was soon at home among his peers. For the first time in his life, Lord Holybrooke knew what it was to be sought out by gentlemen of similar birth and temperament. It was heady to his lordship, and he threw himself enthusiastically into enjoying what society had to offer. He listened politely and with deference to his uncle's sage advice, and steered clear of certain unsavory characters whose primary goal in life was to clean out the pockets of unwary young gentlemen. He boxed at Jackson's Saloon, shot out the pips at Manton's Saloon, attended his first cockfight, and was initiated into the intricacies of whist. After two weeks, Lord Holybrooke could not imagine anything more gratifying than to continue living in London.

His lordship recounted his adventures in the most open

way to his mother and sister. Guin was very interested in all that her brother had to say, and told him wistfully that she wished she could accompany him. "For it sounds very jolly, Percy."

Lord Holybrooke laughed, his eyes gleaming at the picture his imagination summoned up. "Somehow, Guin, I don't think you would be comfortable at Jackson's Saloon," he said.

"No, I suppose not," said Guin, also laughing as she was struck by the absurdity of what she had said.

Naturally enough, Guin had not expressed her wish within her mother's hearing. That would have called down on her head a sharp rebuke for foolishness, which indeed, once she had thought about it, Guin realized would have been entirely deserved. However, she still wished that she could be more in her brother's company. She missed him terribly during that first fortnight, the more so because her own life was shifting beyond recognition since coming to London.

Mrs. Holland was naturally gratified that her son was being accepted so readily by gentlemen of the *ton*. However, after seeing Lord Holybrooke safely away on another of his sprees, she turned to express concern to her brother.

"Cockfights! And fisticuffs! What next, Arnold?"

When Mrs. Holland went on to say that she feared for Lord Holybrooke's moral character, Colonel Caldar burst out laughing. "Come, Aurelia, you wouldn't want to keep the boy wrapped up in cotton. It is doing him a world of good to learn how to go on in polite society."

"Polite society! I scarcely call it that when he is rubbing shoulders with commoners at a cockfight!" exclaimed Mrs. Holland.

"But it does sound as though Percy is enjoying himself," said Guin quietly.

Mrs. Holland glanced swiftly at her daughter, a thoughtful expression entering her eyes. "Indeed, it seems so from all Percy has said."

"Aye, and he is making a place for himself amongst

the young bloods. You wouldn't want it said that Percy lacked spirit, Aurelia," said Colonel Caldar. "Why, it would be the kiss of death to him socially."

At once perceiving where Lord Holybrooke's best interests laid, Mrs. Holland abandoned all of her objections. She nodded her head. "Of course I quite see how it is, Arnold. I haven't the least desire to hinder either Percy's pleasure or his social acceptance. He must do what is proper and befitting to his station. I suppose I must thank you for introducing him around, Arnold."

Colonel Caldar was stupefied by his sister's rare expression of gratitude. "Aye, well, I told you that I'd do my best by Percy," he said gruffly. "He goes on very well. Percy has his head straight on his shoulders. I don't fear that he'll run aground."

"You have relieved my mind of all care, brother," said Mrs. Holland with her lovely smile.

Colonel Caldar bowed, more in charity with his sister than he had been for some time.

Though Colonel Caldar could provide entree to his nephew to select clubs and generally aid Lord Holybrooke, he could not do the same for his niece. And since Mrs. Holland was at a disadvantage in not having close acquaintances in London, she and Guin did not immediately soar to such heights as had Lord Holybrooke. Their entry into society was accomplished far more slowly and quietly.

However, the very fact that the Earl of Holybrooke, along with his family, was in residence acted as a spur on the *ton*. Not wanting to be backward in any attention, and having already heard from their spouses and sons about the young earl, the ladies began to call and to leave their cards.

Guin's days became filled with all those things that were necessary to bring a young miss to the notice of the *ton*. Making calls, taking tea, and walking or driving in the park were all considered proper activities by her mother.

For nearly any other sheltered young lady, such obligations would have been vastly exciting. However, unlike most of her peers, Guin's life had been so insulated that to be thrust suddenly into society was torturous to her.

When she and Lord Holybrooke had a few minutes to themselves, a much rarer occurrence than had once been their custom, Guin expressed something of her feelings. "I-I am just so afraid of doing or saying the wrong thing, Percy," she said glumly. "I am not like you! I cannot converse easily with strangers or strike up friendships on the basis of a few minutes."

"Oh, you'll soon grow more comfortable with it, Guin. I know it is fairly difficult for you now, but I daresay after a bit of time and adjustment, you'll go on in famous style," said Lord Holybrooke reassuringly.

They were in the front parlor, where Guin had gone to do some embroidering because the light was brighter, and Lord Holybrooke had wandered in a few minutes before to keep her company. He had cast himself down in a wing chair and was flipping through a racing journal, yawning over its pages.

"But there is Mama, too. She is not at all pleased with me," said Guin, revealing her most pressing anxiety.

"Oh, you know how Mama is! She comes on cross as crabs, but all you have to do is turn her up sweet and everything will be fine," said Lord Holybrooke in a careless fashion.

Guin dropped the embroidery hoop to her lap and stared over at her brother in astonishment. "Percy! As though I have ever been able to turn Mama up sweet! You know I can't."

Lord Holybrooke looked up quickly. He had the grace to give a sheepish smile. "I suppose that's true. I'll tell you what, Guin, I'll make a point of doing the pretty more often. You won't be so nervous if I escort you and Mama around, will you?"

"Oh, no! It would be the very thing, for—"

The door opened and the butler entered. "My lord, here is Lord Tucker to see you."

A brash young gentleman, starting to speak before he

was properly inside the room, entered on the butler's heels. "Percy, old fellow! I was hoping to find you at home! I've had word of a famous race taking place within the hour. Can you come?"

Lord Holybrooke stood up and with a grin shook his companion's hand. "Of course I can, Chuffy! What's to keep me from it? Chuffy, you've met my sister, haven't you? Guin, this is Lord Tucker, the best of fellows."

Lord Tucker made a belated bow in Guin's direction. His lordship was an aspiring dandy. His coat was very tight, so it was obvious he had to be helped into it, and it could not be buttoned across the front. His waistcoat and the top of his frilled shirt were thus on display. "Honored, Miss Holland!"

Guin smiled and made a determined effort to make a good impression on one of her brother's new friends. With that laudable ambition, she said brightly, "Good afternoon, Lord Tucker. Pray, what sort of race is it?"

Lord Tucker cleared his throat and rolled his eyes toward Lord Holybrooke for help. "Not the sort of thing you would be interested in, ma'am, I assure you. It's to do with geese."

"Geese?!" exclaimed Guin in astonishment. She turned her widening eyes toward her brother. "Racing geese?"

Lord Holybrooke laughed, delighted by this revelation. "Oh, by all that's famous! I wouldn't miss it for the world." He clapped his friend on the shoulder. "Let's be off, Chuffy. You'll not want to keep your team standing, I daresay. There's a stout wind blowing."

"No, indeed. Miss Holland, your most obedient," said Lord Tucker with another graceful bow.

The two young gentlemen left the front parlor, animatedly discussing the upcoming treat. Guin stared after them until the door closed, shutting off their cheerful voices. She began plying her needle again, but slowly, rehearsed in her mind what had just transpired. Lord Holybrooke had virtually promised to spend more time with her, but then at the first opportunity, and without giving the least thought to her concerns, he had run off with a friend to a goose race.

It was lowering to reflect that one did not rate even so high as a goose.

With a heartfelt sigh, Guin wondered whether things would ever be the same between herself and her twin brother. Since coming to town, it seemed they were drifting farther and farther apart. All of a sudden, she recalled with a flash the comment Colonel Caldar had made on their first evening in London, about her having to do without Percy.

Guin began to have a glimmer of what her uncle had meant for indeed, she was seeing less and less of her brother. Lord Holybrooke was gone from the town house as often as he was in residence. Simply because he was the Earl of Holybrooke and she was a young lady just coming out, their paths had inevitably begun to diverge. They were no longer living quietly in the country, dependent upon one another for amusement and shared confidences. Lord Holybrooke had a widening circle of friends and acquaintances now, which was serving to push Guin away. She was intelligent enough to realize that there was nothing she could do to arrest their estrangement.

"I detest London and everything about it!" she exclaimed, thrusting her needle almost viciously through her embroidery hoop.

The door opened and Mrs. Holland entered with a swish of silken skirts. "There you are, Guin! I have been intending to have a word with you."

There was an undercurrent in Mrs. Holland's voice that instantly banished all thought of Lord Holybrooke's defection from Guin's mind. She anxiously regarded her mother's expression as Mrs. Holland approached. "Yes, Mama?"

Unlike her daughter, Mrs. Holland was not at all retiring. She was thriving on her growing circle of acquaintances. She was in her element, and if she noticed how backward her daughter was in social situations, she blamed Guin for being so entirely stupid.

"I do hope you learn to overcome this embarrassing awkwardness, Guin," she said, seating herself across from her daughter. "I scarcely knew where to look when you simply stared at Lady Beasely in such an idiotic way when she so graciously addressed you during our drive yesterday."

"I-I was woolgathering, Mama," said Guin guiltily, knowing full well the excuse would not be well received. The nervous flutter in her stomach, one she was hardly ever without, intensified.

"Pray confine your woolgathering to your own bedroom," said Mrs. Holland with asperity.

"Yes, Mama. Would you like me to read to you now?" asked Guin quickly, setting aside her embroidery in order to pick up the novel that she had started the evening before.

Mrs. Holland shrugged, artfully arranging her skirt to her satisfaction. "I don't know why I should allow you to do so when your voice sets my teeth on edge. But there is nothing else to do until the ball at Lady Smythe's this evening. I am told that your uncle and dear Percy have gone out again. How I wish Percy was here! He does not fret me like you do."

"I wish Percy was here, too," said Guin quietly, turning to the page where she had left off. Indeed, she thought, at times it was almost more than she could bear to be without her twin's support. Without his timely interventions, their mother was more wont to chide her. She understood that her mother was feeling Lord Holybrooke's neglect, just as she was herself dealing with loneliness, but it scarcely made Mrs. Holland's oft-expressed displeasure more palatable.

"We are going to tea with Lady Beasely tomorrow, Guin. Pray try to behave with some semblance of intelligence," said Mrs. Holland. "And I trust you will do the same this evening. Listen to me, Guin! I do not wish to hear that idiotic stammering. It does not make you in the least interesting, which I suspect you believe it does."

"Yes, Mama," whispered Guin, her heart sinking. Her

stomach started churning as she thought about the inevitable mess she would make of everything.

Guin never uttered a word of complaint over her mother's social plans. Often she was made sick with apprehension at being thrust into social situations for which she was ill-equipped by her upbringing. She had been taught from childhood that her place was to be a silent support to her mother.

Her lack of polish was the least of it, however. She stammered much of the time in company, despite her best efforts otherwise. She knew she was a dismal failure. No matter how hard she tried, Guin felt that she always fell short of her mother's expectations.

Guin began to read aloud a chapter from one of the popular romance novels that her mother favored. Her mind was not on it, however. She was nervous about the engagement that evening. Lady Smythe's invitation was the most important that they had yet received.

However, Lord Holybrooke would be accompanying them, so she could at least present a show of calm at the prospect of her first dress ball. If Percy meant to stay close by, Guin thought hopefully, she might possibly scrape through the evening without incurring her mother's wrath.

However, the visit with Lady Beasely was an entirely different matter. Anxiously, Guin hoped her brother would not have a prior commitment so that he could also accompany her and Mrs. Holland to the Beaseleys. She felt certain that otherwise her genius for gaucherie would undoubtedly draw down on her head another of her mother's dreaded lectures.

Guin lacked confidence, and it was pathetically obvious to anyone of the meanest intelligence. It was a crippling handicap to a young miss embarking on her first Season. She had singularly failed to make a favorable impression with any of their new acquaintances. The ladies had tried to coax her into conversation, but when their efforts did not meet with unqualified success, for the most part, they dismissed Miss Holland.

Never one to exercise patience, Mrs. Holland expressed herself in biting criticisms of her daughter's manners, her speech, and her appearance. It never occurred to that lady that she was herself at least partially to blame for Guin's backwardness.

Unhappily reflecting on all this, Guin came to an inevitable conclusion. She had never been so miserable in her life until they had come up to London for the Season.

Chapter Four

The elopement of a certain Russian prince and a young Irish miss at the end of the previous Season had become generally known and set the *ton* on its ears. Sir Frederick Hawkesworth grinned to himself when he heard it. Since in a sense he had helped the prince prosper in his suit, Sir Frederick congratulated himself on a job well-done.

He glanced around the large elegant ballroom as he took a chilled glass of champagne from the lavishly outfitted refreshment table. Lobster and cold cuts vied with delicate pastries of all descriptions, but nothing stirred his interest. Nor was he impressed by the sparkling of jewels or the bright glow of candlelight captured in mirrors and crystal chandeliers, or even by the well-bred company which had gathered that evening. During a somewhat colorful career in the diplomatic corps, he had become immured to such ostentatious displays of wealth. As for social connections, Sir Frederick knew the greater half of royalty on two continents. It would take much to impress one so cosmopolitan in experience.

Sir Frederick was a well-built gentleman of average height, his lean muscular physique showing to great advantage in a finely tailored dark blue evening coat and buff pantaloons. He was generally considered to be a handsome man, though his face was square rather than aquiline. Often the pronounced twinkle in his eyes and his quick smile had led him to be described as engaging in personality.

Sir Frederick thoughtfully sipped the excellent champagne. Trust Lady Smythe to have nothing but the best served to her guests. However, Sir Frederick was not thinking of wines. There came a somber expression into his brown eyes. In truth, he was at a crossroads. He had been offered a new post in Paris. His good friend Lord John Stokes, who was already stationed in the French capital, had urged him to come. He had declined, but it was not because he was still in love with Lady Sophia Wyndham Stokes. His heart had suffered a terrible blow when the lady had chosen Lord John over him. However, he had recovered. As he had once told Sophia, the experience had tempered him as only fire could do to precious metal.

Sir Frederick knit his dark brows, reflecting. No, it was nothing to do with the past that had made him hesitate to take the plum of a post in Paris. Rather, it was the dry future that he was beginning to envision. The recent elopement of the prince and Miss O'Connell merely pointed up the reality of his own barren circumstances.

Simply put, his was an old and honorable name, and he had yet to bestow it on anyone.

Sir Frederick stared with suspicion at the half-empty wineglass he held with one tanned hand. "Rotten stuff. It's making me maudlin," he muttered. He set the glass down decisively, the gold signet on his left hand clicking against the crystal rim.

"Freddy!" Mr. Henry Duckwood clapped him on a solid well-built shoulder.

Sir Frederick turned to greet one of his oldest friends with a few bantering words and firm handshake. "Henry, I am devilish glad to see you."

"We haven't seen much of you at White's of late. How are you, old fellow?" asked Mr. Duckwood. He was a gentleman given much to fashion. His coat was very tight, his starched shirt points were very high, his stark white cravat was always exquisitely tied, and he sported a number of fobs and seals dangling from black ribbons at his waist. A cherubic countenance, enlivened by his fawn-colored eyes, stamped him as an amiable soul. He had only one passion, and that was gaming of any kind.

Sir Frederick glanced over his shoulder, making certain that he would not be overheard, then returned his earnest gaze to his friend. In a lowered voice he confided, "I am not at all sure, Henry. Here I stand in one of the most influential hostess's ballrooms, attended by every high political figure necessary to my future career, and all I can think about is marriage!"

Mr. Duckwood whistled, giving Sir Frederick a thoughtful glance. "That's bad, very bad. You oughtn't to do it, Freddy. You won't like it. Take it from me, I have it on the best authority—the example of my uncle— the wedded state is miserable indeed. Why, he isn't allowed to blow a cloud in his own library or to have a few cronies over to break a bottle or two over a few hands of whist. As for the dinner fare served up at his table now, I shudder whenever I think of it. I tell you, my uncle isn't the same man. He's a mere shadow of his former self."

"Barbaric," said Sir Frederick sympathetically.

Mr. Duckwood conceded it with gloom. He took out a lace-edged linen handkerchief and blew his nose in an excess of emotion. As he tucked the square away, he said, "Close to my uncle, you know. Don't know what possessed him to get leg-shackled so late in life."

"Caroline Richardson," said Sir Frederick succinctly. "I heard she had her hand in it."

Mr. Duckwood sighed and nodded. "Too true; my uncle never had a sporting chance. I tell you, Freddy, if ever Mrs. Richardson turned her sights on me, my knees would begin to knock together from fear."

A dark-featured tall gentleman sauntered up. He waved negligently to Sir Frederick, but addressed Mr. Duckwood. "What ails you, Henry? I've never seen a longer Friday-face than yours."

"It is Freddy, here," said Mr. Duckwood, heaving a sigh. "He is thinking about marrying."

Sir Peregrine Ashford swung a startled blue gaze

toward Sir Frederick. "Good God! Er-have you anyone particular in mind, Freddy?"

"Devil a bit! I was merely thinking about the recent elopement, and one thing led to another," said Sir Frederick, gesturing vaguely. He was somewhat embarrassed to have generated such interest in his private affairs from his friends.

"Oh, the Kirov affair!" Mr. Duckwood's countenance cleared. "That explains it, then. It is no wonder your thoughts took such an erratic turn, Freddy. Perfectly understandable, for everyone is talking about it."

"Indeed, it is a small cause *célèbre,*" said Sir Peregrine, with the merest hint of a smile. He shrugged a good pair of shoulders. "However, I for one am quite willing to allow the topic to die of natural causes. I am far more interested in the chances of the latest champion at the Fives Court."

Mr. Duckwood's gaming instincts were instantly roused. "Do you go, then, Peregrine? I shall accompany you."

"As you will, Henry. You should put that man of yours into the ring, Freddy," said Sir Peregrine. "I suspect he would display to advantage."

"Who, Will? He'd like nothing better, I daresay," said Sir Frederick with a laugh. "I've never known a man who takes to a good turnout the way Will does, but he is retired from the ring."

"Just as well, I suppose. I doubt he could sport his canvas against the talent these days," said Mr. Duckwood thoughtfully.

Sir Frederick instantly leaped to the defense of his pugilist henchman. "Nonsense! I'd back Will against any latecomer."

"I don't know, Freddy. That's going a bit far. Henry may have the right of it," said Sir Peregrine, shaking his head.

Sir Frederick denied it. The trio heatedly compared the rival merits of various pugilists until a lady dressed in the height of fashion glided up to them, interrupting their debate.

Mrs. Caroline Richardson shook her head in reproof at them, her eyes glinting with humor. "Well! All of you standing about without partners and deep in a sporting discussion! I have been commissioned by our hostess to bring you back into the fold, gentlemen."

"I was on my way to the card room, ma'am," said Mr. Duckwood hastily. His fawn-colored eyes bulged a little as he regarded the lady, giving him a startling resemblance to a frightened stag. He grasped Sir Peregrine's sleeve urgently between thumb and forefinger. "We are to play a hand of whist, aren't we, Peregrine?"

"If you say so, Henry," said Sir Peregrine with a grin. He bowed politely to Mrs. Richardson and sauntered off with Mr. Duckwood toward the card room.

Laughing, Mrs. Richardson turned her knowing gaze on Sir Frederick. "You are surely too seasoned a diplomat to abandon your duty to your hostess, Freddy."

Sir Frederick laid a hand over his heart in exaggerated fashion as he declared dramatically, "Lady Smythe's wish is my command, Caroline."

Mrs. Richardson tucked her slender gloved fingers into his crooked elbow as he offered it to her. She cast a smiling glance at her companion's face. "That is one of the things I like best about you, Freddy. You are so utterly agreeable and charming."

"Stock in trade for a diplomat, Caroline," said Sir Frederick with an easy grin. "Obviously my particular talents are wanted, or you would not have let Henry and Peregrine off so easily. What hatchet-faced dragon am I to charm?"

"No such thing! There is a certain widow, Mrs. Holland, who has come this evening and—"

"A widow!" exclaimed Sir Frederick, stopping abruptly. His dark brows peaked over the alarm in his brown eyes. He paid no heed to the curious glances that were directed toward them. "You aren't up to your old matchmaking tricks, are you, Caroline? Pray tell me the worst! This Mrs. Holland is perfectly respectable and perfectly handsome and has a perfect number of offspring requiring a new papa!"

"Oh, Freddy! Don't be ridiculous," said Mrs. Richardson on a rich ripple of amusement. She urged him to continue on with her, and he complied with a show of reluctance. "Mrs. Holland is by far too old for you, and she has two grown children. In fact—"

Sir Frederick groaned. "It's worse than I thought! The widow has two daughters. One is undoubtedly horse-faced and possesses a squint. The other is carrot-topped and has rabbity teeth. I should have known. But I can't marry both of them, Caroline, so don't think it."

Mrs. Richardson laughed at his nonsense. Her voice still quivered with amusement as she said, "Really, Freddy! One would think that you are terrified of my matchmaking. I've never done anything but good, I assure you."

"Oh? Look at Hedgewight. He's so nutty over that girl that he won't go anywhere without her." Sir Frederick waved his hand in the general direction of a young couple out on the dance floor. "He practically lives in her pocket. I have it on the best authority that Hedgewight won't dance with anyone else unless she urges him to do so."

"Isn't it the sweetest thing," commented Mrs. Richardson with a pleased expression. "They make such a delightful couple. And their steps are so perfectly matched. I am sure it is no wonder they prefer to dance with one another."

Sir Frederick felt he hadn't made his point adequately enough, but then inspiration struck. "Yes, and there's Henry's uncle, now that I think of it! According to Henry, his uncle is but a shadow of his former self."

"And a good thing, too. Alphonse Duckwood was by far too fat. I am happy to hear that Mrs. Duckwood is overseeing his diet so strictly, for undoubtedly her efforts will add years to his life," said Mrs. Richardson firmly.

Sir Frederick gave up the fight for the moment and resigned himself to his fate. He saw that they were approaching a matron seated just off to the side of the dance floor. A slim gentleman of average height leaned over the back of the matron's chair. There was another woman with them, but her chair was half-hidden by the others, and she could not be clearly observed. However, from what he was able to discern of her form, she appeared to be a young woman. Sir Frederick instantly concluded that this lady would be the object of his friend's matchmaking efforts.

His suspicions were truly aroused. Despite his drollery, he had a healthy and wary respect for Mrs. Richardson's abilities. She had been too successful in matching up couples in the past. He might have been reflecting on marriage earlier not many minutes before, but he balked at the thought of being pitchforked to the altar. "I warn you, Caroline, I'll run off to Paris first," he muttered.

Mrs. Richardson pinched his arm through his coat sleeve. "Behave, Freddy!" She drew him around to the attention of the small group. With her attractive smile, she made the introduction. "Mrs. Holland, may I present Sir Frederick Hawkesworth? He is a dear friend of my husband and myself. Sir Frederick is one of our most distinguished diplomats."

"I am delighted, Mrs. Holland," said Sir Frederick, none of his inner perturbation in evidence. He made one of his graceful bows, his glance at once cataloging Mrs. Holland. The widow was a striking woman, dark of hair and eyes with pale skin and still possessed a relatively good figure. However, there was a petulance in her eyes, and tiny lines of temper at the corners of her thin-lipped but well-shaped mouth, that spoke volumes to one of his wide-flung experience. Mrs. Holland had obviously once been a society beauty, but was now a fading rose. Her age was indeterminate, but since she possessed two grown children, Sir Frederick felt safe in placing her at forty at least. Sir Frederick had a shrewd notion that Mrs. Holland would never willingly divulge her actual age to any living soul.

Mrs. Holland inclined her head, simpering slightly. "Sir Frederick." She waved her fan slowly, the movement drawing attention to her deeply rounded *décolletage*. The lady wore a silken gown in the new style, cut low over her shapely bosom and gathered close underneath, so that the resulting display of her charms was one that would irresistibly draw any gentleman's gaze.

Sir Frederick looked hastily away. Dangerous, this one, he cautioned himself. Beside him, he thought he heard a soft choking sound. He realized with an instant flash of amusement that Mrs. Richardson had been neither blind nor approving of the byplay. He had seen much of the world, and there was not much that could any longer disgust him, but he rather thought Mrs. Richardson's tolerance for vulgarity was somewhat lower than his own.

Mrs. Holland smiled, her teeth very white and even. She snapped shut her fan and indicated the young man standing beside her gilt-edged chair. "My son, the Earl of Holybrooke, Sir Frederick." There was a wealth of pride in her voice and in the glance she cast up at her offspring.

Sir Frederick looked swiftly at the handsome young gallant. "The Earl of Holybrooke?" He recovered swiftly from his surprise and made a short bow. "It is an honor, my lord."

The dark young gentleman, who had straightened at the outset of the introductions, flushed slightly. His gray-blue eyes met Sir Frederick's with a steady gaze. He held out his hand. "I am pleased to make your acquaintance, sir."

Sir Frederick accepted the younger man's handshake, liking him for his humility. Like everyone else, he had heard how the old earl had died after dispossessing his firstborn and leaving the title and estate to the son of a younger son. It was an unusual story, and the gossipmongers had delighted in it. His recollection was that it was a year past since this serious-faced boy had inherited.

Sir Frederick's glance passed swiftly over the widow and her two children. Of course, they were out of black gloves now and were taking their place in society.

Sir Frederick smiled at the last of the party, who had not yet been introduced to him. It was obvious that the young lady was related, for there was no mistaking her resemblance in face and coloring to Mrs. Holland and the young earl.

Though he had teased Mrs. Richardson about what the young lady might look like, he had seriously never thought to be brought face-to-face with an antidote. Mrs. Richardson knew too well that gentlemen preferred some aspiration to beauty in the ladies to which she introduced them.

However, Sir Frederick had not anticipated that Miss Holland would be an out-and-out beauty. Black ringlets, a cupid's bow mouth, pale translucent skin and a slim but well-rounded figure were not at all difficult to look upon, he thought appreciatively. In addition, there was no sign of the spoiled vanity that marred the widow's fading claim to beauty. There was humility and a quality of innocence in the younger woman's extraordinarily dark blue eyes that caused Sir Frederick, that jaded cosmopolitan, to stare.

The young woman blushed under his intent gaze and cast down her black lashed eyes. Her slim gloved hands entwined together in her lap. Obviously she was unused to open admiration and was thrown into confusion by his pointed attention. Sir Frederick pulled himself together, silently scolding himself for the momentary lapse in his generally unflappable insouciance.

Sir Frederick sent an inquiring glance at Mrs. Holland, but it was the earl who stepped forward. His lordship dropped a hand on the young woman's slender shoulder. "My sister, Miss Guineveve Holland."

"Oh, yes. My daughter, Sir Frederick," said Mrs. Holland shortly, gesturing with her fan without glancing around in the direction of her daughter.

Sir Frederick was somewhat disconcerted by the widow's negligent attitude. In general, matrons with daughters were all too eager to bring them to his notice. He had a comfortable fortune and owned an estate, besides having a brilliant career. Mrs. Holland had given the impression that she did not care whether her daughter was introduced to him or not. Banishing the puzzling impression, Sir Frederick returned his attention to the young lady. He made an elegant bow. "Miss Holland, I am happy to make your acquaintance."

Miss Holland cast a swift glance upward at him, then slid her gaze toward her mother as though seeking direction. It was swift to come.

"Well, girl, have you not anything polite to say to Sir Frederick?" asked Mrs. Holland sharply, turning around to stare disapprovingly at her daughter.

"Mama, pray—!" muttered the earl, obviously embarrassed.

Miss Holland flushed hotly. With a bad stammer, she said, "H-how do you do, sir?"

Sir Frederick was taken aback by Mrs. Holland's stinging rebuke of her daughter. Public humiliation was never easy to witness. At that moment he felt Mrs. Richardson's fingers close on the back of his arm. Suddenly, he knew why she had introduced him to the Hollands. It was not because she was trying to get up a match between himself and Miss Holland. It was because Mrs. Richardson pitied the young woman. Undoubtedly Mrs. Richardson had already witnessed something of the widow's lack of simple courtesy toward the daughter. He knew Caroline Richardson well enough to understand that it had set up her back, as it had certainly done his.

Sir Frederick, to his own rueful recognition, had never been able to resist the urge to aid a damsel in distress.

Chapter Five

Sir Frederick stepped forward and gently pried loose one of the tensely held hands in Miss Holland's lap. Clasping her reluctant fingers, he smiled down into her startled eyes. He had heard the striking up of the orchestra, and now used it to his advantage. "May I have the honor of this dance, Miss Holland?"

Miss Holland turned paper white. The deep pools of her eyes widened in a panicked expression. "I-I don't know! That is—"

"Don't be a dolt, Guin. Of course you will dance with any gentleman who asks. You haven't a single name on your card, to your shame," snapped Mrs. Holland. She returned her attention to Sir Frederick, her face magically transforming with a gracious smile. "You must forgive my daughter, Sir Frederick. She is rather backward, I fear. We have just come up from the country, and Guin is still overawed at the thought of her come-out."

"Shyness is most becoming in a young miss," said Mrs. Richardson in a cool voice. "Don't you think so, Sir Frederick?"

Mrs. Holland was still smiling, but at Mrs. Richardson's words a decidedly unfriendly light came into her eyes. She stared at the lady as though trying to decide whether or not to reply.

"Eminently so," said Sir Frederick, slightly turning his head to respond to Mrs. Richardson. He had not let go of Miss Holland's hand, and so he was standing close enough to hear her desperate whisper.

"Percy!"

Out of the corner of his eye, Sir Frederick saw how the young earl's long fingers tightened comfortingly on his sister's shoulder. Miss Holland drew a steadying breath, almost as though she was going to trial, he thought pityingly. He saw that it was only with the earl's encouragement that Miss Holland felt able to accept his invitation to dance. Truly the young lady lacked countenance, and he had no hesitation in ascribing it to a selfish, uncaring mother.

"I-I should be honored, Sir Frederick," she said, rising gracefully from the silk-covered chair, her fingers still clasped in his hand. She stood there a second, heightened color in her face as she gazed up at him. Sir Frederick smiled at her encouragingly.

"I just saw Lady Smythe beckoning to me," said Mrs. Richardson briskly. "Pray excuse me, my lord. Mrs. Holland, you must bring your daughter driving with me in the park one day." She walked away, but not before she had bestowed a particularly satisfied smile on Sir Frederick as he drew Miss Holland forward onto the marble dance floor to join one of the sets forming up for a country-dance.

Sir Frederick discovered that he had acquired the most wooden partner of his entire career. Miss Holland performed each turn and movement with perfect accuracy but without heart. She held herself stiffly and not once did she look up at him.

Sir Frederick wondered what he had gotten himself into, concluding that if Miss Holland meant to discourage him, or any other gentleman, for that matter, she was going about it just right. It was no wonder she did not have any names on her dance card, which could perhaps explain in part her mother's open irritation.

However, he was not one to give up on even a lost cause. When the music brought them together the next time, he remarked, "You are supposed to at least pretend to enjoy my company, Miss Holland."

At that, her eyes flew up to meet his smiling gaze. A

painful flush leaped into her pale face. "I-I am so sorry! Pray forgive me!"

"I shan't eat you, ma'am," said Sir Frederick with a slight grin. He had the satisfaction of seeing her acute embarrassment change to an expression of confusion as the dance once more separated them.

When they came together again, he said, "You need not be afraid of offending me, Miss Holland. I have a very thick skin. I should like to think it comes from running in diplomatic circles; but honesty compels me to admit that I am simply too obtuse to recognize an insult."

He was rewarded with the smallest of smiles, one that brought a sparkle into Miss Holland's extraordinary eyes. Sir Frederick considered it to be quite an improvement. He did not know how old she was, but if he was any judge of the matter, she could scarcely be out of the schoolroom. Miss Holland's ill ease testified of her youth, as did the simple gown she wore. Her dress was dusky blue, and the modest neckline boasted only a touch of white lace. A gold chain and locket around her slender neck were her only ornaments.

"I shouldn't think a diplomat could be at all stupid," said Miss Holland in a soft hesitant voice. She glanced up at him, a half-scared, half-speculative expression in her eyes.

Sir Frederick was satisfied. He had at last cracked through whatever was imprisoning the young woman's spirit. "Ah, but you would be surprised, Miss Holland," he said lightly. Thereafter he addressed such remarks as were calculated to put a very self-conscious miss at ease. By the time the country-dance came to an end, Miss Holland behaved almost as naturally as any other young lady in the ballroom. She had lost her woodenness, and all of her movements were gracefully executed.

"Would you like to go to the refreshment room for an ice, or shall I escort you back to your mother?" asked Sir Frederick. Instantly he regretted the question, for all animation fled from Miss Holland's face.

Her eyes cast down, she murmured, "Oh, I must return at once to Mama."

"Of course," said Sir Frederick politely. He walked as slowly as he dared, speaking pleasantly on this and that. Once or twice, Miss Holland's eyes rose to his face but just as quickly sank again. Her small gloved hand lay limply on his arm, and she did not remark at all on anything that he said. Sir Frederick noted that though she gave little indication of enjoying his conversation, she did not seem adverse to remaining in his company, for her pace was just as lagging as his own.

When at last they returned, it was to find Mrs. Holland's cushioned chair vacant and only the earl waiting for them. His lordship looked keenly at his sister's apprehensive face. With a wonderfully casual air, he said, "Mama is enjoying a mild flirtation with an old beau. I assured her that I would look after you, Guin."

Miss Holland's countenance lightened at once. "Thank you, Percy." She turned to Sir Frederick and demurely held out her hand. Her eyes met his steadily, though with a hint of timidity in their depths. "And thank you, Sir Frederick. I have never enjoyed a dance more."

Sir Frederick was astonished. Miss Holland spoke with perfect sincerity and without even the hint of a stammer. He took her hand for a short moment, studying her beautiful countenance. She was an enigma to him and therefore of interest. "The pleasure was mine, Miss Holland. I shall look forward to our next meeting."

A blush stole into Miss Holland's face, and a shy smile touched her naturally pink cupid's bow lips. The thought flitted into Sir Frederick's mind that Miss Holland had a very kissable mouth. He was startled. What maggot had got into his brain that such an extraordinary thing should leap to life about this insignificant little creature?

His expression showing nothing of what was passing through his mind, Sir Frederick bowed to the lady. He said a polite word or two to the young Earl of Holybrooke and sauntered away. He did not see how Miss Holland's eyes rose to follow him, the glow of gratitude in their brilliant blue depths.

Sir Frederick danced several more times, accomplishing his duty with graceful ease. When at last he was satisfied that he had fulfilled his obligation as a dutiful guest, he sought out Mrs. Richardson. He had a small score to pay off, he thought with a hint of mischief in his grin.

He found the lady standing beside a well-breeched gentleman, whom Sir Frederick nodded to with a casual air. "Hello, Richard, old fellow. I didn't expect to see you here."

"Oh, did Caroline tell you that I was off on a medical call? Fortunately, it was a small matter, so I was able to come and lend support to my wife after all," said Richard Richardson cheerfully, exchanging a hearty handshake with Sir Frederick. He wore his ball dress with careless ease, as though he set no great store by his appearance. Indeed, the gentleman's time was taken up with many more important things than fashion. His glance was keen and assessing as he looked at Sir Frederick. "We don't see enough of you, Freddy."

"I fear that if your wife has her way, you'll see me at the altar," said Sir Frederick suavely, sliding a glance at Mrs. Richardson.

Mrs. Richardson was not at all put out of countenance by his pointed reference, as he had hoped. She laughed, her eyes alight with adoration as she glanced up at her husband. "You know how firmly I believe that every gentleman deserves to be wed to a good woman, Richard."

"It was certainly true in my case," said Richard Richardson, returning her smile in full measure. He covered her hand, which lay possessively on his arm. However, curiosity had entered his gray eyes. "But what's this? Have you decided on someone for Freddy, my love?"

Mrs. Richardson shook her head with a small laugh. "No, I haven't. I merely asked Freddy to be kind to the poor Holland girl. I told you about her, Richard. Freddy very dutifully stood up with her. Isn't Mrs. Holland frightful toward her, Freddy?"

"I rather thought so," said Sir Frederick, nodding. "If

I am not mistaken in the matter, Miss Holland has a lively dread of incurring her mother's displeasure. That's the cause of that awful stammer.''

"Do you think so?" asked Mrs. Richardson, interested. She wondered how he had come to that conclusion. She smiled warmly at Sir Frederick. "However, I feel positive that you were able to charm her."

"Whom, my dear? Mrs. Holland or Miss Holland?" asked Richard Richardson mildly.

"Both, of course," replied Mrs. Richardson promptly. "Freddy is the consummate diplomat."

Sir Frederick and Richard Richardson laughed, while Mrs. Richardson twinkled up at them, an attractive smile curving her full lips.

"I fear my powers are vastly overrated," said Sir Frederick. "Actually, I came over hoping you could point me in the direction of Lady Smythe, Caroline."

"Freddy! You're not leaving now! Not before supper!" exclaimed Mrs. Richardson in dismay, almost dropping her fan. "Why, I made sure that—" She recovered herself quickly at the expression of polite inquiry on Sir Frederick's face. "Well, it is your own business, after all." She held out her hand to him in civil leave-taking.

"Why, thank you, Caroline," murmured Sir Frederick, taking her hand and saluting her with a flourishing kiss. "And I promise to be more accommodating the next time you wish to set me up to dance with Miss Holland or some other colorless girl!"

Richard Richardson cracked a delighted laugh, while Mrs. Richardson had the grace to appear slightly ashamed. Nevertheless, the quiver of a dimple touched her smooth cheek. "I shall hold you to that promise, Freddy," she said lightly. She gestured with her fan. "I do believe I last saw Lady Smythe over near the west windows."

Sir Frederick excused himself in a casual fashion and went in search of his formidable hostess. He found her soon enough, just turning away from some of her other guests. Lady Smythe was a tall, spare woman. She carried herself with all the assurance of one who had always possessed wealth and breeding. An elegant dresser and an outstanding hostess, her ladyship had ruled her social bailiwick for decades.

When the elderly dame's gaze lighted on Sir Frederick, her expression became one of gracious welcome. She held out a blue-veined hand, diamonds flashing in the candlelight. "Sir Frederick! I am glad to see you. In fact, I am always glad to see you. You know how to pay court so handsomely to an old woman!"

Sir Frederick made a deep bow, one hand clasping hers while the other well-shaped member was pressed over his heart. "My dearest lady, I perceive you are in fine trim." As he straightened, he cast an awed glance upward at the lady's elaborate headdress, which consisted of several blond ostrich plumes and a purple turban encrusted with emeralds and diamonds.

Lady Smythe complacently twitched her fine Norwich silk shawl so that it draped more fluidly over her elbows. "Fine feathers for an old woman, you mean!"

"I would never say anything so deplorably gauche," said Sir Frederick promptly.

Lady Smythe chuckled, her shrewd blue eyes twinkling. "Never mind! We'll not split hairs! Have you come to tell me that you have another engagement to make an appearance at?"

"Alas, it is true. Otherwise I would not be able to tear myself away," said Sir Frederick in a mournful voice, taking the hand that she had again held out to him and raising it to his lips.

"Ah, if I were but twenty years younger! I'd snatch you up, dear boy," said Lady Smythe, totally disregarding that her arithmetic was off by at least two decades. She gave him a curious look, then dug the folded point of her fan into his chest. "Stay a moment, Sir Frederick. I saw that Caroline Richardson had you in tow earlier. Has she made you her latest project?"

"Indeed, I hope not, ma'am," said Sir Frederick fervently. His hostess chuckled wickedly. He responded with a smile. "Actually, I do not believe so, though she did introduce me to a young lady that has not come in my way before."

Lady Smythe nodded, causing her plumes to wave majestically to and fro. "The Holland chit. The only reason I invited them was because the boy has gotten the earldom. Lord Holybrooke is well enough. His sister is a nonentity, of course, but what can one expect with such a one for a mother?"

"Tell me about the Hollands," said Sir Frederick. He felt a mild curiosity to establish what lay behind Miss Holland's extraordinary turnabout in manner. It had been like night and day. He had been trained to seek out the cause of mystery, and his interest was borne purely of habit.

Lady Smythe glanced at him rather sharply. "What maygame are you getting up to, Sir Frederick?"

"Why, none at all," said Sir Frederick, shaking his head and smiling. "I just wondered about the family. I had heard, of course, of the scandal attached to the ascension."

"Scandal seems to follow the Hollands," said Lady Smythe, amused, before shrugging her indifference regarding his query. "Very well! It is quickly told, after all. Mrs. Holland was a Caldar, one of our families of the minor nobility. There is a brother who went into the army. From all accounts he was content with his lot and has done very well. He did not come tonight. I have heard that Colonel Caldar is the bear leader of his nephew until the boy gets his feet under him. He sounds to be a sensible gentleman."

"What about Mrs. Holland and her daughter?" asked Sir Frederick casually, twirling his quizzing glass between his fingers.

Lady Smythe shrugged again. "Oh, as for Aurelia Caldar, the present Mrs. Holland, I recall when she had her come-out. She was a diamond of the first water. She had no portion to speak of, of course, but it was nonetheless expected that she would make quite a respectable match simply because she was so very beautiful."

"Mrs. Holland is still a beautiful woman," remarked Sir Frederick, as unbidden came an image into his mind of the lady's ample charms.

Lady Smythe snorted derisively. "No doubt, as much good as it ever did her! Aurelia Caldar had high aspirations and made it pretty well-known that she looked for a brilliant marriage. She was a vain, beautiful, spoiled girl and, as I have observed this evening, the years have not improved her."

"So I infer that she held out for a title. It seems odd that she did not receive at least one acceptable offer," said Sir Frederick idly.

"Oh, there were offers! But none of them came up to Aurelia Caldar's expectations, and she refused them all, and in such a public fashion that everyone felt quite sorry for her suitors. She became something of a byword as a result," said Lady Smythe. "At the end of the Season, the beauteous and tiresome Aurelia Caldar had the ignoble experience of returning to her birthplace without becoming betrothed."

"How did she meet Holland, then?" asked Sir Frederick. "And why did she choose a younger son if she was so set on a title?"

Lady Smythe smiled, a trifle grimly. "The outcome of a bad progress, I fear. Her second Season was quite uncomfortable for her. She had already spurned the most eligible gentlemen, quite out of hand, and the rest wanted little to do with her. Imagine what she must have felt when she was left, function after function, with scarcely a name to her dance card when others possessing only a tenth of her physical charms were solicited to stand up."

Sir Frederick whistled soundlessly, fully cognizant of the ramifications. Most gentlemen were civil enough to stand up even with the plainest or most boring of ladies. His standing up with Miss Holland was but an example. A beauty such as Mrs. Holland must have been in her prime should have been besieged by partners every time she stepped into a ballroom. "She did make of herself a byword, didn't she?"

"Quite!" agreed Lady Smythe dryly.

"How is it, then, that Holland fell into her toils? Surely he was as disenchanted as the rest?" asked Sir Frederick. He was fascinated now by the history that Lady Smythe was recounting simply because it was so fantastic.

Lady Smythe shook her head. The huge diamond earrings in her ears threw fire. "Robert Holland had not been up the previous Season, you see, having broken his collarbone in a carriage accident. When he returned to town, Holland became utterly smitten with Aurelia Caldar, and she, no doubt because she saw few other worthy possibilities by that time, shamelessly encouraged him. The upshot of it all was that she managed to snare the youngest son of the Earl of Holybrooke and eloped with him. There was a hideous scandal, naturally."

"I can well imagine," said Sir Frederick emphatically, his mind boggling at the thought of what it had meant to the young couple socially. "I don't see how they dared show their faces in London afterward."

Lady Smythe's smile was thin. "They didn't. By all accounts, the Hollands found themselves exiled to a minor holding outside a quiet hamlet." She waved her fan to and fro, looking over the top of it at Sir Frederick. "But this is all ancient history and matters little now. What is your interest in the Hollands, Sir Frederick? Have you a personal stake, perhaps?"

Sir Frederick glanced swiftly at her ladyship's shrewd expression. "None at all, my lady. I was merely curious. I met Mrs. Holland for the first time this evening, as well as her children. I was instantly struck by Mrs. Holland's manner toward her daughter. It seemed to me—" He paused, a frown creasing his well-formed dark brows. "You will think it odd of me, Lady Smythe, but I came to genuinely pity Miss Holland in the few minutes I was in her company."

Lady Smythe nodded. "I understand completely, Sir Frederick. It is a pity, of course. I expect the girl will languish through the Season and at the end sink out of sight, no doubt to become one of those faded female relations who are afraid to open their mouths for fear of offending the ones who keep them."

Sir Frederick's frown deepened with his reflections. "And yet there was something about Miss Holland—"

Lady Smythe laughed. Over the top of her languidly waving fan, her eyes showed tolerant amusement. "Never say you have been smitten, sir!"

"Not that," said Sir Frederick with a swift smile. "At least, not in the sense you mean. I was struck by the difference in her expression, her whole demeanor, when she was not beside her mother. It was like a sleepwalker had opened her eyes, just for an instant, and recognized her surroundings."

Lady Smythe stared at him, her fan stilled. "My word, Sir Frederick. You have made Miss Holland sound as though she is a Sleeping Beauty."

"Perhaps she is just that," said Sir Frederick slowly, turning it over in his mind. "Perhaps, if given the opportunity, Miss Holland would surprise us all."

Lady Smythe's eyes took on a speculative gleam as he had spoken. "You think the nonentity could be turned into the toast of the town? Despite the handicap of that woman for a mother? And that I could do it?"

Sir Frederick was startled. He looked at her ladyship, his brows quirking upward with his surprise. "You, ma'am?"

"Why ever else would you gabble on about it to me?" asked Lady Smythe reasonably. She closed her fan with a decisive snap. "I have always delighted in a challenge, Sir Frederick. Ah, I had resigned myself to a Season as dull as any other, and now I perceive how it could be quite otherwise! We shall have to disengage the girl from her mother, of course, to test your theory properly, Sir Frederick."

"But my lady—!" exclaimed Sir Frederick, astounded at the way his reflections had been taken up and stretched out of all shape.

Lady Smythe tapped her fan against his forearm. "Leave it to me, Sir Frederick. I know how to get around a woman like Aurelia Caldar. An appeal to her vanity will do quite nicely, I should think. And then we shall see whether this Sleeping Beauty of yours has the stuff to become the toast of the town." She swept away, leaving Sir Frederick to look after her with a good deal of astounded consternation.

Chapter Six

Sir Frederick left Lady Smythe's ball still shaking his head in amazement over how her ladyship had misinterpreted his remarks. However, the demands of the remainder of his evening engagements sufficed to put it all out of his mind. He gave no more thought to Lady Smythe's eccentricity, nor to the peculiarities of Miss Holland's position, until the following morning when he sustained a visit from Henry Duckwood.

It was just short of dawn when the door was opened to Mr. Duckwood by Sir Frederick's amazed porter. Upon a demand to see Sir Frederick, the servant showed the gentleman upstairs and then went away, shaking his head.

Sir Frederick was fortunately an early riser, so he had already put off his frogged dressing gown in favor of a dark green riding coat and buff breeches when Mr. Duckwood was ushered into his chambers.

"Henry! You are just in time to join me for breakfast," said Sir Frederick, waving his hand in the direction of the covered dishes on the sideboard. With a knowing eye, he had already assessed his friend's condition and judged that a good meal might do wonders for Mr. Duckwood's state of minor inebriation.

"Don't mind if I do," said Mr. Duckwood, setting aside his ornamented cane and helping himself generously to steak and kidneys. He was still attired in full ball dress, and his eyes showed signs of bloodshot. Otherwise, he was remarkably untouched by what had obviously been a night spent gaming.

"It's an early hour for you, isn't it, Henry?" asked Sir Frederick, eyeing his friend's heaping plate and the large tankard of ale that Mr. Duckwood carried to the table.

Mr. Duckwood sat down. He replied around a mouthful of steak. "I haven't been to bed yet, Freddy. I just popped around when I left White's, hoping to catch you before you went riding." He swallowed the steak, washing it down with ale. "Ah, that's the ticket! My head was swimming a bit, you know."

Sir Frederick regarded him with deep amusement. He watched while Mr. Duckwood made swift inroads on what was on the plate. "This isn't like you, Henry. I never knew you to leave the cards before cockcrow."

Mr. Duckwood shook his head. He took another swallow of ale, before saying, "Don't I know it! And I was having a run of luck, too! But I felt compelled to come round this morning. A matter of friendship, you see. I came to warn you, Freddy."

Sir Frederick was startled. He stared at his friend's somber expression in liveliest astonishment. "Warn me? Of what?"

"Why, Caroline Richardson, of course. I thought and thought about it all night over the cards. I asked myself why did she let me and Peregrine go so easily?" Mr. Duckwood waggled a wise finger. "I'll tell you why! She has lowered her sights on you, dear fellow, that's why!"

Sir Frederick laughed. "Perhaps you're right, Henry. In fact, I suspected as much for all of ten minutes. But I've got her measure, believe me! I'm not one to be cajoled and maneuvered to the altar."

"So you say, Freddy, but I've seen it happen before," said Mr. Duckwood, shaking his head. "That's why I've come, to give you fair warning." He sat back from the table, the plate in front of him showing little of its original overburdened state except for a few bits of fat.

"I shall keep it in mind," promised Sir Frederick. He rose, picking up his riding whip and hat from where they had been laid on a chair. "I'm off to the park. Do you care to join me?"

Mr. Duckwood shook his head. A yawn caught him unawares. "I never ride in the mornings, as you know. Besides, I'm not dressed for it. I am unaccountably sleepy, to boot."

"You're welcome to bed down here," said Sir Frederick hospitably. "My man will take care of you."

"Very kind of you, Freddy. I think I will rest a few minutes on your sofa, if that is all right with you," said Mr. Duckwood with another prodigious yawn.

Sir Frederick assured his friend that it was quite all right, and before he left the room, he had the satisfaction of seeing that Mr. Duckwood was curled up on his sofa and stenoriously snoring.

Mounted on a well-gaited hack, Sir Frederick guided his horse to the park, where he meant to have a good gallop. It was early in the day, the sun barely brushing the treetops with gold, so he was confident of meeting little traffic or other equestrians.

He was a good deal surprised, then, when he saw two other riders out so early. As they cantered toward him, he recognized the Earl of Holybrooke and Miss Holland. They were mounted on good-looking geldings and both appeared at home in the saddle.

As he came abreast of them, Sir Frederick drew up. "Good morning, my lord, Miss Holland!"

"Sir Frederick!" The chance-met riders also reined in and entered into polite conversation with him. Eventually the commonplace gave way, upon the earl's reference to a particular function that they were attending, when Sir Frederick said courteously, "I shall hold myself honored if you will hold a dance for me, Miss Holland!"

A tinge of color rose in her lovely face. She threw a swift glance toward her brother before saying somewhat hesitantly, "I will gladly do so, Sir Frederick."

Sir Frederick smiled and turned to Lord Holybrooke, engaging him in a discussion about horses with a casual question about his lordship's mount. Before many minutes, Sir Frederick and Lord Holybrooke were on the best of terms. Sir Frederick asked Lord Holybrooke and Miss Holland to extend their ride and join him.

The earl and Miss Holland turned their horses to accompany Sir Frederick back into the park, Lord Holybrooke assuring him of their mutual pleasure in accompanying him.

"How do you like London?" asked Sir Frederick as an opening gambit.

Lord Holybrooke's expression immediately became animated. His gray-blue eyes sparkled. "Oh, I like it above all things! I have been very well received, and I have done any number of things that had not previously come in my way."

Sir Frederick encouraged the young earl to expound in this vein for a few minutes before turning to the silent lady who rode between them. "And you, Miss Holland? Is there anything of note that has struck you about London?"

"The metropolis is very large and quite noisy," said Miss Holland in a polite voice.

Sir Frederick's mobile brows rose, and he said sympathetically, "Yes, and it is filled with any number of personages with whom one really does not wish to converse, isn't it?"

Miss Holland's eyes flew to meet his understanding gaze. Her color heightened, she said with the slightest of smiles, "How did you guess, sir?"

"Oh, but I am a well-traveled diplomat. I quite understand the drawbacks of an evening spent in company when what one really wishes is to be with one's closest family or friends," said Sir Frederick flippantly.

"Sir Frederick has characterized you perfectly, Guin!" said Lord Holybrooke, laughing.

"Indeed he has," said Miss Holland, also laughing. She glanced across at Sir Frederick and the previous tension that he had discerned in her expression was gone.

"I trust that I may be considered one of your friends, Miss Holland," said Sir Frederick with a quick disarming smile. "I should not like to think that I am to be lumped together with all the rest!"

"I should like that, Sir Frederick," said Miss Holland with a rising blush.

Sir Frederick considered that he had played the gallant enough. It was his intention to draw the young lady out of herself, not to cause her to develop a *tendre* for him. He casually changed the direction of the conversation into safer channels, and Lord Holybrooke quickly followed his lead.

Though Miss Holland did not converse as readily or as easily as Lord Holybrooke, she did not neglect to put in a word here and there. Her former stiff manner had vanished. She seemed quite comfortable as they rode leisurely through the park. Sir Frederick took note that she never stammered nor betrayed more than the normal hesitancy that a shy young lady might feel when engaging in conversation with a new acquaintance. His curiosity was even more piqued by this girl who possessed such a contradictory manner.

Just then, Miss Holland turned her head to reply laughingly to something her brother had said, offering Sir Frederick an opportunity to study her. Her lovely face was lit by animation, and her deep blue eyes glowed with liveliness. She had a touch of rose in her cheeks that could not all be attributed to the sedate equestrian exercise. Miss Holland was an undoubted beauty, he acknowledged to himself. She appeared to be altogether a different young woman than the timid mouse he had met the evening before.

Sir Frederick wondered whether Lady Smythe's notion of turning Miss Holland into the toast of the town could actually be done. From that idle thought, it was an easy step to feel the unexpressed hope that he could watch it happen.

When he actually made the decision to aid and abet Lady Smythe he could never afterward recall, but by the time he had parted company with Lord Holybrooke and Miss Holland at the gates of the park, Sir Frederick had decided that he would pay a call on that redoubtable old lady.

Mr. Duckworth was gone when Sir Frederick returned to his lodgings, which was just as well because his friend would have demanded to know why he was changing his raiment to that of a Bond Street beau. However, Sir Frederick knew just what was due to an elderly lady. When he sauntered forth again he was attired with all modishness in a blue superfine frock coat, a lightly colored waistcoat and biscuit-colored pantaloons. His Hessian boots were polished to mirror-brightness, and he carried an elegant cane.

It occurred to him that he would not ingratiate himself by calling too early on an elderly lady who had spent the night hostessing a ball. Sir Frederick's facile mind instantly suggested an alternative. He changed his direction and walked around to the Richardsons' town house.

He was fortunate enough to catch Mrs. Richardson just as she was coming out of her front door. Her carriage was waiting at the curb, and the coachman stood ready to hand Mrs. Richardson into it. With a comprehensive glance at the carriage, Sir Frederick realized that Mrs. Richardson was on her way to run some errands or to make her social calls. Otherwise she would have called for a phaeton and driven herself if she intended to tool around.

"Caroline! I am glad that I chanced to catch you before you left," said Sir Frederick, running up the few narrow steps toward her.

Mrs. Richardson looked surprised to see him. "Freddy!" Then she took in his attire, and she blinked at his sartorial elegance. "My word, Freddy."

Sir Frederick grinned up at her, one knee bent and his booted foot resting on the top step where she stood. With exaggerated formality, quite ruined by the amusement dancing in his eyes, he said politely, "Good morning, Caroline. May I have the favor of a few minutes or are you all in a rush?"

"No, of course not! Come back in with me," said Mrs.

Richardson. Very curious, she turned to him at once after she had led him into the sitting room. She tossed aside her silver-knotted reticule and ermine muff without a thought. "What is toward, Freddy? You're very early today." She glanced again at his attire, a question in her eyes.

Correctly interpreting her look, Sir Frederick said, "I am making a visit to Lady Smythe this morning."

Mrs. Richardson at once understood. She sank gracefully down on a settee and made a civil gesture toward the chairs opposite her. "I see! Pray sit down, Freddy. Have you breakfasted? Shall I call for refreshment?"

"No, thank you. I shall not keep you many minutes when I know you are going out," said Sir Frederick, availing himself of his hostess's invitation to be seated and settling in a wing chair. "The thing of it is, Caroline, I've come to ask a favor of you."

Mrs. Richardson's brows rose, and there was genuine interest in her green eyes. "Really! Of course I shall aid you in any way that I might, Freddy. What is it about?"

"What did you think of Miss Holland?" asked Sir Frederick baldly.

Nonplused, Mrs. Richardson stared at him. "Why, I don't know! What should I think about her? She is a pretty thing, of course, but atrociously backward. She'll never make a success of this Season, I fear, not when she is so desperately afraid that she might make a slip in front of that mother of hers!"

Sir Frederick nodded. "I, too, pitied her. I suspected you did as well."

"Well, naturally I did! Anyone of sensibility could see that she is horridly browbeaten," said Mrs. Richardson. She paused, her gaze holding mingled curiosity and speculation. "Why do you ask, Freddy?"

"I am going around to Lady Smythe's this morning because her ladyship told me last night she intends to bring Miss Holland into fashion. Her ladyship says it will be a gratifying challenge," said Sir Frederick in a bland voice.

Mrs. Richardson looked at him in speechless astonishment. She could only shake her head at his revelation.

Sir Frederick stood up, taking a few steps away and coming back again. With a straight look, he said, "Caroline, if her ladyship is of the same mind, I should like to help her to do just that. What do you say? Would you be willing to lend your support to such a harebrained scheme?"

"Harebrained indeed!" exclaimed Mrs. Richardson, finding her voice. "What claim does Miss Holland have on Lady Smythe? Or indeed, on any of us! What possible reason could Lady Smythe have for taking on such a thankless task? And believe me, it would be thankless where Mrs. Holland is concerned."

Sir Frederick flashed his quick grin. "I don't pretend to understand the workings of Lady Smythe's mind, Caroline! As for myself, I am urged to action simply because I cordially dislike Miss Holland's parent."

"That alone is certainly enough," agreed Mrs. Richardson with a distasteful grimace. "I have never met anyone quite like Mrs. Holland." She quickly made a decision. "Very well, Freddy. If Lady Smythe is of the same mind, I shall help. But what is it exactly that you wish me to do?"

Sir Frederick frowned because his thoughts were only half-formed on this point. He had sought out Mrs. Richardson on the spur of the moment and had no very clear picture of what he actually wanted of her. Slowly, he said, "I pitied Miss Holland from the bottom of my heart, Caroline. She is an entirely different person when she is not influenced by her mother. My fear, perhaps irrational, is that Lady Smythe may indeed bring her into fashion, and then where will she be?"

"I am not certain I am following you, Freddy," said Mrs. Richardson

Sir Frederick shook his head as his conclusions came sharper into focus. "Caroline, what will be accomplished by a social success if nothing comes of it? I should think it would only point up a starker contrast for Miss Holland between what could have been and the reality of her life when the Season is over. What she really needs is to escape the tyranny of her mother and become mistress of her own establishment."

Mrs. Richardson broke into surprised laughter. "Freddy, are you asking me to *scheme* on this girl's behalf?"

"Yes, I am. Think of it, Caroline. Here is a challenge worthy of your scope." He flashed a grin. "Besides, if you are working on Miss Holland's behalf, you will be too caught up in it to bother with anyone else. I shall be able to reassure poor Henry that he will escape your toils yet one more Season!"

Mrs. Richardson laughed again, her eyes dancing. "Horrid, Freddy! What if I should decide Miss Holland will be the perfect wife for Henry Duckworth? Or for you, even?"

Sir Frederick laughed and shrugged his broad shoulders. "We shall have to take our chances, of course!"

"All right, Freddy, I shall help Miss Holland make a respectable match," said Mrs. Richardson, rising and holding out her kid-gloved hand to him. "It will be amusing, in any event."

Sir Frederick bowed over her hand. When he straightened, he smiled at her. "Thank you, Caroline. I thought I could count on you. You are the best of friends."

"Abominable creature! Now, do go away, for I must fly if I am to make my appointment," said Mrs. Richardson, shooing him toward the door.

Chapter Seven

Sir Frederick left the Richardsons' town house fairly well pleased. He was just a few doors away from his original destination, and he sauntered down the walkway, nodding to acquaintances as he met them.

At Lady Smythe's residence he sent in his card and was immediately shown up to her ladyship's private parlor. Lady Smythe reposed in style in a large stuffed chair with her feet propped up on a padded stool and her gaunt figure wrapped in several Norwich shawls.

It could not be said that Sir Frederick's pains over his wardrobe stood him in the least stead, for her ladyship's expression did not lighten on perceiving his handsome figure. Instead, Lady Smythe welcomed him with a somewhat acid smile. "What, pray, brings you here at such an ungodly hour, sir? I'll have you know that I have not yet had my Bohea tea and toast."

Without a blink, Sir Frederick said, "I would be delighted to join you in tea, my lady."

Lady Smythe gave a short bark of derisive laughter. "Oh, aye! And no doubt you take weak tea and toast every morning."

"Only when I have a head," said Sir Frederick blandly and quite untruthfully.

Lady Smythe stared at him very hard. "You do not appear to be foxed, nor suffering from the effects of a late night. And I know very well you have not come to enjoy my company, for I am a tartar before noon and I always look a fright, besides. Very well, Sir Frederick! You have made me curious. You may stay."

"Thank you, my lady," said Sir Frederick meekly. He seated himself in a wing chair appearing completely at ease.

Lady Smythe regarded him suspiciously for a moment, but then snorted. By the time she had finished with her tea and toast, and somewhat maliciously watched Sir Frederick politely choke down some of the same, her good humor was completely restored.

Lady Smythe waved away her servants and prepared herself to be entertained. She rearranged the expensive shawls that she could reach and settled more snugly into the chair's soft cushions. "I can now see why you are so highly regarded in diplomatic circles, Sir Frederick. There aren't many gentlemen who would be able to stomach Bohea tea and toast," she said in congratulatory accents.

Privately wondering if he could stomach it, Sir Frederick smiled and bowed from his chair. "I hoped to bring myself securely into your good graces, my lady," he said.

Lady Smythe chuckled, her shrewd eyes alight with amusement. "Well said, Sir Frederick! Now, out with it! What has brought you to my door before noon?"

Sir Frederick allowed his expression to sober. "I went riding in the park this morning, ma'am, and our conversation of yesterday evening was brought forcibly back to my mind. You see, I met Lord Holybrooke and his sister out riding."

Lady Smythe raised her thin brows. Her frosty blue eyes regarded him unblinkingly. "So? What of it?"

Sir Frederick gave his quick smile. "So, I wondered if you were completely serious in what you said to me."

"I am not in the habit of uttering empty words, Sir Frederick," said Lady Smythe sharply, slightly affronted.

"I did not think you were, my lady. Hence my visit to you at such an unseemly hour of the morning," said Sir Frederick.

"I see." Lady Smythe drummed her fingers on the pad-

ded arm of her chair. "I stand by my word, Sir Frederick.
I'll take that girl and make her the toast of the town, if
I can."

"I should like the privilege of helping you to do just
that, ma'am," said Sir Frederick. "When I saw Miss Holland this morning, I was all the more convinced that it
could be done."

"Acquitted herself well, did she? I take it that her
mother was nowhere in sight?" asked Lady Smythe,
bending forward with her interest.

"You have guessed correctly, my lady. Miss Holland
was escorted by only her brother, Lord Holybrooke,"
said Sir Frederick. "I own, it is not my usual arena, but
it is a challenge from which I suspect I should derive a
good deal of satisfaction. That is, of course, if you were
to enlist my help."

"Sir Frederick, I ask you again, and I wish you to be
completely honest with me, are you in love with this
girl?" demanded Lady Smythe.

"Not at all, ma'am," said Sir Frederick promptly.
"However, more than a year ago I discovered in myself
a disconcerting tendency to rush to the defense of the
helpless. It is a trait better suited to the days of chivalry,
I willingly admit, and one that has in the past led me
into severely uncomfortable situations."

"In this instance, it will likely thrust you headlong into
trouble," said Lady Smythe roundly.

"I trust if that is so, you will be able to extricate me,
Lady Smythe," said Sir Frederick with his quick disarming grin.

"Oh, very well! You may as well do whatever it is you
have it in mind to do," said Lady Smythe. "I shall call
on Mrs. Holland this week. You may rest assured that I
shall leave there with that woman's permission to sponsor her very backward daughter. I suppose you intend to
cultivate a friendship with Lord Holybrooke?"

"Just so, my lady," said Sir Frederick, nodding. "As
well as pursue my acquaintance with Mrs. Holland and
her daughter. I see my role as teaching Miss Holland to

handle herself well in the company of a gentleman, so I shall establish myself in an avuncular light."

"Be careful that you are not entrapped by that woman for her daughter," said Lady Smythe in abrupt warning.

"I am too old a hand at such games, my lady," said Sir Frederick, his composure unshaken. He laughed suddenly. "I have far greater fear of Caroline Richardson's subtleties than those of Mrs. Holland!"

"And with greater cause!" retorted Lady Smythe. "I observed how she drew you up like a banked fish and presented you to Mrs. Holland and her daughter!"

"Not a fish, ma'am!" exclaimed Sir Frederick, for once startled out of his suavity.

"Just like a gasping carp," said Lady Smythe, with malicious satisfaction. She saw that she had momentarily thrown him off balance and smiled. "I have just realized, Sir Frederick, how we might put Mrs. Richardson's talents to good use in our little conspiracy."

Sir Frederick eyed Lady Smythe with some misgiving and a good deal of wariness. Though he had already enlisted Mrs. Richardson, he could not help wondering what exactly Lady Smythe might have in mind. As well acquainted with her ladyship as he was, he thought he knew better than to believe it would be simply a matter of requesting Mrs. Richardson's aid in finding a husband for Miss Holland, as he had done. His suspicions were confirmed when he asked, "And what do you propose, my lady?"

Lady Smythe chuckled, her eyes gleaming. "Never mind that now! You do your part of making yourself agreeable, and I shall do mine. Between us, we should have the Holland chit set firmly on her way to social success by the end of the month."

Shortly thereafter, Sir Frederick took civil leave of Lady Smythe.

Sir Frederick did not wait on Lady Smythe's offices to begin his campaign to bring Miss Holland into fashion. After discharging his own obligations that day, he returned to his chambers to change into driving attire and gave orders that his phaeton be brought round from the stables. Then, with his groom up behind him, he drove over a few streets. That morning while riding in the park, Lord Holybrooke had mentioned the general vicinity of his lordship's residence. Once Sir Frederick turned down the street, it was an easy matter to discover which town house was the Earl of Holybrooke's from a loitering urchin, who was eager to supply the information in exchange for a guinea.

Sir Frederick was surprised by the modest size of the town house. He had expected something quite different since coming into contact with Mrs. Holland's overweening pride in her son's attainment of the title. It occurred to him that the simplest explanation was that Lord Holybrooke had leased the town house. From all accounts the former earl had squandered most of his fortune and had sold or mortgaged the better part of his holdings. Most likely, any permanent London residence had been disposed of long since.

After giving orders to his groom to walk the horses for a few minutes, Sir Frederick mounted the steps of the town house. Sir Frederick was confirmed in his opinion when his card was taken and he was ushered inside to a front parlor. He cast a single comprehensive glance around him at furnishings that had been in fashion ten years before. He had no doubt that if the town house had been Lord Holybrooke's own residence, Mrs. Holland would have seen to it that it was refurbished for the Season.

The door opened and Mrs. Holland entered, followed by her daughter. Sir Frederick turned and gave more particular attention to their dress than he had at Lady Smythe's ball. His practiced eye at once discerned what he had previously overlooked. The ladies were attired fashionably enough, but their daydresses had not come from the hands of a haute couture. Shrewdly, Sir Frederick guessed that Mrs. Holland, at least, chafed at the restrictions that a depleted estate had placed upon her. This town house, not in the first stare of fashion, and a wardrobe that did not include many extravagances would scarcely be palatable to one of Mrs. Holland's cut, he thought.

Mrs. Holland would have been vastly annoyed if she had known how accurately Sir Frederick had summed up her situation. Fortunately, the lady was not privy to Sir Frederick's thoughts, and so she was able to greet him with every appearance of pleasure. She bustled forward, a lovely smile lighting her countenance, one hand hospitably extended. "Sir Frederick! What a perfectly delightful surprise. You asked to see my son, Lord Holybrooke. The earl is not here at the moment, but I could not send you away without seeing you."

Sir Frederick gracefully bowed over Mrs. Holland's shapely hand. "I am disappointed to have missed his lordship. When we struck up a conversation this morning at the park, we discovered a mutual interest in good horses. His lordship had mentioned in particular his intent to acquire a neat hunter. I had hoped Lord Holybrooke could be persuaded to accompany me to Tattersall's. However, I daresay there will be another time."

He turned and smiled at Miss Holland, able to acknowledge her at last. "Miss Holland, your obedient servant." He was rewarded with a shy smile that lit up her countenance.

"Sir Frederick," said Guin quietly, nodding to him.

Deciding that the pleasantries had been adequately observed, Mrs. Holland chose a yellow-silk-covered chair and waved her daughter to another. Her mind was on Sir Frederick's errand. "Won't you be seated, Sir Frederick? Tattersall's, I believe you said! That is where all of the gentlemen purchase their mounts, is it not? Indeed, I am certain that Percival will be sorry to have missed you, for it sounds just the sort of thing he would enjoy."

"I haven't a doubt of it, Mrs. Holland, for from what Lord Holybrooke let drop, I gathered that he is used to riding and has been brought up to appreciate good horseflesh," said Sir Frederick.

"Oh, yes! Percy, and my daughter Guin, too, were wont to career all over the countryside for hours. Now their riding together has been severely curtailed. It is the one drawback of living in town, I fear," said Mrs. Holland with a regretful shake of her head.

Sir Frederick commiserated before turning to Miss Holland. "I know that you must feel it, Miss Holland, being cooped up indoors when you are used to going out."

"Oh, yes. That is, Mama and I do go driving often in the park," said Guin, looking at him with a slight smile. Her hands were clasped loosely in her lap.

Sir Frederick laughed. "You will never persuade me that a sedate drive can compare with a good gallop in the country, Miss Holland!"

"I should not try to persuade you, sir," said Guin. A tinge of color had come up into her face, and there was warmth in her eyes. "The countryside at home and at Holybrooke is beautiful when seen from horseback and—"

"Guin, I am certain that Sir Frederick isn't interested in a bucolic description," said Mrs. Holland lightly, but with a meaningful glance at her daughter.

At once Guin fell silent and slightly bowed her head. Her fingers clenched tight in the folds of her skirt. Before Sir Frederick's eyes, she actually seemed to wilt with dejection.

Sir Frederick drew in his breath, scarcely able to contain the swift remonstrance that rose to his lips. He determined to exert every ounce of his much-vaunted persuasive powers to pry the young woman loose from her prison, if only for an hour. "It seems a pity to waste the afternoon. Mrs. Holland, may I crave a boone? I have my groom and phaeton waiting, naturally having hoped that I might take up Lord Holybrooke. However, failing his lordship's company, might I request permission to take Miss Holland for a drive? I would take the most particular care of her, ma'am, I assure you."

Guin's head came up. She stared at Sir Frederick with

half-parted lips, a blaze of open astonishment on her face.

Mrs. Holland was equally taken aback. "Why, Sir Frederick! I scarcely know how to answer you!"

The door opened and Colonel Caldar entered. "I heard you had called, Sir Frederick. I am glad to see you again."

Sir Frederick stood up to shake the colonel's hand. "As I am you, sir. Do you go to the club this evening?"

Colonel Caldar nodded. The two gentlemen stood talking for a few minutes, before Colonel Caldar inquired what had brought Sir Frederick on a visit.

"I thought I might find Lord Holybrooke at home and take him up with me to Tattersall's," said Sir Frederick easily.

Colonel Caldar nodded again. "Aye, the boy has been mad about acquiring a hunter for the winter months at Holybrooke. He is not here?"

"No, indeed, brother! I have just been telling Sir Frederick that Percival will be sorry to have missed him," said Mrs. Holland, asserting herself. She disliked at any time to be ignored or to be obliged to listen to a conversation that was not of interest to her.

"When you came in, I was soliciting Mrs. Holland's permission to drive out with Miss Holland," said Sir Frederick smoothly.

"Capital! A bit of fresh air will be just the thing for you, Guin," said Colonel Caldar with a nod and a smile at his niece.

"Arnold, I am not at all certain—" began Mrs. Holland, with the gathering of a frown.

"Nonsense! Guin will not come to any harm. I am persuaded Sir Frederick is a capital whip," said Colonel Caldar. He gestured with his hand for his niece to get up from where she was sitting. "Well, come on, Guin! Run upstairs and put on your straw. It will not do to keep Sir Frederick's horses waiting."

"Yes, Uncle!" Guin obediently leaped to her feet. She purposefully did not glance at her mother's face as she hurried across the room toward the door. She did not want to see Mrs. Holland's expression, fearing that she would be denied the treat so surprisingly held out to her.

Colonel Caldar opened the door for Guin, giving her a wink as he ushered her out. Guin realized that she and her uncle had become coconspirators. She was quite breathless at her own, as well as her uncle's, audacity.

Before Colonel Caldar closed the heavy paneled door behind her, Guin heard him say, "I understand that you have enjoyed a brilliant career, Sir Frederick. You must tell my sister and me something about your travels."

Guin gave a small almost hysterical laugh as she picked up her skirts and ran up the stairs.

Chapter Eight

Once Colonel Caldar and Mrs. Holland had seen Guin off with Sir Frederick, Mrs. Holland immediately rounded on her brother. "I am not pleased, brother! I do not know what you were about to push Guin into driving out with Sir Frederick! Anyone could see that she had no wish for it. And I scarcely knew where to look when you told her to run upstairs like some hoyden! I shall have something to say to her when she returns, I assure you."

Colonel Caldar regarded his sister thoughtfully. "You would do better not to, however, Aurelia. Has it occurred to you that this is the first gentleman who has ever bestowed any attention on Guin? I don't think it will suit your plans to discourage her when someone as well connected as Sir Frederick chooses to make her an object of his gallantry!"

"But Sir Frederick is a mere baronet, Arnold," said Mrs. Holland, her frown deepening. "I do not wish to encourage that connection in the least!"

"Perhaps not! However, it will do Guin a world of good to learn how to conduct a polite conversation with a gentleman. Sir Frederick is just the sort to overlook her awkwardness. He is a diplomat, recall! And she will do better, then, with the next gentleman," said Colonel Caldar.

By the time he had finished speaking, Mrs. Holland's frown had disappeared and she was regarding him with a half-opened mouth. With a tinge of respect, she said, "Why, Arnold, what a clever notion. I did not expect it of you, to be sure! I quite see how Sir Frederick could be very helpful to Guin. And he is very well connected, isn't he? My head positively reeled with the names of I don't know how many princes and noble families he has been associated with." She gave a decisive nod. "Yes, I think we shall encourage Sir Frederick's friendship. I shall invite him to our rout."

Colonel Caldar left his sister in the front parlor, complacently revising her seating plan for the upcoming evening party. He was smiling to himself and felt something like that he had beaten the enemy on all points.

Guin was positively dazed by her good fortune. She sat quietly, her kid-gloved hands resting in her lap, as Sir Frederick set the team in motion and the neat phaeton pulled away from the curb. She still could scarcely believe she had been allowed to go driving with him. She was utterly grateful that her uncle had come into the front parlor at just that moment, for it had looked very much like her mother would have turned down Sir Frederick's generous invitation.

She slid a glance at Sir Frederick's handsome profile. It seemed so incredible to her that he had actually extended such an invitation to *her,* when he could have chosen anyone else he had wished. A warm feeling suffused her heart. She did not believe that there was anyone kinder or more handsome or noble or—

"A penny for your thoughts, Miss Holland," said Sir Frederick, glancing down at her with a smile lurking in his brown eyes. His firm full-lipped mobile mouth was slanted upward.

Guin's face pinkened with embarrassment. "Oh!" She averted her head, her thoughts in a turmoil. She couldn't possibly tell him that she had been thinking about him, and in such a way, too!

At once Sir Frederick began to talk about things of passing interest, his voice pleasant and impersonal. At length Guin was able to regain her complexion. She thought she should apologize, but she feared that it would sound awkward. She nervously pleated her pelisse skirt, knowing that the silence on her part was stretching to the point of incivility.

Once more Sir Frederick came to her rescue. "I seem to have a disconcerting habit of putting you out of countenance, Miss Holland," he commented pleasantly.

Guin glanced up quickly and what she saw in his expression encouraged her. "It—it is not your fault, sir, but my own. I am not very skilled at—at dalliance," she said breathlessly.

"Dalliance?" he asked lightly. He admired the translucent quality of her complexion, which was still betraying a touch of rose. "Is that what we are doing? I thought we were merely driving, Miss Holland!"

Sir Frederick saw that she had colored again and castigated himself for this carelessness. He had forgotten again how inexperienced this young lady actually was. He transferred both reins to his right hand and then reached over with the other to cover her hands in her lap. "Forgive me, my dear. I am a shocking tease. You must believe me when I tell you that I wish you no harm, nor do I desire to place you at a disadvantage when you are in my company."

"I do believe you, Sir Frederick," said Guin, raising her eyes and looking straight into his with scarce-concealed adoration. "You are quite the nicest gentleman I have ever met, excepting my brother and uncle, of course."

Sir Frederick burst out laughing. He withdrew his hand and got hold of the reins properly again. "I am relieved, Miss Holland! And honored, as well, for I am definitely in good company if I measure up to Lord Holybrooke and Colonel Caldar in your estimation!"

"Oh, you do!" said Guin quickly, anxious to reassure him.

He laughed again, his friendly glance inviting her to share in his amusement. She started to laugh, too, though she couldn't be certain if she did so because of how silly she had made herself sound or because she was simply so happy.

Sir Frederick glanced down at his companion again. She was looking up, a bright smile on her lips and a laughing expression in her extraordinary dark blue eyes. He thought he had never seen such eyes before, deep midnight pools ringed with black lashes, expressive of her every emotion. "You are altogether charming," he said unthinkingly.

She blushed and turned her head away. After a pause she asked in a carefully neutral voice, "Have you been a diplomat long, Sir Frederick?"

And that was as neat a setdown as he had ever received, he thought ruefully. A polite and impersonal question in response to a flourishing compliment. He had deserved it, of course. He had already promised her that he would not place her at a disadvantage while she was with him, and at once he had then turned around and uttered what must be guaranteed to put her out of countenance again.

Sir Frederick meekly accepted his companion's lead. "I have been employed in that capacity since I finished at university. My last post was in St. Petersburg. Since then I have been attached to the Foreign Office, and there is some talk of a post in Paris."

"Russia? Paris! Oh, how I envy you, Sir Frederick," said Guin, clasping her hands together in front of her breast as she turned impulsively toward him. Her eyes shone with enthusiasm. "Pray describe to me something of those places, for I have always longed to travel."

"Where would you like to go?" asked Sir Frederick, amused. "Besides Russia and Paris, of course."

A tiny frown formed between her slender black brows, so that she bore a strong resemblance to a puzzled kitten. "Well, I have always thought I should like to see Greece because of the stories that Percy and I read under his tutor. And I should very much like to see Rome. I was quite fascinated with Julius Caesar, you see. He was such an interesting man."

Sir Frederick was startled, so much so that he allowed the reins to drop in his surprise. The phaeton surged forward. It did not need his groom's hoarse exclamation to make him realize the possible consequences of bounding along through the heavily trafficked streets. Sir Frederick modified the pace of his team. He regarded his companion with raised brows. "Miss Holland, am I to infer that you have had a classical education?"

She returned his look with mingled surprise and puzzlement. "I don't know what you mean."

"Latin? Hebrew? Greek?" quizzed Sir Frederick.

Guin's expression cleared. "Oh! Well, you see, I had lessons with Percy. He told Mama that he was lonely without me and that I could help him with his books. I daresay I learned all sorts of things that females don't usually. Percy's tutor was very kind to me, too, so that I felt quite comfortable."

Sir Frederick rattled off a simple Latin phrase and then looked at her curiously. "Can you translate that, Miss Holland?"

Guin obediently did so, the puzzlement in her expression beginning to give way to amusement. "That was an easy one, Sir Frederick. You must do better than that to stump me."

"Let's try one in Greek, then." Sir Frederick quoted a familiar passage from a well-known ancient Greek play.

Again, Guin found no difficulty in translating what he had said. She looked at him inquiringly. "Why are you asking me these things, sir?"

Sir Frederick drew in his breath. "My dear Miss Holland, you are amazing. You are probably better educated than most ladies of my acquaintance."

She burst out laughing and shook her head. "But how absurd! You must know that I have no accomplishments at all, Sir Frederick! My governess despaired of ever teaching me to draw or watercolor, and I am the merest dab at playing the harp."

"Thank God!" said Sir Frederick swiftly, flashing his quick grin. "I positively detest the harp, Miss Holland."

"Oh, you are always so kind, Sir Frederick," said Guin, her white straight teeth flashing in a quick shy smile.

"Did your governess succeed in teaching you French?" asked Sir Frederick, still smiling. He was fascinated with what he was learning about Miss Holland. She had been nothing but a lovely shrinking mouse when he had first met her, and chivalry had stirred in his breast. Now he was learning that she had intelligence sharpened by education.

"Poor Miss Rhodes! Yes, she did and also a little Italian. But Mama would much have preferred that I had learned to paint instead. I fear that I was a disappointment to Miss Rhodes," said Guin on a regretful sigh. "Mama turned her off in the end."

"I doubt that she was disappointed in *you*, Miss Holland, as much as she must have been with her employer," said Sir Frederick. He saw that she was looking puzzled again, and he casually turned the conversation.

Soon he judged it to be time to return Guin home, and he drove back to the town house. "Take their heads, Spencer," he said to his groom, springing down from the phaeton. He was just giving a hand to Guin to help her down when Lord Holybrooke came strolling around the corner.

"Oh, here is Percy!" exclaimed Guin, her face lighting up at the sight of her twin brother. She jumped down to the pavement and ran to meet Lord Holybrooke. As the two walked back toward Sir Frederick, she was animatedly telling her brother about being able to drive out with Sir Frederick.

"Sir Frederick, I am glad to see you again," said Lord Holybrooke with his easy dignity.

Sir Frederick returned the greeting, shaking the younger man's hand. He at once reiterated his offer to take Lord Holybrooke to Tattersall's with him. The young earl civilly declined, though with obvious regret.

"I came home only to change since I am engaged to a party of friends and must meet them within the hour," said Lord Holybrooke. He grinned boyishly at Sir Frederick. "The thing of it is, sir, there is to be a mill."

"Oh, no, Percy! You cannot be going to a horrid fist-fight!" exclaimed Guin, stepping back so that she could look into her brother's face. "How can you like such a thing?"

The two men exchanged glances, complete understanding passing between them. A lady could not be expected to comprehend the fascinated draw that a round of fisticuffs had on the male of the species.

"Another time, then, my lord," said Sir Frederick easily. He said good-bye to Guin and her brother, and climbed back up into the phaeton. His groom let go of the horses' heads and leaped up behind. Sir Frederick nodded his head in farewell and drove away.

He had been given much to ponder about Miss Holland. She was a surprising female, he reflected. He had originally taken her for little more than a lovely dormouse. Then he had perceived there was more to her personality and had attempted, with a modicum of success, to draw her out. Today he had discovered that she had a well-educated mind. Not only that, but she was probably every bit as versatile as he was himself in several languages.

A few streets over, he saw his friend Mr. Henry Duckwood standing on the walkway. Mr. Duckwood was waving to him, so Sir Frederick pulled over to the curb. "Going my way, Henry?"

"Wherever you wish, dear fellow," said Mr. Duckwood, stepping up into the phaeton and disposing himself comfortably on the narrow leather seat.

Sir Frederick guided the phaeton back into the traffic. Casting a knowledgeable gaze over his friend, he said, "You are looking elegant today, Henry. Is that a new coat?"

Mr. Duckwood sprawled carelessly on the phaeton's seat. He lovingly smoothed his sleeve. "You've discerned it, Freddy. I had it from Weston this morning. I am very pleased with it. Where are you headed? If you are going to Tattersall's or the park, I have half a mind to accompany you."

"Tattersall's it is, then, for I have already exercised my

horses by driving with Miss Holland," said Sir Frederick, turning a corner with neat skill.

Mr. Duckwood abandoned his lazy attitude and sat up. His fawn's eyes were at once filled with concern. "Holland? Isn't she the chit that Caroline Richardson introduced you to?" He shook his head. "Freddy, Freddy! I warned you, and what must you do but run your head straight into the noose."

Sir Frederick shook his head. "It isn't like that, Henry. I feel sorry for Miss Holland. Mrs. Holland is a regular tartar and abuses her. So I have been paying Miss Holland a bit of attention, just to get her confidence in herself built up a trifle."

Mr. Duckwood morosely shook his head. "Dangerous, Freddy, very dangerous. What's to say that Miss Holland isn't setting you up for a facer?"

Sir Frederick laughed. "If you knew her, Henry, you would recognize that Miss Holland hasn't an ounce of coquetry in her. She's a sweet innocent who doesn't know the first thing about how to go on. On top of it all, I discovered this morning that she can translate Latin and Greek and speaks French and Italian."

"A bluestocking, is she?" said Mr. Duckwood, pursing his lips as he turned it over in his mind. He shook his head. "She'll never go off in style if that becomes known. A pity, but there it is."

"You're right," said Sir Frederick thoughtfully. He glanced at his companion. "Miss Holland has more than enough to overcome as it is. I'd appreciate it if you wouldn't tout this about, Henry."

"Oh, I'm not one to spread damaging tales. You may count on me to keep quiet, Freddy," said Mr. Duckwood amiably.

"I knew I could," said Sir Frederick casually.

A good understanding being established, the two gentlemen dismissed the subject of Miss Holland from their minds and began discussing horseflesh.

Chapter Nine

Sir Frederick accepted the invitation to Mrs. Holland's rout with mixed feelings. Though he had committed himself to lending a helping hand to Miss Holland socially, he had the feeling that he was letting himself in for just the sort of entertainment that he most disliked. Within minutes of entering the town house, he realized that he was right.

Mrs. Holland had filled her guest list with as many notables as she could possibly lay claim. Since she was not acquainted with the sort of personages that made up diplomatic or government circles and was on terms with very few fashionables, the result was a majority of many of the same sort of pretentious personalities that she was herself.

Sir Frederick recognized most of the guests and exchanged polite nods or bows with several of them, though privately deploring the necessity. His dark brows rose when he saw two or three gentlemen present that he would have hesitated to introduce to any of the ladies of his acquaintance. He particularly disliked the gushing familiarity of one lady whom he cataloged as an encroaching mushroom. He would probably hear it rumored before the week was out that she was quite one of his closest acquaintances, he reflected disparagingly.

"My, my, aren't we vicious this evening," murmured Sir Frederick to himself disgustedly. He regarded the assemblage through his quizzing glass in an aloof manner calculated to give pause to anyone else who did not know him well. Even altruism stopped short of encouraging the sort of toadeating he found singularly deplorable. Dropping the glass, he decided he would make the opportunity to leave early. Having already spoken to his hostess and to Colonel Caldar, it but remained to do his duty toward Lord Holybrooke and Miss Holland.

A drawling, cheerful voice broke into his thoughts. "Is that what happens to diplomats when they are kept dangling at the Foreign Office without assignment? Do they gibber madly to themselves?"

Sir Frederick turned swiftly. He threw out a hand. "Thank God! A friendly face."

Sir Peregrine Ashford laughed and shook Sir Frederick's outstretched hand. "Not your style of thing, is it?" He glanced around them and grimaced slightly. "Truth to tell, it isn't mine, either. But when young Holybrooke invited me, I thought I should accept. I didn't like to disappoint him, especially when he told me how devilish it would be and that it was some sort of coming-out party for his sister."

"I didn't know you and Lord Holybrooke were on such friendly terms, Peregrine," said Sir Frederick, surprised.

"We had met before, of course, but I fell into conversation with him at a mill last week. I liked him. He is very unaffected, quite unlike what one might have expected," said Sir Peregrine with a shrug.

"You mean, after one had had the doubtful pleasure of a few moments spent in Mrs. Holland's company," said Sir Frederick suggestively.

Sir Peregrine laughed, his dark features lighting up. "Quite, though I wasn't going to say so." He eyed Sir Frederick curiously. "What brings you tonight?"

"I come at personal invitation, my dear fellow," said Sir Frederick, assuming a lofty tone. "Mrs. Holland apparently approved of my tender care of her daughter when I invited Miss Holland out for a drive. I did not feel myself able to deny myself the pleasure of attending."

Sir Peregrine gave a skeptical glance. "I shan't bother pointing out that you have, without a doubt, larger experience than anyone else I know in sliding out of unwelcome invites!" He shook his head at Sir Frederick's quick grin. "What I don't understand is this sudden devotion to Miss Holland's interests. Freddy, you haven't gone nutty on her, have you?"

"Have you been talking to Henry?" demanded Sir Frederick suspiciously.

"No, should I be?" asked Sir Peregrine mildly.

"Henry would have it that I am dancing to a tune of Caroline Richardson's making," said Sir Frederick with a negligent shrug.

Sir Peregrine's brows rose. "And are you?" he asked with every expression of interest.

"Damn your eyes," said Sir Frederick without heat. "If you must know, it is Lady Smythe's coil more than anyone else's." He saw that Sir Peregrine was looking at him with polite astonishment, and he sighed. "I suppose I shall have to explain it to you, now that I have said this much."

"Quite, dear fellow. Er-would it be tactless to suggest you have been deuced indiscreet?" said Sir Peregrine.

Sir Frederick recommended that Sir Peregrine could keep his unsolicited opinion to himself, and in a few sentences outlined his conversation with Lady Smythe and the astonishing upshot. "And I have pledged myself to do whatever I can to help Miss Holland along."

Sir Peregrine heard him out in silence, then shrugged. "Well, you know your own business best, Freddy. However, if you find yourself at point-non-plus, I hope you know that you may count on me."

Sir Frederick begged him not to be melodramatic and to come meet Miss Holland. "Since you are so eager to sport your canvas on my behalf, you might as well make yourself useful and help me bring her into notice."

"You've got windmills in your head, Freddy," said Sir Peregrine calmly. He allowed himself to be led over to where Lord Holybrooke and Miss Holland were standing. He greeted Lord Holybrooke, before turning to the earl's sister while Sir Frederick performed the introductions.

"Sir Peregrine is a particular friend of mine," said Sir Frederick.

"Oh, then I am persuaded we shall be friends, Sir Peregrine," said Guin with a shy smile, extending her hand to him.

Sir Peregrine was taken aback. As he bowed over the lady's hand, he glanced swiftly upward at Sir Frederick. However, there was nothing on that gentleman's face to hint that he had found Miss Holland's avowal at all discomposing. Sir Peregrine smiled at Miss Holland and returned a civil reply, before turning again to the earl.

Lord Holybrooke quickly bore Sir Peregrine off with him toward the refreshment room, saying, "I warned you that it would be devilish. It is the fault of that screeching violin. Why my mother must hire an orchestra at all is beyond my comprehension, for there will not be anything but country-dances, since my sister hasn't been presented at Almack's yet."

Sir Frederick and Guin laughed as the two gentlemen left them. "Percy does not care for musical evenings," observed Guin.

"No, I can see that he doesn't. For myself, I look forward to the dancing. I asked you before if you would stand up with me, Miss Holland," said Sir Frederick.

"That was for quite a different function, sir," said Guin, scrupulously fair.

"I know it, but will you stand up with me this evening also, Miss Holland?" said Sir Frederick.

"Of course I shall. However, I should like it if you would stand up with someone else first, if you please," said Guin.

"But I don't please," said Sir Frederick gently. "There is not another lady in the room whom I wish to dance with more."

"Oh!" Guin dropped her fan. She smiled up at him. "That—that is quite the nicest compliment anyone has ever paid me!"

Sir Frederick obligingly picked the fan up for her and handed it back. "Have I put you out of countenance again, Miss Holland?" he asked with amusement, taking note of her blush.

"Yes—no! Yes! Oh, you mustn't say such things where someone might overhear you," said Guin, glancing uneasily around. "Someone might think I was fl-flirting with you, and Mama might hear of it."

"Then I shall flirt with you in Greek, and no one will know," said Sir Frederick, and promptly said something both outrageous and provocative. He watched with interest as her cheeks brightened even more. "Did you understand that, Miss Holland?"

"Fairly well, I believe," said Guin breathlessly. She had cast down her eyes, but now she looked up at him with a trembling smile. "I think you are very ungallant, sir. But—but I like you to tease me, I think!"

Sir Frederick laughed. He was about to reply when Mrs. Holland rustled up with a gentleman in tow. Sir Frederick bowed to his hostess. "Mrs. Holland, your servant." He glanced toward her cavalier, keeping his face impassive.

"Sir Frederick, how good it was of you to come. You must know Lord Holloway, of course," said Mrs. Holland, indicating her companion with a swift lovely smile. Her hand was laid proprietarily on the gentleman's bent arm.

Sir Frederick acknowledged that he did, suppressing all sign of his scorn for one whom he knew for a fop and profligate. The two gentlemen exchanged polite civilities. It was evident to anyone interested in such nuances that no spark of friendship lay between them.

Mrs. Holland waited with a touch of impatience for the gentlemen to be through with their pleasantries, then at once introduced Lord Holloway to her daughter. His lordship bowed low over Miss Holland's hand, kissing her gloved fingers with a flourish and perhaps holding her hand an instant too long.

"Guin, Lord Holloway tells me that he has estates in the north," said Mrs. Holland, with another smile for his lordship.

Lord Holloway nodded and in a mincing voice said, "I am fortunate to have inherited vast responsibilities." He waved a laced handkerchief in a negligent fashion and scent bathed the air.

Sir Frederick discreetly coughed.

"How—how nice, to be sure," said Guin colorlessly. She had dropped her eyes and was staring at the floor.

A small silence ensued. Sir Frederick made no attempt to fill it and waited to see how his hostess would manage to overcome Miss Holland's patent withdrawal.

"And Lord Holloway is very fond of horses. You must know, my lord, that Guin is quite a notable horse-woman," said Mrs. Holland, plowing on determinedly. Her smile had tightened, and a rather hard look had come into her eyes as she narrowed her gaze on her recalcitrant daughter.

Lord Holloway bowed, a smile of acknowledgment on his thin lips. His heavy-lidded gaze ran boldly, thought-fully, over Miss Holland. "Indeed? Perhaps we shall try our mounts against one another in a race, Miss Holland."

Sir Frederick felt himself stiffen at the undercurrent in his lordship's tone.

Guin looked up swiftly to meet the gentleman's lazy gaze. Color flew into her face. "Oh, I don't think—" she began, before catching her mother's eyes. After a pause and in a much more subdued tone, she said, "I have heard that racing in the park is considered very fast, my lord."

Sir Frederick silently applauded. Miss Holland had caught herself up very well and come up with a com-pletely neutral and unoffensive objection to Lord Hol-loway's swift bid for familiarity.

Mrs. Holland might be all eagerness to marry off her daughter, but she was not willing to sacrifice her daugh-ter's reputation in pursuit of her goal. She knew what was due the sister of an earl. "Indeed it is, my lord! Fie on you for putting such improper notions in my poor daughter's head. Why, I daresay nothing could suit her better than to go riding with a notable horseman such as yourself, but it must be with a respectable party," she said with just the right touch of amusement.

Lord Holloway returned a graceful, if rather languid, reply. Mrs. Holland once more made mention of his lordship's northern assets and begged Lord Holloway to describe the country in which his estates were located. "We have never traveled so far north, my lord. I am certain that my daughter will be quite interested," said Mrs. Holland enthusiastically.

Sir Frederick could see which way the wind was blowing and adroitly excused himself from the group. He caught the forlorn expression in Guin's eyes when he stepped away, but assuaged his conscience by reminding himself that he was pledged to stand up with her in a country-dance. In the meantime, he thought grimly, his time would be well spent in dropping a bug in young Percy's ear.

With that thought in mind, Sir Frederick wandered with seeming lack of purpose through the ballroom to the refreshment room. As he had hoped, Lord Holybrooke was still standing near the well-appointed tables, a glass in one hand and deep in laughing conversation with a young sprig that Sir Frederick recognized to be Lord Tucker. Sir Peregrine Ashford was nowhere in sight.

With very little difficulty, Sir Frederick disengaged Lord Holybrooke from Lord Tucker without either young gentleman realizing that they had been dealt with by the hand of a master. He drew the earl a little apart so that they would be free of being overheard.

"Lord Holybrooke, I wished to put a question to you concerning Lord Holloway's depth of acquaintance with your sister," he said gravely and without preamble.

"I believe they have not met before tonight," said Lord Holybrooke. He eyed Sir Frederick curiously. "Why do you ask, sir?"

"I hesitate to trod where I have no business, but I felt that I should say something to you as head of your family, as it were. You have but recently come to London,

and your acquaintance may not yet be so wide as to
have brought certain things to your attention," said Sir
Frederick, idly twirling his quizzing glass by its black rib-
and. He was speaking carefully so that he did not offend.

Lord Holybrooke looked at him with slightly narrowed
eyes, alertness in his gaze. "I beg you to bare your
thoughts, Sir Frederick. I count you among our friends.
I take it that there is something of ill repute connected
to Lord Holloway?"

"Not precisely that, no. However, I would suggest that
you inquire around about his lordship's habits and his
fortune," said Sir Frederick with quiet authority. "Unless
I miss my guess, you will not deem him an eligible *parti*
for Miss Holland."

"I understand you, Sir Frederick, and I shall do just
as you suggest," said Lord Holybrooke with a nod and
tightening of his lips. There was a steely look in his gray-
blue eyes. "My sister is very dear to me, as you may
imagine. I shall do all in my power to protect her from
pain."

"She is fortunate to have you for her champion," said
Sir Frederick. "Ah, I hear a set being struck up. Excuse
me, my lord."

"Of course. And thank you, Sir Frederick. I suspect
that I stand in your debt," said Lord Holybrooke in a
slightly stiff manner that spoke louder than words of his
awkwardness associated with their conversation.

Sir Frederick nodded, said a quick laughing word to
turn off the young earl's mild embarrassment, and went
off to find Miss Holland. He was surprised to discover
that she was already being led into the set by none other
than Sir Peregrine Ashford.

"Well, well! Peregrine's curiosity has been piqued," he
murmured, smiling. He settled himself to one side to
watch the dancing and was glad to see that Miss Holland
was acquitting herself rather better than she had done in
her first dance with him. At the end, he sauntered over
to claim Miss Holland's hand from his friend.

"You stole a march on me, Peregrine," he complained.
"The lady was promised to me."

"It was your own fault, Freddy, as well you know," said Sir Peregrine with an expressive grin. He stepped away, leaving Sir Frederick only nominally in control of the field.

"Whatever did Sir Peregrine mean by that? And he was wearing such a droll look, too," asked Guin.

"Never mind," said Sir Frederick hastily. "Let's take our places, Miss Holland."

Chapter Ten

Invitations and morning calls began to descend with gratifying regularity upon the modest town house off Albemarle Street. Mrs. Holland happily received them all. It became one of her chief pleasures to read through the invitations and to write out the RSVPs herself. She seldom rejected any entertainment, and where there was a conflict due to date, she decided always in favor of the more prestigious invitation.

Engaged in addressing RSVPs early one morning in the back sitting room, she remarked, "It is shaping up very well, very well indeed."

"You'll have us all knocked into flinders if we attend even the half of those," said Colonel Caldar from his chair, waving his hand at the stack of gilt-edged cards sitting at his sister's elbow.

"While I admit it will be difficult for one of my delicate constitution, I shall not begrudge any effort on my children's behalf," said Mrs. Holland dramatically. She dipped the pen again in ink and hummed a little tune as she wrote.

Colonel Caldar looked as though he might have wished to say something in reply. Instead, he only shook his head and straightened out his newspaper again.

Guin sighed as she watched her uncle disappear behind the pages of the newspaper. She had hoped her uncle would make a firmer objection to the number of social engagements her mother deemed essential to accept. It was doubtful that Mrs. Holland would have actually attended to anything Colonel Caldar said, but one never knew, after all.

Guin strongly wished that she could cry off now and again, but it was utterly impossible. She knew her mother would never allow her to do so. Mrs. Holland herself too much enjoyed the social gatherings, and she had not let go of her original intention to snare a husband for her daughter, both facts which Guin knew very well.

The Holland ladies were never denied to visitors. Mrs. Holland was especially fond of welcoming eligible gentlemen who might conceivably make an offer for her daughter. There had been a mere sprinkling of the latter since Guin's come-out party, and the gentlemen's interest in her thus far was lukewarm at best. Miss Holland was known not to be an heiress, after all.

However, Lord Holloway had called more than once. The gentleman had a disconcerting habit of watching Guin while he directed the majority of his conversation to Mrs. Holland. His lordship's sly regard gave her an uneasy prickle down her spine, and she disliked the way he held her hand overlong whenever common civility demanded that she give it to him. On one occasion he had even lightly stroked her wrist with his thumb. She had snatched her hand away, feeling the heat come instantly into her face when she met his heavy-lidded gaze.

Guin said nothing about her discomfiture in Lord Holloway's presence to her mother. She knew well enough what would be Mrs. Holland's reaction. However, she did mention it to her brother, and she was surprised when he forcibly recommended that she maintain as much distance between herself and Lord Holloway as possible.

"Why, Percy, of course I will. But why should I?" asked Guin, surprised by his vehemence.

Lord Holybrooke had frowned. "I can't tell you that yet. But don't let Mama bullock you into encouraging Lord Holloway."

Guin had agreed to it, but with the slightest sinking of her heart. If Lord Holloway requested permission to pay court to her, she knew precisely what would be her mother's answer. Mrs. Holland would leap at the opportunity to see her daughter betrothed to such a distinguished *parti*. Guin wasn't at all certain of her own strength of will in withstanding her mother's wishes. She could only hope that Lord Holloway would continue to hold back a declaration of any sort.

Guin couldn't imagine actually becoming betrothed, but she had come to view the probability with almost fatalistic resignation. If Mrs. Holland had anything to say about the matter, it must be the inevitable conclusion to the London Season. She just hoped that it would be someone other than Lord Holloway.

Not for the first time, Guin reflected that the only gentleman with whom she was acquainted, excepting her brother and Colonel Caldar, of course, that she had ever felt completely comfortable with was Sir Frederick Hawkesworth. However, she thought of that gentleman as so far beyond her that it would be idiotic to ever pretend that he would come to care for her.

Sir Frederick was polished, worldly and a member of the diplomatic corps, whereas she was naught but a tongue-tied provincial. It was marvelous that he had not taken her in instant disgust. Strangely enough, Sir Frederick seemed to like her.

Guin sighed. Liking was not the same as caring. Even she knew that. She wondered, and not for the first time, whom her husband would be. If she knew anything at all about her mother, Mrs. Holland would make certain that the gentleman was a touted catch. If it was not Lord Holloway, it would be someone else equally distinguished in position and title.

Guin wondered what other unacceptable gentleman could be expected to capture her mother's ambitious gaze. It was a worrisome thought that she could not easily overcome. She had long ago accepted that her own opinion counted for nothing in her mother's scheme of things.

If she had but known it, Guin's apprehension over her future was echoed in full measure in her uncle's own mind.

Hidden behind the newspaper and not comprehending a word of what he was staring at, Colonel Caldar reviewed for the thousandth time his unpalatable reflections. He was becoming gravely troubled on his niece's behalf, for he had observed disturbing signs that his sister had turned the sights of her large ambition on achieving a spectacular match for Guin. Mrs. Holland's infatuation with Lord Holloway's northern assets was merely an example.

Indeed, from certain things his sister had let drop, the colonel began to regret that he did not have any right to question what was to be done with his niece's future. He had actually begun to fear that Guin might be thrust into a marriage that she did not care for.

Later, when he broached the matter to his sister, Mrs. Holland merely laughed away his concerns. "My dear brother, Guin will naturally be guided by me. She would never disoblige me by rejecting any suit which *I* found acceptable!"

Colonel Caldar took a turn about the sitting room, his hands clasped behind his back. With a deep frown, he threw over his wide shoulder, "That's just it, Aurelia. My niece is a biddable girl. She is too pliant for her own good. I am not saying that you would force her into a distasteful marriage, but, seeing that you are the stronger personality, you might override her preferences."

"These are mere phantasms, Arnold. I assure you that I shall take the greatest care in choosing a proper husband for my daughter," said Mrs. Holland. She smiled, a somewhat malicious gleam coming into her eyes. "I never took you, a soldier!, to be of a nervous disposition, Arnold."

Colonel Caldar also smiled, but there was little humor in his expression. Somewhat cryptically, he replied, "There are battles and then there are battles, Aurelia. Some have the power to make my blood run cold."

"I don't pretend to understand you," said Mrs. Holland, lifting a shoulder in a dismissive gesture.

"No, you wouldn't," said Colonel Caldar heavily, his unhappy thoughts on his niece's situation.

Mrs. Holland promptly forgot the interview, viewing her brother's concern to be unimportant. She had weightier matters to consider. Mrs. Holland had rarely bothered with her daughter except to take for granted that Guin was always available to fetch and carry for her. However, for several weeks before their removal to London, Mrs. Holland had begun to give some thought to her daughter's future.

She had never had much affection to spare for Guin, not when her son Percy had always commanded the greater portion of her tepid emotions. That had not changed, of course, but it had occurred to Mrs. Holland that her daughter had also gained stature through her son's good fortune.

Driven as always by ambition, Mrs. Holland started to plan for a brilliant marriage for her daughter. It never occurred to her to inquire what Guin's wishes might be, or indeed, to question whether Guin's desires coincided with her own. It mattered nothing. What was of paramount importance to Mrs. Holland was the social and financial status of the gentlemen who could be considered eligible suitors.

With that laudable thought in mind, Mrs. Holland took long, considering stock of her daughter. She concluded that Guin was attractive enough, though woefully inadequate in social skills. That was the fault of having retained an inferior governess, but what she could have done differently when she had had to hire a good tutor for Percy, all on a widow's pension, she didn't know. There was one thing she could do to enhance Guin's chances and, little though she cared for the notion of the expense, Mrs. Holland decided that the investment had to be made.

Mrs. Holland told her daughter of her decision while they were out driving in the park. "We must make the best of you, Guin. I've decided to provide you with a new wardrobe. There must be day dresses and a walking dress or two, a new pelisse, and several gowns. Later, of course, there will be the cost of your court dress to bear."

Guin was completely taken aback. She had never had an extensive wardrobe, and she could not imagine owning even half of what her mother had outlined. Her initial surprise was followed at once by the recollection of what her brother had said about the resources of the estate. She did not want to add to her brother's burden by commanding a large outlay on clothing.

"I really don't need so very much, Mama," said Guin hastily. "I have three day dresses and a perfectly adequate pelisse, so indeed I wish you will not spend a fortune on me."

Mrs. Holland's expression was faintly contemptuous. "My dear Guin! What nonsense you talk! As though you know anything about it, which you don't. I assure you, there is not a gentleman worth the name who would give you a second glance dressed as you are. You give all the appearance of being a schoolgirl in those plain bonnets and gowns, and you are already nine-and-ten! I don't know why I didn't see it before. Much though I grudge the necessity, I shall have to retain the services of a respected modiste."

Guin swallowed nervously, knowing herself to be greatly daring in questioning her parent. "But, Mama, the expense—!"

Mrs. Holland gave a genteel laugh. "Really, Guin, I do not know where you have picked up these bourgeois notions of yours. When I had my come-out, I never gave a thought to the expense, for it was all for the object of making a good match."

"But I do not know that I wish to make a match just yet," blurted Guin. At once, she realized she had made a mistake in airing exactly what was in her mind. She quailed under the gathering wrath in her mother's snapping brown eyes.

"Really, Guin! Sometimes I wonder how I could ever have given birth to you! You are all that is stupid and ungrateful."

The wounding words flowed for several minutes, and by the end Guin felt sick and it was all she could do not to disgrace herself. She no longer even cared that the coachman had probably heard every word and would no doubt repeat the sum of her humiliation to the rest of the household.

"I—I am sorry, Mama," whispered Guin miserably, twisting her gloved hands in her lap.

"So I should hope! I'll not hear another word from you, Guin! You'll do as I say," said Mrs. Holland in a harsh voice. "I will dress you as befits your new station, and you will go to every function that I decide upon, and you will be as conformable as one could wish with whatever gentleman I choose for you! Is that quite understood?"

Mutely, Guin nodded, her tear-burned eyes downcast. Her stomach was tied in knots, and all she wanted was to escape from her mother's displeasure. How much she wished for her brother Percy's comforting presence!

Late that afternoon, when Mrs. Holland was laid down for her habitual hour, Guin had the opportunity to pour out her anguish to her brother. The enormity of her plight made her start to cry again. She searched wildly for a handkerchief, and when she found it, attempted to dry her streaming eyes. Making a valiant effort to choke back her sobs, she exclaimed, "And it's no use saying I must turn Mama up sweet, Percy! I cannot! You know I can't!"

Lord Holybrooke was appalled at the depth of Guin's unhappiness. He had had no notion of it. Having known since childhood that he was the favored one, he had acted as a buffer between Mrs. Holland and his twin sister. Guilt struck him full in the face, for he was uncomfortably aware that he had made himself too scarce to protect her.

"Here, Guin! It will be all right, I swear it! Didn't I tell you that I wouldn't let you be bullied into anything you didn't want?" he said, putting a comforting arm around her shoulders.

"But you're never here anymore!" cried Guin, looking up at him with eyes awash with tears. "And Mama will make me accept someone's offer even if I don't want to!"

Nothing could have been more calculated to deepen Lord Holybrooke's guilt than his sister's unthinking reproach. Of course, Guin didn't intend it to sound that way, but nevertheless a fellow had to read between the lines.

Since that first evening upon their arrival in town, the young Earl of Holybrooke had made swift strides into popularity. Indeed, Colonel Caldar joked that his nephew had left all of them behind, so fast had the invitations come. All of the family were included in invitations from hostesses. However, many times Lord Holybrooke was pressed to join other young nobles in their manly pursuits in activities that naturally did not include the females of one's family.

At first, the earl had been reluctant to leave his mother and sister so often, but Mrs. Holland and Guin had both urged him not to turn down invitations on their account. He thought now, and with what he felt was justifiable irritation, that the present crisis was what came of accepting those assurances so blithely.

"I should have known something like this would happen," he muttered. "You and Mama have never been able to be in the same room for an hour without some rumpus being kicked up."

Guin was quick to catch the bitter note in his voice. She drew back slightly, staring wide-eyed at him. "Are—are you angry with me, Percy?" she faltered, almost in disbelief.

"No, of course I am not! I just meant that I know what Mama is, and I should have been here to take care of you. I shall say something to her, Guin," said Lord Holybrooke.

Guin sighed, gesturing almost despairingly with her hand. "I am sorry to be such trouble, Percy. Indeed, if I could do anything else, I would not even tell you! But I haven't anyone else, except our uncle, and Mama will never pay the least heed to anyone but you."

Lord Holybrooke's mouth firmed, and there came a steely flash into his eyes. "I promise you that I shall take care of you just as I always have, Guin. And I will speak to Mama directly, too. I'll tell her that I will want to approve any offer made to you. How will that be?"

Guin looked at him, hope leaping into her drowned eyes. "Oh, will you, Percy?"

"I will as soon as I find the proper moment," he said resolutely.

Guin snatched up his hand and caught it against her damp cheek. "Thank you, Percy!"

"Don't be such a goose, Guin," said Lord Holybrooke, somewhat embarrassed, as he regained possession of his hand.

Chapter Eleven

Guin nervously regarded herself in the mahogany cheval glass. Obedient to her maid's injunction, she stood still while the finishing touches were put to her toilette. She was attired in one of her new carriage dresses, which was vastly becoming to her. The dark green admirably showed off her trim figure. Her straw bonnet, trimmed with matching green ribbons, was a charming frame for her black curls, deep blue eyes and heart-shaped face.

However, Guin's thoughts were far from the pretty picture she made. Her heart pounded and she could scarcely breathe. It was always so when she was required to attend her mother on social calls. She dreaded it. However, it would never do to let her mother see it. Her one consolation was that her brother Percy had agreed to accompany them that afternoon.

At the thought of her twin brother, Guin took a steadying breath. Her tumbling thoughts stilled. She could rely on Percy. He wouldn't leave her to drown in her own inanity.

"There you are, miss." The maid eased back on her heels and looked admiringly at her mistress's reflected image. "My, you look a real treat, Miss Guineveve."

Guin gave a fleeting glance at herself, but it did not give her confidence. The paramount thought in her mind at that moment was not even the pending social engagement, but her mother. She had not yet been summoned to join Mrs. Holland.

"Has Mrs. Holland sent for me yet?" she asked, looking at her maid in the glass.

Morgan pursed her lips. She got up and began busying herself with putting away discarded articles of clothing. "Yes, miss. This five minutes past."

Guin gasped in dismay, whirling away from the mirror with a rustle of fabric. "And you did not tell me!"

Morgan's face was wooden, though there was a spark of sympathy in the glance she shot her mistress. "You were not turned out decent, miss."

"As though that mattered!" exclaimed Guin. She snatched up her reticule and hastily crossed the small room to the bedroom door.

"Indeed, and the mistress would have scolded you had you made such unseemly haste that you neglected any part of your toilette," said Morgan. "She'll be more content now that you're ready, miss."

Guin faltered, her hand on the brass knob, and glanced back at her maid. She knew well enough that it was true. Her mother would have condemned any sign of untidiness. Yet she still wished that the message had been delivered to her. "I must go downstairs at once," she said, and left the bedroom.

Guin flew down to the front parlor, dreading the inevitable scold she would receive for keeping her mother waiting. Her stomach was already churning. However, Mrs. Holland was not in evidence, and only Lord Holybrooke was in the front parlor. "Thank God," murmured Guin to herself, trying to calm her quickened breathing.

The earl rose upon his sister's precipitate entrance. He gave a low whistle of appreciation as he looked her over. "Very fine, Guin, I must say!"

Guin gave a small laugh. Her nervous tension dissipated under her brother's teasing smile. "Thank you, Percy! But I am not nearly as smart as you, dear brother."

"Oh, well! Not everyone in the family can aspire to becoming a Tulip of fashion," said Lord Holybrooke on a laugh. He was wearing a new superfine coat over a pair of pale pantaloons. The high gloss of his boots shone not a speck of dust. He put his hand up to his snow-white cravat, which was tied in an intricate fashion. "I have attempted a new way of tying my neckcloths. Do you like it, Guin? Sir Frederick Hawkesworth put me in the way of it."

"Indeed, Percy, it is very dapper dog," said Guin, twinkling at him. "I must dash off a note of thanks to Sir Frederick for his kind offices."

"You wouldn't! No, of course you wouldn't. Lord, Guin, don't even joke about such a solecism. You don't know him very well yet, I daresay. Well, it stands to reason. You stood up with him at Lady Smythe's ball, and a handful of other times since, and have been driving with him only once," said Lord Holybrooke.

"I met Sir Frederick again at Mama's rout last week. He—he was very kind," interposed Guin, delicate color tingeing her cheeks.

"I daresay he was. What I meant to tell you, Sir Frederick is a great fellow, not one to look down on one because he is older or more knowing," said Lord Holybrooke. "I have met him any number of places, and he always has a civil word to say to me. I have asked Mama to put his name on her guest list for that dinner ball she is throwing for you."

"Have you?" asked Guin, her color mounting. "I am glad, for I like him very well."

Lord Holybrooke looked keenly at her. "Guin, do you—"

Mrs. Holland bustled into the room. She was pulling on her gloves. She glanced at her son, smiling with patent fondness. Then she turned her glance on her daughter to look her over, nodding in critical approval. "Well, I perceive that you are both waiting for me, so let us not tarry a moment longer. I am glad you decided to accompany us to the Beasely's for tea, Percival. It is so gratifying to have a male escort when one goes to call."

"I am certain my uncle would be happy to fill that

place, Mama," said Lord Holybrooke blandly, slanting a mischievous glance toward his sister.

Guin smothered a smile with her hand. She knew without any word said that her brother was bent on teasing their mother. Mrs. Holland could always be aroused to protest whenever Lord Holybrooke announced his intention to abandon her to Colonel Caldar's escort.

For once Mrs. Holland did not rise to the bait. She had already garnered the earl's promise to accompany her that afternoon, and nothing could ruffle her equanimity. "Your uncle's escort can hardly compare with yours, dearest," said Mrs. Holland complacently. "After all, you are an earl!"

Lord Holybrooke rolled his eyes in exasperation, his amusement suddenly extinguished. A frown shadowed his face as he said woodenly, "May I offer you my arm, Mama?"

Sublimely unaware that she had offended her son, Mrs. Holland agreed that he could. Lord Holybrooke left the front parlor with the two ladies most dear to him on either side.

It was left to Guin to feel every sympathy for his frustration. More than anyone, she knew how often her brother had remonstrated with their mother about her constant references to his title with little effect.

Lord Holybrooke did not offer much more than monosyllabic replies to Mrs. Holland's stream of light conversation during the carriage ride. Guin made an effort to fill the gap to cover up her brother's withdrawal. Her efforts met with an unexpected and unprecedented commendation from Mrs. Holland.

"I am glad to see that you are in such good form, Guin. I trust that you will be able to carry it forward during our call on Lady Beasely," said Mrs. Holland over her shoulder as she got out of the carriage.

"I hope so, too, Mama," said Guin, descending from the carriage on her brother's extended hand. Lord Holybrooke muttered something under his breath, a rather pointed reference to his mother's behavior. Guin pinched his arm warningly as they accompanied Mrs. Holland into the town house and were ushered upstairs into Lady Beasely's presence.

Lady Beasely was a widow, apparently left with considerable funds so that she was able to live in the first style of elegance. She was an aristocrat to her fingertips, cool and gracious and superior. Guin still remembered how annoyed her mother had been with her earlier in the Season when she had been too preoccupied to respond to an inquiry made by Lady Beasely. Mrs. Holland set store by her acquaintance with Lady Beasely. The thought of committing a faux pas while partaking of Lady Beasely's hospitality, and under her mother's eye, filled Guin with renewed foreboding.

However, it wasn't going to be half as dreadful as Guin thought it might be. She realized quickly that Lady Beasely scarcely noticed her existence. Her ladyship was not uncivil, but she did little to recognize Guin except to address a polite remark now and again to her that did not require an answer.

It was Lord Holybrooke who garnered most of the attention, allowing Guin to more easily fade into the background. Lady Beasely had greeted Mrs. Holland and her daughter with a few welcoming words, but from the outset she reserved her widest smile for the young Earl of Holybrooke.

"My Lord Holybrooke! I had extended my invitation through your mother to include you, but I scarcely dared hope that I would see you this afternoon. It is a pleasure, my lord. Allow me to introduce my eldest daughter, Miss Margaret Beasely, who is coming out this Season!" said Lady Beasely, bringing forward the young lady standing beside her.

Lord Holybrooke gravely acknowledged the introduction, an unreadable expression in his gray-blue eyes. He bowed over Miss Beasely's slim hand when she presented it to him. "Miss Beasely, I am honored to make your acquaintance."

"Oh, the honor is entirely mine, my lord, I assure

you!" said Miss Beasely, gazing at the earl with brilliant green eyes. Her smile was an attractive flash of white, even teeth. She was a handsome redhead, pale-complexioned with a delicious sprinkle of golden freckles across her well-shaped nose. The expression in her face was lively. Guin thought with an inward sigh that Miss Beasely would have little difficulty in filling her dance cards.

After urging her guests to make themselves comfortable, Lady Beasely turned to her daughter. "Margaret, will you pour?"

"Certainly, Mama," said Miss Beasely, at once taking competent command of the tea tray. As Guin watched, Miss Beasely poured tea and added just the right amount of cream and lumps of sugar to each cup before handing them round.

Guin sighed enviously. How she would like to be able to acquit herself so well. The one time Mrs. Holland had told her to pour tea, she had overturned the cup into her mother's lap and had her ears soundly boxed. Guin still did not understand how she had come to do such a hideous thing.

Lady Beasely and her daughter set themselves to entertain. Guin sat quietly by, carefully sipping from her porcelain cup, while her mother and her brother conversed. She was content to listen. She knew her own conversational skills to be sadly lacking, and hesitated to take part when she knew her mother would judge every syllable coming out of her mouth.

Guin glanced with a fond smile at her twin brother. It was otherwise with Percy, of course. He had always possessed a glib tongue. Whereas she was awkward and ill at ease in making conversation, he had the ability to converse easily with practically anyone.

At last Mrs. Holland rose to take her leave, giving cue to her children that the visit had come to an end. Lady Beasely and her daughter expressed their mutual regret, but pressed Mrs. Holland to be certain to call again and promised to reciprocate very soon.

As the Holland ladies and Lord Holybrooke were ushered toward the door, Miss Beasely said warmly, "Miss Holland, I am determined that we are to become friends."

Guin would have been flattered if Miss Beasely's eyes had been focused on her instead of on her brother. She started to murmur a polite civility, when her mother interrupted her.

"How kind of you, Miss Beasely! I am positive my daughter is as conscious of it as I am," said Mrs. Holland. She directed a pointed look at her daughter. "Are you not, Guin?"

"Yes, Mama," said Guin obediently. "It—it is very kind of you, Miss Beasely."

Miss Beasely bestowed a dazzling smile on Guin and squeezed her hand. Guin was surprised that Miss Beasely had actually met her eyes; indeed, she had actually looked at her and seen her. A small warm feeling fleeted through Guin. Perhaps Miss Beasely had been sincere in her offer of friendship, after all. It was something nice to think about.

"We shall send an invitation to our dinner party next month," said Lady Beasely. She held out her hand to Lord Holybrooke, her smile glinting. "I hope you will not be otherwise engaged, my lord."

Lord Holybrooke bowed with a smile, uttering something civil and noncommittal, before ushering out his mother and sister. When he had handed them up into their carriage and climbed in himself, he threw himself back against the upholstered seat squab with an exhausted air. "Mama, I beg you will hold me excused from the Beasely affair. Perhaps my uncle can escort you and Guin that evening."

"Naturally, if you do not wish it, there is nothing more to be said," said Mrs. Holland equably, though, with an inflection of surprise.

Guin glanced at her brother with a teasing smile. She had observed how well received the earl had been and formed her own conclusions. "Miss Beasely will be gravely disappointed if you were to cry off, Percy."

Lord Holybrooke grimaced wryly. He thrust his hands deep into his pockets. "Have done, Guin, I pray you."

"Whatever can you mean, Guin?" asked Mrs. Holland with a hint of pique. She did not like that her children shared some understanding to which she was not privy.

"Come, Mama, surely it was as plain to you as it was to Guin and me," said Lord Holybrooke with a touch of impatience. "Lady Beasely and Miss Beasely have decided I am an eligible suitor for Miss Beasely's hand."

Mrs. Holland stared. Blinded by her own bias, she had seen nothing extraordinary in the attention lavished upon her son. Now she swiftly recovered herself, unwilling to appear wanting in her son's eyes. "Of course I noticed! Why, the very idea is absurd! You are too young to wed. And when it is time, we shall look much higher for a suitable bride than Miss Beasely!"

Guin glanced down at her hands clasped in her lap. According to her mother, Percy was too young to be wed; but she was not. Perhaps it was different for females, she thought dismally, for surely her mother must know best.

"It won't do to cut Lady Beasely and her daughter from our acquaintance, however. They are very well connected, and I would hesitate to offend them. After all, there must be any number of scheming females wishing to throw their daughters at your head, Percy, and we cannot avoid them all," said Mrs. Holland reflectively.

"That's not a comforting thought, Mama," said Lord Holybrooke with a quick grin.

"However, I feel that you need not dance attendance on Miss Beasely," said Mrs. Holland decisively. "Or any other young lady, if it comes to that. I shouldn't like to see you leap into any entanglement which you might later regret!"

"I heartily agree with you, Mama," said Lord Holybrooke. The earl glanced swiftly at his sister's downcast face. "And don't you think that we should go slowly with Guin, as well? After all, we wouldn't wish her to make a mistake in her choice, either."

Guin looked up quickly, hopefully, glancing from her brother to her mother. She awaited with fast-beating heart for her mother's reply. The vivid memory of the unpleasant interlude earlier in the week still had the power to make her shudder. She had not dared to proffer an opinion on any of her mother's subsequent decisions concerning her wardrobe. She had agreed with everything, even the cutting of her hair in a smart crop. She was vaguely aware that she had never appeared more attractive, but her overwhelming anxiety to please her mother overrode all other considerations. She felt like a tricked-out doll, nodding and smiling and silent, even though her heart quailed inside her breast at her mother's continued allusions to eligible suitors.

Now Lord Holybrooke had seized the opening offered, just as he had promised he would, and spoke up in her defense. Guin thought Percy had been very clever. She waited with baited breath for what her mother might say to her brother's carefully constructed question.

Mrs. Holland smiled and shook her head in a tolerant fashion. Without even glancing at her daughter, she said, "Well, it is a bit different for Guin, dear Percy. Young females should be wed as soon as possible. That is really why we have come to town for the Season. I wish to see your sister suitably established."

"I shouldn't want Guin to accept the first offer made to her, Mama. I wouldn't be easy in my mind," said Lord Holybrooke firmly. "I should like to get to know some of these gentlemen before we begin encouraging any of them."

"Well, of course!" Mrs. Holland laughed. "How nonsensical you are, to be sure, Percy! And that is a very good notion of yours. I would be very interested to hear whatever you may tell me about the gentlemen which might be considered eligible for your sister's hand."

"Rest assured that I shall do my best to further Guin's interests," said Lord Holybrooke earnestly.

Mrs. Holland bestowed a fond smile on her son. "You have always been my greatest consolation, Percy."

Guin stole her hand into her brother's and squeezed his long fingers gratefully. With Percy on her side, she knew that everything would work out as well as could be expected, for their mother never denied Percy anything he wanted. And if he objected to her marrying someone on the score that he didn't like the gentleman, Guin rather thought their mother might listen.

"I think you are the best of brothers, Percy," she said, conveying her feelings as best she could without betraying the trend of her thoughts.

"I am glad to see that you are properly grateful, Guin," said Mrs. Holland.

"On the contrary, I am grateful to Guin. Her company has always been good for me; you know it has, Mama," said Lord Holybrooke casually, but returning the pressure of his sister's hand to show he understood.

"Yes, I am fully persuaded of Guin's loyalty to you. She has always been willing to fetch and carry and bear you company whenever you have been bored," said Mrs. Holland. She gave a rare smile to her daughter. "It is the best thing I know of you, Guin."

"Thank you, Mama," said Guin, quick tears starting to her eyes. She was overwhelmed by her mother's generous comment.

"Then, you must see, Mama, that I do not wish Guin married off entirely at once," said Lord Holybrooke in a persuasive tone. "I should miss her company."

There was a short silence, while Mrs. Holland began to frown. Of a sudden she tossed her head. Somewhat pettishly, she said, "Well, we shall see what comes of the Season. I anticipate a positive whirl of engagements once it is more widely known the Earl of Holybrooke is in residence. And I have every intention of making the most of our opportunities! So pray put your best foot forward, Guin!"

"Yes, Mama," said Guin, breathing a small sigh of relief. She glanced at her brother and caught his conspiratorial wink. Her heart was warmed, just by knowing her brother was willing to help her.

However, Mrs. Holland had the last word. "In any event, I should think with an earl for a brother that you won't lack for opportunity."

Chapter Twelve

Guin counted heavily on her brother's continued support. When he had spoken up for her after their morning call to Lady Beasely, she had felt quite hopeful. However, Lord Holybrooke's social engagements commanded more and more of his time. He tried to cry off from various invitations, but it was difficult to extricate himself when his friends urged him to reconsider.

Guin quite understood the dilemma that her brother found himself in even before Lord Holybrooke took her aside to explain it to her, but it was difficult to assure him that she did not mind. She watched, her hope dwindling, as her brother seemed once again to forget her.

Once more, Guin was at the mercy of her mother's overweening ambition. Mrs. Holland was cultivating Lord Holloway with such blatant encouragement, Guin did not believe his lordship could possibly misunderstand that an offer from him would be accepted.

Guin thought the Season could hold no greater apprehension for her until a fresh alarm raised up suddenly in her face.

Lady Smythe finally made good on her pledged word to Sir Frederick Hawkesworth by paying a morning call on the Holland ladies.

When her ladyship's card was taken up, Mrs. Holland exclaimed with pleasure. She at once directed the butler to show Lady Smythe up to the front parlor. "Depend upon it, Guin, her ladyship has come to pay her respects because Percy has stepped into the title," said Mrs. Holland complacently.

Since Guin could think of no other reason for someone of Lady Smythe's social standing to recognize them with a visit, she accepted her mother's explanation without question.

As Lady Smythe entered, Mrs. Holland bustled forward to receive her. "My lady! Such a treat for us that you have chosen to call!" She at once offered refreshment, which her ladyship declined in a civil manner on the grounds that she had just breakfasted.

Lady Smythe shook hands with her hostess and nodded casually to Guin, who had also risen to murmur a polite welcome. "I am glad to have found you both at home, Mrs. Holland. I trust that I am not keeping you from an engagement?"

Mrs. Holland laughed to scorn the very suggestion. She urged the exalted visitor to a comfortable chair in front of the fire before seating herself opposite and waving her daughter to the settee. "Of course not, Lady Smythe. We could have nothing more important to do when you have come to call!"

Lady Smythe smiled politely, but she appeared a trifle bored. She turned to Guin. "I trust you enjoyed yourself at my ball, Miss Holland?"

Guin opened her mouth to reply, but her mother forestalled her.

"Of course we did, my lady! How could it be otherwise?" exclaimed Mrs. Holland with a small laugh. "You must forgive my daughter, Lady Smythe. She is sometimes behind in expressing her gratitude for the many kindnesses that have been showered upon her since we have come to town."

Guin sighed. She summoned up a properly grateful smile for Lady Smythe's benefit. In a somewhat wooden voice, she said, "Indeed, I enjoyed myself prodigiously, my lady."

"There! Did I not say so? I am quite sorry that my son, Lord Holybrooke, is not at home, for I am certain that he, also, would like to express his appreciation of your hospitality, my lady," said Mrs. Holland with her lovely smile in place.

Lady Smythe's shrewd eyes held a disconcerting gleam. "I have not a doubt of it being just as you say, Mrs. Holland," she said dryly.

Mrs. Holland, quite unconscious of the gentle sarcasm in her ladyship's tone, again laughed. "Oh, Percy is quite the accomplished gentleman, I do assure you!"

Guin glanced, startled, at Lady Smythe. Her ear was more discerning than her mother's. She realized at once that mockery tinged her ladyship's agreement with her mother, and the knowledge brought a flush to her cheeks. As always, her loyalties emboldened her. "It was a very fine evening, indeed, my lady. We are beginning to receive many invitations, but I trust we shall not have a prior engagement when next you entertain, Lady Smythe!"

It was the longest speech Guin had ever made in company. She was amazed at her own temerity. She sank back against the settee cushions, doubts assailing her as to the wisdom of her contribution.

Guin was not the only one surprised. Mrs. Holland regarded her daughter with open astonishment mixed with dismay. "Why, Guin! Whatever will her ladyship think of you?"

Lady Smythe merely inclined her head. With a definite smile for Guin, she said that she hoped not indeed. "Which brings me in a roundabout way to my business to you today, Mrs. Holland," said Lady Smythe, turning her gaze back to her hostess. "I hope to be of some small service to you."

"Why, of course, my lady!" said Mrs. Holland, the puzzled expression in her eyes at complete variance with her gratified air. "But I really cannot imagine what—"

Lady Smythe smoothly interrupted her. "I chanced to observe Miss Holland's company manners the other evening, which I can no doubt ascribe to your training, Mrs. Holland, and I was impressed by the thought that I should like to take Miss Holland a little under my wing.

As she is just coming out, I am certain you could not object if I were to give her a few hints on how to go on."

"Of course I would not object! It is certainly a kindness which I never looked for, my lady!" exclaimed Mrs. Holland. The throb of excitement in her voice was audible.

Lady Smythe nodded as though she had had every expectation of acceptance. "I have often observed how backward many young misses are upon their come-out. I am certain you know precisely what I refer to, Mrs. Holland."

Mrs. Holland glanced at her daughter, and her lips thinned a little. There was little of maternal pride in her eyes. "Oh, yes, I do know, ma'am." She looked back at her guest, her smile sliding firmly back into place. She said in an earnest voice, "Believe me, I wish every possible advantage for my daughter. Alas, she is naught but a country miss, and I quite despair at times of bringing her into fashion!"

Guin bit her lip and lowered her eyes, feeling the heat of humiliation rise up in her face. She wished she was everything her mother wanted her to be. It was an old yearning, one that she had had from childhood and one that brought with it a depressed feeling of hopelessness. It was made all the worse in this instance because her mother held up her shortcomings to this elegant lady. Guin felt ready to sink into the floor.

"It must be a severe trial, situated as you are with a daughter to be credibly gotten off your hands and a son who is just beginning to appreciate the responsibilities of his new station," said Lady Smythe conversationally.

"Indeed, my lady! It is just as you say," agreed Mrs. Holland. Seemingly overcome, she searched for her handkerchief. When she had found it, she dabbed carefully at the corners of her eyes. "Forgive me! I have always been of a delicate nature, and the circumstances quite overpower me if I allow myself to dwell on them. However, I do not begrudge any effort that will advance the cause of my children!"

"I have always been of a disgustingly strong constitution, nor do I possess any children, and so I have not myself experienced such exquisite sensibility as you seem to possess in such full measure, Mrs. Holland," said Lady Smythe astringently.

Guin gasped, completely shaken out of her self-pity. It had actually sounded as though Lady Smythe had delivered a crushing set-down.

Mrs. Holland apparently thought the same. She stared at her ladyship, the handkerchief suspended in midair.

Lady Smythe seemed to realize that she had lapsed in her manners. She summoned up a polite smile. "Pray do not take me amiss. Many of my friends have lamented to me, Mrs. Holland, of the time and expense involved in bringing out their daughters. It appears at best a tiresome necessity and at worst a plaguey nuisance."

"It is unfortunately too true," sighed Mrs. Holland, drooping gracefully in an affected attitude. She waved her handkerchief. "Why, I have had to completely outfit Guin with a new wardrobe since coming to town. What was proper when we lived secluded simply would not do in London! As for the time I have already invested, I assure you that it exhausts me simply to contemplate it."

"Perhaps I may be of even greater service to you, then. I find myself unutterably bored by the prospect of yet another stale Season. If you felt able to relinquish the responsibility, it would amuse me to bring Miss Holland out under my aegis," said Lady Smythe with a casual air.

"What?" exclaimed Guin. She regarded Lady Smythe incredulously. Her ladyship had dropped the stunning announcement as though it was the merest commonplace.

Lady Smythe appeared totally unaware of Guin's shock. Her ladyship had the slightest smile touching her thin lips, while her rather cold blue gaze was fixed on her hostess. "Well, Mrs. Holland?"

Mrs. Holland had sat bolt upright, her eyes widened to a stare. Her mouth had dropped half open from astonishment. She appeared unable to draw a proper breath, and her reply was faint. "My lady!"

Lady Smythe threw up a bejeweled hand. "Oh, I know

what you will say! You are devoted to your children, and it will be difficult to part with your daughter!"

"Oh, no, no. At least, of course it will be difficult but—"

"And no doubt you find it strange that I should offer to take such a personal hand in what are your affairs!" said Lady Smythe.

"I would never say that it was *strange*! After all, my son is the Earl of Holybrooke, and his rank must certainly excite some interest. Indeed, I would have thought that he— Certainly I never expected that you would take an interest in *Guin*!" exclaimed Mrs. Holland.

Guin glanced at her mother, a familiar hurt plunging into her heart. Momentarily Lady Smythe's stated purpose was overridden by her oft repeated, despair-tinged thoughts. She could never measure up. She would never be found worthy in her mother's estimation of the least consideration.

"Well, I do know something about young ladies and how they should go on, whereas I would not dream of squiring a young gentleman through his first Season," said Lady Smythe smoothly, obviously amused by Mrs. Holland's patent assumption. "I would far rather leave that to your discretion, ma'am!"

"Of course! Indeed, I am more nearly concerned with furthering Percy's interests than anyone else could be!" said Mrs. Holland. Speculation gleamed in her eyes as she thoughtfully regarded Lady Smythe.

"Then, have we a bargain? For I am persuaded that one of your . . . delicate nature would find it far less fatiguing if I took a hand with your daughter," said Lady Smythe, showing her teeth in a somewhat satirical smile.

Guin turned her astonished gaze from Lady Smythe to glance at her mother. What she saw in Mrs. Holland's expression sent a frisson of alarm through her. "Mama! Pray do not—"

"Hush, Guin!" said Mrs. Holland with a minatory frown. Quickly, she said, "Though it pains me to give her up, my lady, I am also cognizant of the kindness of your offer. I do not begrudge the sacrifice of my own sentiments, however, when it is a question of my children's welfare."

"Mama!" exclaimed Guin again, though with little hope that her mother would attend. Indeed, Mrs. Holland did not even glance her way, all of her attention being focused on Lady Smythe and her extraordinary offer.

"Very well!" Lady Smythe rose to her feet, obviously ready to take her leave. "I shall certainly see what I can do on your daughter's behalf. Miss Holland, I can see very well that you are completely taken aback, so I shall not press you for an exchange of civilities over this business. There will be time enough to become better acquainted, I assure you! Good-bye, Mrs. Holland! No, there is no need to show me to the door, for I know my way well enough."

Mrs. Holland nevertheless solicitously accompanied Lady Smythe downstairs. When that lady had departed, Mrs. Holland came back upstairs to the parlor where her daughter was awaiting her. Mrs. Holland was in an expansive mood. Her eyes were alight, and a smile hovered over her mouth. For once, she looked at her daughter with unqualified approval. "Well! What have you to say to this day's events, my dear Guin? I never looked for anything so fortunate!"

Guin found her voice. Suppositions and conjectures had seethed through her brain during her mother's absence. "But, Mama, what does it mean? Surely I am not to go live with Lady Smythe!"

"If that is what her ladyship wishes, you certainly shall. I am utterly astonished at your good fortune, that someone as well connected as Lady Smythe should have taken a liking to you! Of course, if Percy had not become Lord Holybrooke, the case would undoubtedly have been quite different!' said Mrs. Holland.

"Mama, I know you have placed much emphasis on the title having come to Percy, but surely there must be more than that to explain Lady Smythe's incredible offer," said Guin, stammering a little in her haste to get out everything that was in her tumbling thoughts. It was not possible that someone as exalted as Lady Smythe should care as much as Mrs. Holland seemed to think her ladyship did who had ascended to the earldom. Yet it seemed equally impossible to Guin that Lady Smythe, on the basis of a few moments' exchange of civilities during a ball, should have decided to lend her aegis for Guin's come-out.

"Why, are you thinking that Lady Smythe is taking you up on your own account? What absurd vanity is this?" said Mrs. Holland brutally. She shook her head with a pitying look of contempt for her daughter. "I can assure you that it has nothing at all to do with you, Guin!"

As always, Guin was crushed by her mother's denigration. Whatever else she might have voiced shriveled inside her, left unsaid. She made a small, hopeless gesture. "I wished you understood, Mama."

"Understand what, Guin? I find you incomprehensible," said Mrs. Holland with frowning impatience.

Chapter Thirteen

At that moment Colonel Caldar walked into the room. He nodded civilly to his sister, but directed a fond smile at his niece. "Here you are! I was on the point of going out to exercise my team. I thought you might like to drive with me, Guin. You need not tell me that you don't wish to go, Aurelia, for I know it already. You've told me any number of times that you can't abide my driving."

Mrs. Holland paid not the least heed to her brother's statement. Instead she hurried forward to take her brother's arm with both hands in an urgent grasp. "Arnold! You will scarcely believe what has just happened. My breath is taken away by sheer surprise, I assure you!"

"Indeed?" Colonel Caldar noticed that his niece did not appear to be as excited as her mother. Guin had turned away and walked toward the window overlooking the street. There seemed to be some tension in the way she held herself.

Colonel Caldar was all at once concerned. He patted Mrs. Holland's hands and gently pried himself loose from her clutching fingers. "There, now! Pray do not keep me in suspense, Aurelia."

"Lady Smythe came to call, which in itself was quite unusual, for we do not know her at all well. And the purpose of her call! Her ladyship wishes to help me bring Guin out!" said Mrs. Holland in a dramatic rush. She regarded her brother with an expectant air. "What have you to say to that, Arnold! Is it not marvelous?"

Colonel Caldar was as incredulous as his sister could have wished. "Why, what has brought this about?"

Mrs. Holland gave a delighted laugh. She made a dismissive gesture to show she thought the question unimportant. Nevertheless she answered, "Guin would have it that Lady Smythe has some hidden motive, but as you might imagine, I quickly corrected her. It is all because of Percy, of course. Everyone is anxious to become acquainted with the new Earl of Holybrooke, and naturally they will be very obliging toward us all."

Mrs. Holland spoke in self-congratulatory accents that earned her a swift, backward glance from her daughter. If she had seen Guin's doubtful expression, she would have taken instant umbrage. However, Mrs. Holland's attention was all on her brother as she eagerly awaited his comment.

"Naturally," repeated Colonel Caldar, though with a dubious intonation. A crease formed between his sandy brows. "I still do not understand how Percy's good fortune has influenced Lady Smythe to such a high degree, Aurelia."

Guin had turned around to listen. Her uncle's observation made her pluck up her courage. "Nor do I, Uncle. Surely it—it is nonsensical to suppose that Lady Smythe has taken me in such liking on a mere handshake and short introduction at her ladyship's ball?"

"Nothing could be more unlikely, as I have told you," said Mrs. Holland waspishly. "Pray do not pretend, Guin, that out of silly vanity you do not secretly hope it is yourself who has captivated her ladyship's interest!"

"No, Mama, I—"

"Let me reassure you that nothing could be further from the truth," interrupted Mrs. Holland. "Her ladyship is being very obliging so that I might concentrate on Percy's social progress. Lady Smythe has no particular interest in you!"

As Colonel Caldar had seen so many times in the past, his niece did not argue with her mother but merely bowed her head. He spoke more sharply than he intended. "Is that what Lady Smythe told you, Aurelia?"

Mrs. Holland jumped. "Well, not in so many words, of course! But certainly her ladyship implied it. Really, Arnold, I must take exception to your tone of voice. It is very displeasing to me."

Colonel Caldar ignored his sister's offended expression. His mind turned over the meager information he had been given. He wondered if this was not just what would most benefit his niece. After all, Lady Smythe was a famous hostess and possessed élan to the nth degree. There could not be a better example for Guin to emulate. "What precisely has Lady Smythe offered?" he asked slowly.

"Oh, I don't know! What does it matter, really? Lady Smythe has pledged herself to see Guin through the Season," said Mrs. Holland dismissively. "Isn't that enough?"

"Mama says that I am to go live with Lady Smythe if her ladyship wishes it!" said Guin, a quiver in her voice.

"Yes, and why not? It is more than I ever hoped for you," said Mrs. Holland, rounding on her daughter. "Your opportunities will be greatly enhanced by Lady Smythe's generosity, so do not become missish on me, Guin!"

Colonel Caldar had given thought to what he had been told and, with his soldier's training, quickly made up his mind. Now he said, "Guin, much as you might dislike it, it might be the very thing for you."

Guin reacted as though she had been struck, swaying back on her feet. "Uncle! How can you say so?" She took several rapid steps toward Colonel Caldar, her wide eyes riveted on his square face. Her own face was white. "I should have to leave Percy!"

"My dear, I rather think that Percy has already left you," said Colonel Caldar with brusque gentleness. He watched, not without sympathy, as his niece's eyes grew wider and more apprehensive. He closed the distance between them and lifted one of her unresisting hands, folding it between his own square ones in a comforting hold. "Did you not realize it would come to this, sooner or later, Guin? Why, Percy has been jauntering about town for weeks now. We all see less and less of him. Perhaps your mother is right. Perhaps this is a happy solution to an unhappy circumstance. I doubt that Lady Smythe will actually require you to take up residence with her, but even if it is so, I urge you to consider it carefully."

Mrs. Holland nodded agreement. "You see, even your uncle, who is not at all beforehand with the fashionable world, is able to see all the advantages."

"No, no! I will not go! I will not!" exclaimed Guin, wresting her hand from her uncle's clasp. She covered her cheeks with her hands, half turning away. Unshed tears shimmered on her lashes. Her mind was in a whirl. She didn't blame her uncle, but how she wished he had upheld her! More than anything, however, she was unutterably hurt by her mother's easy relinquishment of her to a virtual stranger.

"Guin, you will stop this nonsense at once! I vow I could shake you!" exclaimed Mrs. Holland, extremely displeased by her daughter's unreasonable attitude.

"Be kinder, Aurelia," said Colonel Caldar in a warning voice.

Mrs. Holland shot an angered glance at her brother. "Guin is my daughter, Arnold. I shall speak to her just as I ought."

Colonel Caldar's face hardened, but he bit back what he dearly wished to say.

Mrs. Holland advanced on her shrinking daughter and grabbed her arm. She pulled Guin around. Her expression was furious. "I have already pledged my word to Lady Smythe and, indeed, I think it high time that you were weaned a little from your brother! Such freakish airs are highly unbecoming, let me tell you!"

"Why not go out driving with me, Guin. The fresh air will cool your head," said Colonel Caldar quickly. He had taken a hasty step forward, but caught himself back from actual physical interference.

"Yes, brother! Take her with you, for I am out of all patience," said Mrs. Holland, flinging away her daughter's arm. "Pray do not keep your uncle waiting! Go fetch your hat, Guin!"

Guin fled from the parlor, the tears running down her cheeks.

It was nearly a quarter hour later when Guin returned downstairs. She had changed into a becoming carriage dress with mother-of-pearl buttons and put on a bonnet. Her eyes were dry, but she wore a woebegone expression. Her mother was nowhere in evidence, for which Guin was grateful.

Colonel Caldar was waiting in the deserted entry hall. He glanced at his niece quickly as he offered his elbow. Guin said not a word as her uncle escorted her out of the town house, down the front steps to the carriage, not even to thank him when he helped her up onto the seat.

Colonel Caldar climbed up on the other side, the seat shifting on the springs with his weight. He said a quiet word to the groom, who was set to jump up onto the back of the equipage, and the servant stepped back up onto the walkway. Colonel Caldar took up his whip and started the team. Once the horses were moving, he glanced over again at his niece.

Guin was gazing straight ahead. Her bonnet was a delightful poke with a broad brim, so Colonel Caldar could not see all of her face as she looked forward. He uncomfortably cleared his throat. "Guin, I know how you must feel."

At that, she turned her head. The anguish was plain in her darkened eyes. "No, how could you? Mama is tossing me aside as though—as though—" Her voice became wholly suspended. She searched frantically in her reticule for her handkerchief.

Colonel Caldar very kindly pulled a large linen square from out of his coat pocket and proffered it.

Guin snatched the handkerchief from him and defiantly mopped her streaming eyes. "I was so determined not to cry!"

"You certainly have every reason to cry, my dear," said Colonel Caldar sympathetically. He shook his head.

"I don't know how you've withstood it this long. Aurelia is a wretch to treat you so."

"No, no! It is not Mama's fault. It is just that I am so stupid and awkward and have no conversation," said Guin tightly, twisting the dampened handkerchief between her slim gloved fingers. "I don't blame Mama for having so little patience with me. Or—or for wanting to be rid of—of me!"

Colonel Caldar growled something beneath his breath. He turned to her and said earnestly, "Guin, you must listen to me! You are none of those things. You are a lovely girl with many fine qualities, but you haven't been allowed to discover that."

Almost unheeding, Guin whispered, "I wish Percy was here!"

"Percy be hanged! This is about you, Guin!" said Colonel Caldar explosively.

She stared at him, almost frightened by his vehemence. Guin had scarcely ever heard her uncle raise his voice. "I—I am sorry, uncle! I did not mean to anger you."

"You haven't angered me!" Colonel Caldar made an effort to control his emotions. "Guin, I must tell you something, and you must believe me. One day Percy will marry, and his wife will then more than likely become his closest companion. He will eventually have a family and an intimate circle of friends. It won't be just you and Percy anymore, ever again, no matter how much you wish it."

He saw that she was looking stunned. He gentled his voice even more. "You've grown up, Guin, and so has Percy. You can't expect things to remain the same. I don't know when it will happen; but you can't continue to rely on Percy to protect you or enter into your confidences."

There was a flash of comprehension in her eyes. Still she said nothing, however, and he added urgently, "You must think, Guin! What will you do?"

Guin stared at her uncle for several more long moments. Her dazed look dissipated and various emotions flitted across her face, denial and fear predominating. But eventually she sighed and nodded her head. Her shoulders slumped in defeat. There was a wealth of sadness in her voice when she spoke. "I know you have but spoken the truth, Uncle. Percy and I were always together. I even shared his lessons with him, because Percy told Mama he needed me to hold his books for him and wipe clean the slate when he copied his letters. But ever since he became Earl of Holybrooke, we—we have become forced apart! Percy had so much to learn about his duties and responsibilities, you see, and—and I could not help him anymore. Then we came up to London, and it is much, much worse!"

"I know it. My conscience has troubled me, for I must bear some responsibility for Percy's defection," said Colonel Caldar heavily.

"Oh, no, no! You must not blame yourself, Uncle," said Guin quickly. She laid her gloved hand on his arm, saying earnestly, "It is not your fault, sir, that Percy became an earl."

Colonel Caldar burst out laughing. "No, indeed! You make me feel much better, Guin!"

She smiled at her uncle. "I am glad, sir!"

His amusement faded as he looked down into her brave face. Colonel Caldar shook his head. "It won't do, Guin. We must still talk about what is best for you."

Guin managed another, smaller smile. "I shall do very well, I expect! Mama intends to find me an eligible husband, and I have decided just now that is the very thing for me. I quite see that Percy will someday wed, and I should not wonder at it if he did *not* wish to be forever providing for my support!"

"That's all very well, my dear," said Colonel Caldar, somewhat dryly. "However, I should wish you to make a match with a gentleman with whom you shared a mutual attraction. I do not think it wise to accept the very first offer made to you."

"Oh, no, I shouldn't do that," said Guin. She continued almost wistfully, "For it would be ever so much more agreeable to like one another."

Colonel Caldar looked out over his horses' flickering ears. "What if your mother insisted upon your accepting an offer from a gentleman whom you disliked?"

There was a short silence. He glanced down again and saw a meditative expression on his niece's face. She seemed to feel his regard, for she looked up to meet his eyes, and sighed. "Perhaps it would be better if I were to seek some eligible post, Uncle, for I suspect that I should do exactly what Mama thought best."

Colonel Caldar nodded, somewhat grimly. "Aye, you would indeed, for you are a biddable girl. As for seeking a post, I don't think it would suit you, Guin. I have a better thought than that."

"Could I perhaps come to live with you?" asked Guin hopefully. "I know you have a snug little property in the country. You have spoken of it many times. And—and I could become your housekeeper, for I do know how to order a house!"

He looked down swiftly, touched equally by her troubled gaze as by her offer. "There is nothing I'd like better, my dear, but it wouldn't do. For one thing, your mother would never allow it. For another, I could not reconcile it with my conscience to bury you in the country without all the advantages a lovely, worthy girl such as you are deserves."

"I wouldn't mind, dear sir. At least I would be happy," said Guin quietly.

Colonel Caldar's heart was torn by the melancholy in her softly spoken words. Guin! Now, you listen to me! I am only a rough soldier, but I know this much," he said sternly. "There is a better way for you, I know there is. I have got a feeling about this arrangement with Lady Smythe. It is the same itch I always got whenever there was a battle brewing, like a current of lightning forking through the air. It is fear and excitement and anticipation all at once."

Guin stared at him, absorbing what he was saying as well as the conviction in his voice. She felt a stirring of hope in her breast in response. "Do you really, Uncle?" she said hardly daring to believe that he might be right.

Colonel Caldar gave an emphatic nod. "I do, indeed!
Now, I know you don't wish to go live with Lady Smythe.
That part of it seems a bit hazy to me, so I wouldn't
refine too much on it. Lady Smythe is a stranger to us,
after all, and it makes no sense to me that her ladyship
would open her house to someone she has just met.
However, I believe your mother in that Lady Smythe
has offered a splendid opportunity to you, whatever her
ladyship's reasons for it. You mustn't be so anxious,
Guin! Rest assured that I shall continue to watch over
you."

Guin gave a small laugh. "I am being rather goose-
like, am I not? It was just such a shock, you see, especially when Mama— But I shall not refine too much on
that! I shall take your advice, sir, and accept Lady
Smythe's obliging offer."

"That's the spirit! Now, before we are both of us quite
knocked up by all of this emotional folderol, what do
you say to having an ice at Gunther's?"

"I should like it above all things," said Guin, making
an effort to appear more carefree. She politely inquired
what her uncle's plans were later that evening. "We are
to go to the theater, and if you are not engaged already,
I would like it if you came with us, sir."

"Well, I will," said Colonel Caldar with decision. He
strove to maintain a spritely flow of conversation and
was gratified when his niece's expression appeared to
be lightening.

Chapter Fourteen

By the time they had arrived at Gunther's and he was helping Guin down from the carriage, Colonel Caldar was encouraged to think that she was in a happier frame of mind. Pushing down his own natural misgivings, he hoped that he was right about Lady Smythe's offer and that Guin would benefit by her ladyship's sponsorship. In any event, her ladyship's benevolence could hardly do worse harm to Guin than had his sister's mismanagement, he thought acidly.

"Miss Holland!"

Guin turned quickly on the walkway, at once recognizing the cheerful voice. "Miss Beasely!" she said in surprise.

She saw that Miss Beasely was accompanied by a tall dignified lady whom she did not know, and she nodded politely. The lady smiled and nodded.

Miss Beasely gave an easy laugh. The expression in her green eyes was friendly. She held out her hand to Guin. "I've startled you! Are you going to Gunther's? Do let us join you! It is already so hot that I persuaded my cousin to stop for an ice before we returned home from our shopping. Oh, this is my widowed cousin, Mrs. Clara Roman."

Guin realized her own social obligations. She said a shy hello to Mrs. Roman. "I—I don't believe you have met my uncle, Colonel Caldar, Miss Beasely. Uncle, may I present Miss Beasely and her cousin, Mrs. Roman?"

Colonel Caldar gravely exchanged civilities with Miss Beasely and her companion. He invited them to join himself and his niece, gallantly insisting that the expense was to be his, so that they had formed a friendly party before entering the portals of the famous Gunther's.

Miss Beasely chatted away in a lively style, drawing everyone else into conversation. Before many minutes, Colonel Caldar discovered that he had known Mrs. Roman's late husband, a major with the army. The major had been a great correspondent, so that Colonel Caldar and Mrs. Roman could talk of many of the same events and people.

Miss Beasely regarded Colonel Caldar and her cousin with satisfaction before turning to Guin and drawing her attention by lowering her voice. "I must say, I am glad that Clara and your uncle seem to have hit it off so well. It makes it ever so much easier to talk to you."

"I fear that I am not a-a *good* conversationalist," confessed Guin worriedly. She was still bemused by Miss Beasely's friendliness and apparent desire to further their acquaintance.

Miss Beasely chuckled. "How droll you are! But that is why we shall get along so amazingly for the next fifty or so years."

Guin was surprised into unthinking comment. "What a queer thing to say!"

"No, why? It is quite true, you know! For I shall be your friend and your sister-in-law," said Miss Beasely matter-of-factly. She spooned up some of her lemon ice as though she had not just uttered something fantastic.

Guin regarded Miss Beasely with fascination. "Shall you? I mean, I would be delighted to have your friendship, of course."

Miss Beasely looked shrewdly at her. There was an unsettling gleam in her green eyes. "But you have reservations about me becoming your sister-in-law? How horridly rude, Miss Holland!"

"I—I didn't mean that! It's only that Percy—"

Flustered, Guin bit her lip. She couldn't very well inform the young lady, who was gazing at her with such a calm, interested expression on her pretty face, that Lord Holybrooke had already discerned that Miss Beasely looked upon him as an eligible *parti,* nor how he had reacted to it. She was embarrassed and annoyed all at the same time. How dare Miss Beasely place her in such an uncomfortable spot.

Miss Beasely must have read something of her consternation in her face. She laid a slim gloved hand on Guin's arm. "Forgive me! I was only funning with you a little. I don't think you are rude at all. On the contrary, it is I who has been rude. I shouldn't have sprung it all at once on you like that. However, I do mean what I have said, about becoming your friend and sister-in-law!"

"But how can you? You know nothing at all about me or Percy," said Guin, completely at sea. She knew that she was bungling it badly, but really there wasn't any polite, roundabout way to ask.

A smile hovered over Miss Beasely's face. She did not seem to mind Guin's blunt question. "I knew all I needed to know about Lord Holybrooke the very instant I looked up and saw him enter Mama's drawing room. In short, Miss Holland, I fell quite madly and completely in love with your brother at first glance! And since it must be an object with me to make myself agreeable to my future husband's family, I am determined that we are to become friends."

"Oh, my!" exclaimed Guin faintly. She wondered what her brother would make of Miss Beasely's unblushing declaration if he ever heard it. She certainly had no intention of telling him about it, however. "I mean, how interesting to be sure!"

Miss Beasely went into a peal of laughter. Her cousin glanced over at her thoughtfully, and she hastily rearranged her expression. She leaned closer to Guin and murmured, "Pray don't look so amazed, Guineveve! I may call you that, mayn't I? I know it sounds like rubbish and absolutely fantastical, but it is true. And so I have set my cap at Lord Holybrooke; but you are not to tell him so! It—it would greatly embarrass me if you did. You see, I am already laying open my heart to you, my new friend."

"No, I shan't tell Percy," said Guin, reflecting that since her brother had already realized that the Beaselys had their eyes on him, it would scarcely come as a surprise to him that Miss Beasely was encouraging. As for the rest of what Miss Beasely had shared with her, she rather thought that would be better left between the two of them. However, she could not think of any reason why she could not wholeheartedly accept Miss Beasely's offer of friendship. She had never had a friend before, with the exception of her brother, and she rather liked the possibility. "And you may call me Guin, if I may call you Margaret?"

"Of course you may!" exclaimed Miss Beasely warmly. "And now I see that our tête-à-tête is quite at an end, for Clara is saying good-bye to your uncle. Shall I see you at our *soirée* on Friday?"

"I am certain of it," said Guin positively. "Mama has already sent an acceptance to Lady Beasely."

"Good! I hope Lord Holybrooke will accompany you," said Miss Beasely with a twinkle as Mrs. Roman and Colonel Caldar came up. She turned to hold out her hand to the colonel. "It was a pleasure, sir. I have been assuring myself that Guin will be attending our *soirée* on Friday. I trust that you will come, too? I am persuaded Mama must have included you in the invitation."

Colonel Caldar glanced at Mrs. Roman. There was a smiling expression in his gray eyes. "Perhaps I shall come."

The faintest color tinged Mrs. Roman's cheeks, and a smile flickered across her attractive countenance. The lady did not say a word, however.

"Splendid! And now we must be off. Mama will be waiting for us at the end of the street with the carriage and all our packages," said Miss Beasely, waving gaily as she and her companion took their leave.

Colonel Caldar gave a hand up to Guin into their carriage. He gave a guinea to the urchin who had watched his horses, and the boy ran off clutching the coin tightly. "Miss Beasely is quite a friendly young miss," commented Colonel Caldar as he climbed up into the carriage and gathered the reins.

Guin nodded, a smile on her face. "Yes, and I have come to like her very much. I didn't think I would when I first met her. But she told me today that we are to be the best of friends for the next fifty years!" She did not reveal what else Miss Beasely had said, believing that it would be a singular betrayal of her new friend's confidence.

Colonel Caldar laughed. "I perceive that Miss Beasely is a young lady of decided force of character. It seems you have very little to say in the matter, Guin! You *must* like her!"

Guin laughed, too, more lightheartedly than she had in some weeks. "Yes, I think I must, indeed! Did you like Mrs. Roman? What did you find to talk about for so long?"

"It is a strange world. I served in several campaigns with Major Roman, though I did not know the gentleman well. Roman wrote home often, and so Mrs. Roman and I were able to converse on any number of things. As it turns out, her husband was killed a year before the Peace of Amiens," said Colonel Caldar somberly.

"How terrible! So many have been killed in the war with France, have they not?" said Guin with quick sympathy.

"Quite. War is a bloody, terrible thing. I am glad it is over. Now I am able to forget soldering and set myself to learn to be a retired gentleman," said Colonel Caldar. He was silent for a moment, a faint frown between his brows. "I'll tell you something, Guin, women such as Mrs. Roman are a credit to us all. She is a very brave, admirable lady."

"I am certain she is, sir," said Guin warmly. She glanced sideways at her uncle's profile and said, quite casually, "I suppose Mrs. Roman will be at Lady Beasely's *soirée,* as well."

"Aye, perhaps you are right," said Colonel Caldar with a thoughtful expression.

They drove back to the town house, amiably conversing. Colonel Caldar pulled up the horses and brought the carriage to a stop at the curb. A gentleman, who was about to climb up to the town house door, paused with one foot on the first step and looked around.

Guin recognized him with a flutter of pleased surprise. "Why, it is Sir Frederick Hawkesworth!"

"Why, so it is," said Colonel Caldar affably.

Sir Frederick had by this time recognized those in the carriage, and he came over to it. "Miss Holland! Sir, your servant. I was just on the point of sending up my card. I hope it is a convenient hour to call?"

"Oh! Of course, Sir Frederick! You would be welcome at any time," said Guin quickly, blushing.

Colonel Caldar paused in the act of stepping down from the carriage, surprised alike by his niece's animation and the bloom of rose in her cheeks. All of a sudden, a suspicion shot into his mind. He narrowed his eyes, studying Sir Frederick more closely. He liked what he saw in the baronet's eyes. As Sir Frederick's gaze rested on Guin's face, there was warmth and kindness in his expression, Colonel Caldar thought. At once he made a swift decision.

"Sir Frederick, if you will be so kind to hand down my niece, I shall be able to take this carriage round to the stable," said Colonel Caldar.

"Of course. I am delighted to be of service," said Sir Frederick promptly. He put up a hand and aided Guin to descend to the walkway.

Smiling, Colonel Caldar thanked Sir Frederick and drove the carriage away.

Sir Frederick offered his arm to Guin. "Allow me to accompany you up the steps, Miss Holland. I was hoping to find you, and Mrs. Holland of course, at home."

"Thank you, Sir Frederick," said Guin. She happily if a bit shyly laid her fingers on his elbow. Gathering her skirt with her free hand so that she would not trip on it, she went up the steps and entered the town house with Sir Frederick.

An inquiry of the butler elicited the information that Mrs. Holland had gone out. Guin was disconcerted and disappointed. "Oh, dear!" She looked up at Sir Frederick uncertainly.

Sir Frederick pressed her hand in quick understanding. "I must not stay, then. Pray give my regards to Mrs. Holland when she comes in."

"Of course, Sir Frederick," said Guin politely. She knew well that she couldn't entertain Sir Frederick without proper chaperonage, and it would be some minutes before her uncle returned. For the first time in her life, Guin questioned the wisdom of the proprieties that hedged and protected every young lady.

The library door opened, and Lord Holybrooke stepped into the entry hall. When he saw his sister and her companion, he exclaimed, "I thought I heard voices! Sir Frederick!"

With a welcoming smile, Lord Holybrooke walked forward with an outstretched hand. The two gentlemen exchanged friendly greetings. "Come into the front parlor, Sir Frederick. It is by far the most pleasant room. I only use the library when I am attending to accounts. Barlow will bring refreshments. I don't know what Guin is thinking of to keep you standing in the entry hall." He realized that Sir Frederick still had on his hat, and his gaze narrowed in surprise. "You are not leaving, surely?"

"I came hoping to find both Mrs. Holland and your sister at home," explained Sir Frederick.

Lord Holybrooke looked a question at his sister. "Guin?"

"I have just come in from driving with our uncle and have been told that Mama is not at home, Percy," said Guin. "Our uncle is not yet back from returning the carriage to the stables."

"Oh!" Lord Holybrooke grinned, understanding at

once the problem. "Well, there can surely be no objection about whom I entertain, can there? You'll stay, Sir Frederick?"

Sir Frederick laughed. "If you insist, my lord." He handed his hat to a waiting footman.

Chapter Fifteen

While Lord Holybrooke invited Sir Frederick again into the front parlor and the butler went off in search of refreshments, Guin excused herself so that she could go upstairs to put off her hat. Once she had reached the first landing and turned the corner where she knew she could not be seen by those below, she flew to her room. With her maid's help, she changed quickly out of her carriage dress into a fresh day gown and dragged a brush quickly through her crushed curls.

When she returned downstairs, she found not only her brother and Sir Frederick in the front parlor, but Colonel Caldar as well. They each held a glass of fine brandy and were conversing in a companionable fashion. There was a burst of laughter at some witticism made by Sir Frederick.

Upon seeing Guin enter, Lord Holybrooke said, "Guin! You're just in time. Sir Frederick has proposed a treat. There are to be fireworks at Vauxhall. He has asked us to make up the numbers of his party for supper."

"It does indeed sound delightful, Sir Frederick," said Guin, flashing the smile that was so like her brother's. Her eyes glowed with anticipation as she looked at Sir Frederick. She sat down on the settee, and her brother seated himself carelessly beside her. Sir Frederick took the chair opposite, but Colonel Caldar remained standing near the hearth.

"Then it is something you would enjoy, Miss Holland?" asked Sir Frederick, an answering gleam in his own eyes. There was appreciation in his gaze as he looked at the attractive picture made by the twin brother and sister. However, his eyes rested mostly on Miss Holland. He thought he had rarely seen her look more lovely than she did in the cerulean-blue gown that she had put on. The color deepened the shade of her eyes and was a striking contrast to her dark ringlets.

"Oh, yes!" exclaimed Guin. "There can be no question. I have not been to Vauxhall yet, and I have heard so much about how beautiful and entertaining it is."

Colonel Caldar claimed her attention. "My dear, even though it is rather early in the day, Barlow brought in tea. Would you like some?"

Guin shook her head and smiled across at her uncle. "No, thank you, dear sir. After the splendid ice you treated me to at Gunther's, I don't wish for anything."

"Then it is settled. We shall certainly join your party, Sir Frederick," said Lord Holybrooke, never having lost sight of the main topic.

"And pray allow us to return your hospitality in advance, Sir Frederick," said Colonel Caldar. "We go to the theater this evening. I am certain we shall all be delighted to have you join us in our box."

"What a capital notion!" said Lord Holybrooke enthusiastically. He looked over at Sir Frederick, somewhat diffidently. "I hope you have no prior commitments, Sir Frederick?"

"None that I cannot easily break, my lord. I shall be honored to join your party," said Sir Frederick easily. He glanced toward the earl's sister as though to gauge her reaction.

Guin was aware of Sir Frederick's gaze, but it did not make her feel at all ill at ease. She smiled at him. She was truly glad for her uncle's spontaneous invitation. She could not think of anything she would rather do than spend an evening in Sir Frederick's company. Now she would have the opportunity both that evening and again when they joined him for supper in Vauxhall Gardens.

The door opened and Mrs. Holland entered the front parlor. Guin tensed, anxiously scanning her mother's face as she recalled how they had parted. But it seemed that Mrs. Holland had put off her anger, for she wore one of her lovely smiles.

"Sir Frederick! What a pleasant surprise. I am sorry to have missed your arrival. I trust that Percival has made you suitably welcome?"

Sir Frederick had risen at Mrs. Holland's entrance. With his habitual grace, he bowed over her outstretched fingers. Civilly, he said, "Quite welcome, ma'am. I find you well, I trust."

"Oh, I am well enough for one of my sensitive constitution," said Mrs. Holland, taking a chair and adjusting the folds of her skirts. "I shall do even better now that Lady Smythe has offered to bear some of the burden of launching my daughter into society. You cannot conceive what a comforting thought it is that her ladyship is willing to oblige me in this! I have just come from telling my particular friends about it."

Colonel Caldar spluttered on a mouthful of brandy and began coughing. "Pardon!" he gasped, turning red. He turned away to the hearth, presenting his broad shoulders to the company as he got himself under control.

"Mama, you didn't," exclaimed Guin, dismay and embarrassment rising up in her breast. It was bad enough that her mother had aired her shortcomings to Lady Smythe in the privacy of their own parlor. Now she learned that Mrs. Holland had confided the particulars to all of London.

"Why shouldn't I, my dear? I am sure it is no great thing, and I can conceive of no reason to keep secret her ladyship's kindness," said Mrs. Holland in a reasonable voice, pulling off her gloves.

"What are you talking about, Mama?" asked Lord Holybrooke in puzzlement. He glanced from his sister's coloring face to his mother's complacent expression. "What's this about Lady Smythe and Guin?"

Guin's embarrassment escalated. She avoided Sir Fred-

erick's eyes as she hastened to say, "Mama, I doubt that
Sir Frederick would be much interested in her ladyship's
expression of kindness. May we not discuss it at another time?"

"On the contrary, Miss Holland! I am most interested,
especially since Lady Smythe is quite one of my oldest
friends," said Sir Frederick, his brows quirking upward.
He swirled the brandy in the bottom of his glass.

"Oldest! How droll of you, Sir Frederick!" said Mrs.
Holland on a laugh. She flashed a roguish look at him.
"I shall not betray you to Lady Smythe, on my honor."

"Thank you, ma'am," said Sir Frederick civilly. There
was nothing in his demeanor to hint that he had borne
the least anxiety over the possibility.

Guin jumped up. Hoping to divert her mother's
thoughts, she asked, "Would you like some tea, Mama?
Shall I get it for you?"

Lord Holybrooke looked up at her with a gathering
frown.

"Why, thank you, Guin," said Mrs. Holland, accepting
her daughter's offer to serve her without surprise. She
turned to Sir Frederick. "I don't care to boast, you must
understand, Sir Frederick. However, it is really too good
of Lady Smythe, and I cannot express my gratitude
enough."

"I quite understand, Mrs. Holland," said Sir Frederick
with his charming smile.

Seeing that there would be nothing to save her, Guin
fled with reddened cheeks to the occasional table.

Mrs. Holland needed little encouragement to trumpet
abroad anything she perceived as a social boost. In short
order, she laid out for Sir Frederick the particulars of
Lady Smythe's visit earlier that day. Against her will,
Guin glanced back often and saw that Sir Frederick was
listening with every appearance of interest. He put in a
suitable comment or question now and again, which only
served to spur Mrs. Holland to further disclosure and
boastful speculation.

Guin had rushed to the occasional table, but now she

dawdled over the tea tray. She was embarrassed by her mother's aggrandizement and wished that she was courageous enough to either interrupt or flee entirely from the parlor.

Lord Holybrooke walked over to her and asked in a low voice, "What the deuce is Mama talking about, Guin?"

"You have only to listen, Percy," said Guin with a flash of irritation. She arranged for the fifth time the tea things on the tray.

"One would think to hear Mama talk that Lady Smythe is in a fair way to adopting you, and all because you are the sister of an earl! Next she will be saying that you have wheedled your way into her ladyship's confidence," said Lord Holybrooke, frowning as he glanced over his shoulder.

"Hush!" exclaimed Guin, afraid that her brother's frank speech might be overheard by Sir Frederick. She picked up the tray in trembling hands. The teacups clattered on their saucers while the plate of biscuits slid to one edge of the tray.

Lord Holybrooke deftly took the tray from her. "Better let me have that. You'll tip it over onto the carpet the way you are shaking. You stay here, Guin. I am going to say something to Mama to make her stop making such a cake of herself in front of Sir Frederick!"

Guin plucked at the sleeve of her brother's coat. "Percy, pray do not!"

Colonel Caldar came up in time to hear his nephew's angry mutter. He set down his emptied wineglass and decanted the bottle of brandy. He said calmly, "Don't go off half-cocked, Percy. Think of your sister."

"I am thinking of her, sir. I've no wish for her to figure as a conniving baggage in Sir Frederick's eyes. Or in anyone else's, for that matter," said Lord Holybrooke in a grim voice. "I wonder how many others she has told this stuff?"

"Oh, no!" said Guin, distressed. "Pray do not say anything to Mama in front of Sir Frederick, Percy!"

"Well, I shall! I can correct his impression, at least," said Lord Holybrooke.

"I suspect Sir Frederick is more savvy than you give him credit for, Percy," said Colonel Caldar dryly. He refilled his glass and then poured a measure of brandy into another.

"You're mighty cool of a sudden, sir," said Lord Holybrooke swiftly, "when just a minute ago you choked over it!"

"Take my advice and leave well enough alone for now. It won't harm Guin to be around Lady Smythe and away from your mother," said Colonel Caldar. "Don't queer it for her, Percy."

Lord Holybrooke's eyes met his uncle's, an arrested expression in them. "I see. You're quite right, sir, of course." He threw a glance toward his mother and Sir Frederick, and the frown descended again. "Yet I can't but wish that Mama would not expose herself so."

"Then, perhaps we should join her and Sir Frederick again," said Colonel Caldar. He picked up the two wineglasses. "The poor fellow must be glazing over with boredom by now."

Lord Holybrooke laughed and carried over the tea tray, Guin right beside him. Guin glanced anxiously at Sir Frederick's face. He did not appear in the least bored by Mrs. Holland's boastful confidences. Instead, there was a pronounced expression of amusement in his eyes.

Guin felt ready to sink.

Colonel Caldar had followed with the wineglasses, one of which he now offered to Sir Frederick. "My apologies in taking so long, Sir Frederick. I had a bit of trouble decanting the bottle."

"Not at all, Colonel Caldar," said Sir Frederick, accepting the glass of brandy. The amusement in his eyes deepened. Despite his apparent absorption in what Mrs. Holland was saying to him, he had not missed the intense murmured conference at the occasional table.

"Well! I trust the tea is still warm," said Mrs. Holland pointedly, throwing a disapproving glance at her daughter.

"I imagine it will be found to be just as you like it, Mama," said Lord Holybrooke gravely. "I made certain that Guin fixed it to your taste." He met his sister's fulminating gaze with bland innocence.

"Thank you, Percy. I may always trust you to see to my comfort," said Mrs. Holland, at once in charity with everything around her. She tasted the cup of tea that Guin handed to her. "Quite perfect, Percy."

Lord Holybrooke sketched a bow before lounging over to the mantel and laying an arm along it. "Mama, my uncle and I have invited Sir Frederick to join us this evening in our box at the theater. Sir Frederick has very kindly assented."

For an instant, Mrs. Holland looked startled. Her expression smoothed into a smile. "What a pleasant notion. You must come to dine with us also, Sir Frederick. We are sitting down only twenty couples, but another gentleman can never be counted amiss."

Sir Frederick was too old a hand not to realize when his presence would be de trop. Sensible of the fact that Mrs. Holland had mentioned couples, he made a graceful disclaimer. "I am unfortunately already engaged for dinner. However, I shall certainly present myself later this evening at the theater."

"Excellent," said Colonel Caldar jovially.

Sir Frederick rose to take his leave, and the ladies rose with him. He made a pretty speech to each, then shook hands with Lord Holybrooke and Colonel Caldar.

As Sir Frederick left the front parlor and retrieved his hat from the butler, he was well pleased with his visit. He had gleaned much from Mrs. Holland's disclosures. He had also discovered that Colonel Caldar was willing to advance his niece's interests through Lady Smythe.

It was shaping up very nicely, Sir Frederick thought. Soon Lady Smythe would have the polishing of Miss Holland, and he would naturally do his part.

A reminiscent smile played over his mouth. Miss Holland had been acutely embarrassed in becoming the topic of discussion. He would have thought less of her if she had not shown self-consciousness. He hoped, however, that the young lady would quickly learn to get over much of her tendency toward discomfiture. It was the nature of people to talk about other people.

The toast of the town necessarily had to have more than poise, more than beauty, more than quality. She had to have a thick skin. It remained to be seen if Miss Holland had the fortitude to acquire it.

Chapter Sixteen

Guin had known that Lord Holloway was to be one of the guests that evening. Despite Mrs. Holland's oft-repeated approval, she did not particularly like Lord Holloway. Apparently her brother shared her feelings because Lord Holybrooke was not far distant when Lord Holloway sought out Guin's company. The earl engaged Lord Holloway in polite conversation, his hand resting upon Guin's chair back. Guin was grateful that her brother hovered over her, for she had no ambition to further her acquaintance with Lord Holloway.

Lord Holloway eventually bowed and walked away to join some of the other guests.

Lord Holybrooke watched the gentleman's sauntering progress with narrowed eyes. "I wish you wouldn't have anything to do with his lordship, Guin."

"I don't wish to, Percy, I assure you," said Guin quickly. "But Mama considers Lord Holloway to be a suitable *parti*."

"I have been given reason to believe that he is not," said Lord Holybrooke shortly.

"Whatever do you mean?" asked Guin, turning her head to look full into his face.

However, Lord Holybrooke only shook his head and repeated his statement. Guin assured him that she would do her best not to encourage Lord Holloway. She really did not know how to accomplish that without incurring her mother's wrath, but simply hoped that something would come to mind or that his lordship would lose his seeming interest in her.

Half an hour later, Guin was dismayed when she discovered that her mother had designated Lord Holloway to be her dinner partner. His lordship held out his arm to her, his heavy-lidded gaze on her face. "Shall we go in, Miss Holland?" he inquired in his mincing voice.

Guin hid her consternation and rose to her feet. "Of— of course, my lord," she murmured, her stammer in evidence. Without glancing upward into his long handsome face, she laid her fingers delicately on his elbow.

Lord Holloway escorted Guin toward the dining room. The other couples going before and coming after them were exchanging animated pleasantries. "You are quiet, Miss Holland. But then, it is my observation that you are generally restrained from speech," said Lord Holloway lightly.

"My lord?" Guin looked fleetingly up to meet his inscrutable gaze. She saw the half smile on his thin-lipped mouth. There was something about his expression that made her shiver suddenly. "I—I don't quite understand you."

Lord Holloway waved his scented handkerchief in a languid manner. "Pray do not fear that I am offended, Miss Holland. On the contrary, I think it an admirable quality."

Guin shook her head, still in the dark as to his meaning. She was intelligent enough to realize that there was more underlying the impersonally uttered words than there would seem to be on the surface.

They entered the dining room, and Lord Holloway ushered her to her place, politely pulling out the chair and seating her. Guin felt his fingers brush featherlight across the back of her neck, and she looked around quickly.

Lord Holloway did not glance her way as he pulled out the chair beside her. Guin decided it had been an accidental contact on his lordship's part, and she put it out of her mind.

Guin looked up and down the long elegantly set table. Candlelight lit the scene, catching the gleam of plate and silverware, as the guests settled into their places. Most of the guests were ones Guin had previously met at her mother's rout. There was much loud talk and laughter, the lone exception being the pool of silence existing between Colonel Caldar and his dinner partner.

Colonel Caldar maintained a polite expression, but Guin perceived the boredom that underlay it. She was sorry that her uncle was finding the dinner party so tedious. It was her mother's fault, of course, for saddling her uncle with such a terrible choice of partner. Anyone could have seen that Colonel Caldar and Miss Baker were ill paired. If she had been the hostess, Guin thought, she would have discreetly rearranged matters. However, she understood how her mother's mind worked.

It chanced that Miss Baker was a relation to Lord Holloway and, knowing that her brother was always civil and could be relied upon to make an effort to entertain a guest, Mrs. Holland had assigned Colonel Caldar the task of making the evening agreeable for Miss Baker.

Several days previously, Lord Holloway had told Mrs. Holland of his cousin's visit to London and asked the favor of adding the lady to Mrs. Holland's dinner party. Mrs. Holland had graciously assented, even though her numbers would be uneven, and extended her invitation to include Miss Baker. She told Colonel Caldar that she would not be backward in any attention toward Lord Holloway.

"For I am convinced that his lordship intends to offer for Guin," said Mrs. Holland. "I could wish better, of course, but Lord Holloway will do very well for Guin. He is a peer and his estates are extensive."

Colonel Caldar had frowned, his eyes narrowed. "I wish you would not encourage anything from that direction, Aurelia. There is something about Lord Holloway that I cannot like."

"Nonsense! What is there not to like? His lordship is

a fine gentleman, always well dressed, and he possesses such exquisite manners," said Mrs. Holland, putting up her well-formed brows.

Colonel Caldar barked a laugh. "I would call him rather a pretty gentleman, and his manner is that of a fop! That scented handkerchief he is always waving about! What affectation!"

"You are obviously biased, Arnold. Just because you do not admire the cut of his coat—"

"It is the cut of the man that I do not admire," interjected Colonel Caldar.

"Nevertheless, I trust that I may rely upon you to entertain Miss Baker?" asked Mrs. Holland with a determined smile.

Colonel Caldar had agreed to it, rather impatiently. However, as Guin had seen, he had cause to regret his acquiescence.

Miss Baker was a colorless creature. Though she was dressed elegantly enough, she had no beauty, either of face or of personality. She made little effort at conversation and replied to questions in monosyllables. There was not a hint of animation in her expression or her presence. She sat like a block, mechanically eating what was put before her.

Guin glanced several times during the course of dinner down the table toward her uncle and Miss Baker. Anxiously, she regarded the lines that were gradually forming about Colonel Caldar's mouth. She knew her uncle for an amiable gentleman, seldom roused to wrath, but she got the distinct impression that he had about reached the end of his patience as far as Miss Baker was concerned.

Her assumption was proven correct when the other dinner guests had departed and only Lord Holloway and Miss Baker remained. Mrs. Holland had invited Lord Holloway and his cousin to accompany them to the theater. Colonel Caldar cornered his sister for a private word, which became something of a heated exchange, and ended only when Colonel Caldar returned to the company to make his apologies and excuse himself from making one of the party that was going on to the theater.

At once Guin spoke up, her sympathy fully aroused on Colonel Caldar's behalf. "It is quite all right, dear sir. You will be missed tonight, but there will be another time."

Mrs. Holland darted a wrathful glance at her daughter. There was high color in her face. She started to say something, but she was forestalled.

Lord Holloway smoothly accepted Colonel Caldar's excuses. "I concur precisely with Miss Holland's sentiments, sir." His lordship's cousin sat silent, her hands folded and with not a flicker of emotion in her eyes.

Colonel Caldar eyed Lord Holloway for an instant, almost as though he wanted to retract his decision, before he bowed and went out of the room.

Mrs. Holland made an attempt to smooth over what she obviously felt to be an awkward moment. Lord Holloway seemed perfectly ready to accept whatever platitudes she chose to utter.

Lord Holybrooke bent down to whisper in Guin's ear, "Anyone could see in what direction it was going. What a muff Mama made of it!"

Shortly thereafter a message was received from Sir Frederick, conveying his apologies that his own appearance at the theater would be delayed. Guin put up a brave front, but her spirits sank. The evening was going from bad to worse.

A few minutes later the reduced party set out for the theater in separate carriages. The entire ride was enlivened by Mrs. Holland's bitterly expressed opinion of her brother's defection. Guin was never more glad of anything when they arrived and were able to descend from the carriage. Naturally, Mrs. Holland's whole demeanor changed once they rejoined Lord Holloway and his cousin, and went inside the crowded theater to find their box.

The play was a good one and kept Guin entertained, though she had to lean uncomfortably forward to see the entire stage past the heavy velvet curtain that draped across the side of the box. She was seated in the far corner, her brother slouched in the chair beside her. Lord

Holybrooke yawned from time to time, and Guin once shushed him. Lord Holybrooke shrugged with a rueful smile. He was not a theatergoer, preferring more lively entertainments, as Guin well knew.

When the curtain came down for intermission, the house lamps were lit. A knock sounded on the door, and an elderly admirer of Mrs. Holland's came in. She received him with pleasure, and they swiftly entered upon a light flirtation.

Lord Holybrooke was bored with the company. His mother was engaged in conversation, as was Lord Holloway with his cousin. After exchanging a few observations with his sister about the play, Lord Holybrooke felt that there was little else to inspire his interest.

Looking idly down into the pit, he exclaimed that he saw a couple of his friends and left the box.

The elderly admirer offered to escort Mrs. Holland out for refreshments, and she acquiesced. She glanced over at her daughter meaningfully. "I know that you won't care to come with us, Guin."

"No, Mama," said Guin, knowing full well what was expected of her.

Mrs. Holland stood up and placed her fingers on her gallant's arm. Her gaze swept across Miss Baker's wooden face and lingered on Lord Holloway. "I know that you will be perfectly safe with Lord Holloway and Miss Baker, Guin, so I do not feel guilty for leaving you with them for a few minutes."

"Pray do not feel any need to rush back on your daughter's account, Mrs. Holland," drawled Lord Holloway. "My cousin and I will take very good care of Miss Holland."

"I am certain of that, my lord," said Mrs. Holland with the flash of her lovely smile. She left the box in company with her gallant.

Lord Holloway exchanged a few desultory remarks with Guin. She was civil to his lordship, but she felt unaccountably nervous at being the sole object of his conversation. She felt a flash of irritation toward Miss

Baker, who had subsided once more into silence. Really, the woman was beyond anything.

Guin leaned forward so that she could better see the lady past Lord Holloway. "Do you like the play, Miss Baker?"

Miss Baker stared back at her, before giving a bare nod.

Lord Holloway laughed indulgently. "You must forgive my cousin, Miss Holland. She is not good in company." He gave a slight signal with his head.

Without a word, Miss Baker rose and left the box. The door closed behind her with a small snap.

Guin had watched Miss Baker's exit with astonishment. Surely the lady knew that she was entrusted by Mrs. Holland to enact the role of chaperon. Guin turned her troubled gaze to Lord Holloway "My lord! Your cousin—"

Lord Holloway shook his head. "My cousin is completely rag-mannered, Miss Holland. You must forgive her."

"Of course: but—"

"I fear the torchlight must be hurting your eyes, Miss Holland," drawled Lord Holloway. He had turned in his chair and was regarding her with a half smile.

"Oh, no! I am quite all right," said Guin. She threw a glance toward the door of the box and began to rise from her chair. She was convinced that it was better to brave her mother's annoyance at having her own tête-à-tête interrupted than to remain alone in the box, unchaperoned, with Lord Holloway.

As though he had not heard her, Lord Holloway got up and pulled the curtain partially closed. He was blocking the way toward the door, and Guin sank down again onto the chair.

Lord Holloway did not take his former seat but sat down again beside Guin in the chair vacated by her brother. A smile played over his mouth as his gaze slid over her. "Now we may be comfortable, Miss Holland."

Shielded from view behind the heavy curtain, Lord

Holloway abruptly reached out and took Guin in his
arms, half dragging her from her chair.

Guin scarcely had time to realize what he was about.
With an efficiency quite at variance with his usual lazy
air, Lord Holloway pinioned her arms behind her with
one ruthless hand. With the other he captured her head
to hold her still for a bruising, very thorough kiss.

Guin made an inarticulate protest and tried desperately to free herself. But Lord Holloway's arms tightened
until she was practically bent backward over the chair
back. Tears started to her eyes with the stabbing pain in
her captured wrists and arms. She was utterly helpless as
he possessed her mouth avidly.

When Lord Holloway at last raised his head, he stared
down at her with a hot-white light in his eyes. He was
breathing rapidly. His words were soft, insidious. "You
will not say anything, will you, Miss Holland? You will
not say anything to your dear mother. No, not when she
so ardently wishes me to wed you. She would be so very
angry with you, would she not?"

Instinctively recognizing the truth of what he had said,
Guin exclaimed, "I will tell Percy!" She stared fearfully
up into his handsome face, with its hateful smile, that
was bare inches above her own. She could feel his pant-
ing breath on her skin, and she shuddered suddenly.

"Then he would challenge me to a duel, and I would
have to kill him, my dear," said Lord Holloway, his mincing voice at chilling contrast to the utter coldness of his
voice. "I have killed before, you know. No, you will not
tell Lord Holybrooke. *Will* you?"

He lightly pinched her cheek. She jerked her head
away, giving a sob. He laughed softly. "I thought not.
You and I will deal well together. We shall enjoy several
delicious tête-à-têtes. And when I am done, why, perhaps
I will marry you."

Chapter Seventeen

Lord Holloway released her wrists, freeing her arms, and drew her upright.

Guin shrank against her chair back, staring at him, her breath coming fast. She could not think what to do. She felt trapped. Her heart was tripping over itself with fear. At least he was not touching her anymore.

His eyes glittered at her. "Now, my dear, you will show me that we have come to a perfect understanding. I shall kiss you again, and this time I will not need to restrain you. You understand me, of course."

Guin stared in horror at Lord Holloway. She was trembling uncontrollably, and her flesh was bruised where he had held her wrists. She could not stop the shuddering breaths that shook her. Mutely she shook her head, denying the nightmare in which she found herself.

He encircled one of her wrists, and his powerful fingers closed cruelly about it. "You do understand, Miss Holland, don't you?"

Guin gasped as the bones in her wrist seemed to grind together. She understood. All too perfectly. Lord Holloway meant to use her for his own purposes, confident that there would be none to champion or protect her. He had shrewdly taken Mrs. Holland's measure. That lady was blinded by ambition. She would be more inclined to berate her daughter for missishness than put any stock in a terrified report of unwonted liberties. As for Lord Holloway's threat against Lord Holybrooke,

Guin believed implicitly that his lordship would carry it out. There had been that in his eyes and his cold voice that had utterly convinced her that her beloved twin would be in danger of his life if she were to fly to him.

Lord Holloway nodded as though he could read her tumbling disordered thoughts. "Now, my dear." He slowly slid his hands up her bare arms to her shoulders and drew her trembling body toward him. He lowered his head and took her mouth once more.

Guin shuddered. She felt his repulsive embrace, in all of its loathsomeness. She held herself as immobile as she could despite the gorge that rose up inside her. The musk scent he favored filled her nostrils, surrounding her with proof of his possession. One of his hands slid around to find and caress her breast through the thin silk of her dress. Guin jerked under his fingers, and Lord Holloway raised his head an instant, to laugh softly in her face, before he drove his mouth down hotly on hers again.

An inarticulate cry gurgled in her throat. Something snapped in Guin's mind. She became a snared animal, unthinking, unreasoning. No thought of the threats held over her head could withstand her revulsion and fear. She struggled wildly, twisting in Lord Holloway's arms. He uttered a coarse expletive and tightened his hold on her.

Suddenly the iron arms were no longer about her, the hateful mouth was no longer plundering her own. Abruptly released, Guin fell awkwardly back in the chair. When she straightened herself up, she saw Sir Frederick drive Lord Holloway out of the box, one hand clenched in the back of the man's cravat and the other pinning Lord Holloway's arm painfully across his spine. With a violent shove, Sir Frederick released Lord Holloway to stagger without dignity into the passageway.

Immediately Sir Frederick turned, his breathing slightly elevated. His appearance was impeccable, with not a crease in his coat to play witness to his exertions. His mouth was unsmiling and held in a tight line. "Miss Holland! Are you quite all right?"

Guin's face flamed. She turned her head away from the hard, inscrutable expression in Sir Frederick's eyes. She lifted one shaking hand to her hot cheek. "Yes, thank you, Sir Frederick." Her voice sounded strangled even in her own ears. She swallowed a gasping sob.

Sir Frederick sat down on the chair lately vacated by Lord Holloway. He did not attempt to touch her. "How came you to be here alone with Lord Holloway?"

There was anger in his voice, and Guin assumed it was directed at her. She lowered her head, tears starting to her eyes again. "Percy went to see some friends he saw in the pit. An admirer of Mama's invited her to take refreshments, and she said—she said that she was certain I would be perfectly s-safe if Lord Holloway and his cousin remained with me. Then Lord Holloway sent Miss Baker away and—and—" Her voice became wholly suspended. The tears slipped down her face unchecked.

Sir Frederick reached over and took her chin in a gentle hand. Turning her face toward him, he wiped away the tears with his handkerchief. His voice level, he said, "It is over now, Miss Holland. Your mother and Lord Holybrooke will soon return. You mustn't show them this face."

"No, no! You are right, I must not. There would be questions," exclaimed Guin, hastily wiping her eyes with her hands. She took his handkerchief from him and finished what he had started. Then she blew her nose. Bunching the handkerchief in her hand, she looked into Sir Frederick's concerned face and managed to form a smile. "Is this better, dear sir?"

"Infinitely," said Sir Frederick gravely, though privately thinking that she looked as though she had been shattered. Her face was extremely pale, and her lashes were damply clumped together. There was dazed shock in the depths of her eyes. He urgently wanted to fold her into his arms and reassure her that she was safe. But he could not. He had not the right.

His hand suddenly clenched on his thigh. "I should like to beat him to a bloody pulp!" he said savagely.

Guin gave a low cry of instant protest. "Oh, no, no! You mustn't! It would cause such trouble for me!"

Sir Frederick stared at her, his dark brows snapping together. "Trouble for you, Miss Holland! The boot is on the other foot, I assure you. When you relate to your mother what has happened—"

"I can't tell her! Oh, you don't understand! Lord Holloway is-is—" Guin made a helpless gesture and another stifled sob broke from her.

Sir Frederick grimly surveyed her. His understanding was quick. Obviously Mrs. Holland was still cherishing hopes of an offer from Lord Holloway, and her daughter was petrified at the thought of incurring her mother's displeasure by recounting the pretty scene he had chanced upon. "Then let your brother or your uncle know. They will know how to protect you."

Guin shook her head adamantly. "Lord Holloway threatened—" She covered her mouth, her expression appalled.

For an instant, there was silence while Sir Frederick regarded her with gathering incredulity and wrath. "Are you saying that bastard has threatened the lives of your family?"

Guin fought for self-control, her breast heaving. She clasped and unclasped her fingers in unconscious tension. "I—I have said too much, Sir Frederick. I wish you to disregard it."

"The devil I will," said Sir Frederick flatly. "If you think your brother would thank you for this misguided loyalty, you are mightily mistaken. As for Colonel Caldar, I doubt that a man of his caliber will stand idly by while some cowardly cad takes advantage of his niece!" He looked around with a profound frown. "Where is Colonel Caldar? I thought he was to come tonight."

"I wish he had," said Guin with suspended tears in her voice.

At once Sir Frederick regretted his angry tone. "Forgive me, Miss Holland. I had no right to speak to you in such a fashion." He took her hand in a careful grasp. "If you will allow me, I will handle this matter. Will you trust me?"

Guin looked into his earnest face for a long moment. The anxious kindness that she perceived in his eyes was staggering to her bruised self-esteem. She could scarcely comprehend it. Her heart fluttered in her breast; all at once the dread that had crushed her from the first moment of Lord Holloway's attack lifted from her soul. She smiled tremulously. "I will trust you, Sir Frederick. With all of my heart."

He lifted her hand to his lips. He was deeply moved. "You honor me, Miss Holland."

There was a rustle and a laughing word. Mrs. Holland came back into the box, accompanied by a gentleman of advanced years who was obviously besotted with her. Lord Holybrooke followed in his mother's train.

Mrs. Holland at once saw Sir Frederick. He was sitting at his ease in the chair next to her daughter, one leg straightened out before him. She blinked and glanced around the otherwise empty box. "Why, where is Lord Holloway?"

No one answered her surprised query at once. Sir Frederick rose and greeted Mrs. Holland with a civil bow. He recognized the gentleman with her and nodded and exchanged pleasantries. Lord Holybrooke stepped forward to shake Sir Frederick's hand, welcoming the baronet with obvious friendliness.

Mrs. Holland repeated her question, this time looking at her silent daughter. She was frowning. "Where is Lord Holloway?"

Sir Frederick neatly shifted, placing himself between Mrs. Holland and her view of her daughter. Suavely, he said, "His lordship was forced to leave, Mrs. Holland." He heard a soft gasp followed by a stifled giggle behind him. He did not show by even the quiver of a muscle that he had heard Guin's self-betrayal.

Mrs. Holland pouted petulantly. "I don't understand. Did Lord Holloway say where he was going? Did he have another engagement?"

"Lord Holloway did not say, ma'am," said Sir Frederick with perfect truth.

Mrs. Holland shook her head over it. She was annoyed, and it showed in her expression. "Well! What a very odd thing, to be sure. At the very least I would have thought Lord Holloway and his cousin would leave a message for me."

Lord Holybrooke had been listening closely, his gaze leaving Sir Frederick's bland expression to travel to his sister, where she was still sitting in the shadows of the corner of the box. He was aware of undercurrents he did not understand, but one thing was perfectly clear: Sir Frederick was shielding Guin from a too-searching questioning.

With swift presence of mind, Lord Holybrooke said quickly, "Mama, the curtain is about to go up, and you are not seated! Allow me to pull this chair farther forward so that you and General Layton may converse more readily." He suited action to words, gracefully fielding the general's expression of thanks as well as Mrs. Holland's fond expression of appreciation.

Sir Frederick quietly adjusted the heavy velvet curtain and tied it back to its original appearance. Then he sat down on the chair next to Miss Holland, pulling the seat forward a few inches so that his body would partially hide her from Mrs. Holland's casual glance.

Lord Holybrooke seated himself next to Sir Frederick Hawkesworth. He leaned forward to speak across the gentleman to his sister. He had thought it strange that Guin had not said anything even to him. "Guin! Are you quite all right?"

"Of course, Percy."

Her voice was suspiciously bright and sounded strained to Lord Holybrooke's attuned ears. The young earl muttered under his breath and half rose from his chair.

Sir Frederick swiftly laid a detaining hand on Lord Holybrooke's arm and interjected in a lowered voice. "Your sister has sustained a shock, my lord." On his other side, he felt her convulsive hand on his sleeve. He let go of the earl to reassuringly cover her fingers. Firmly, he said, "You must trust me, Miss Holland."

Lord Holybrooke had sat back down, but his eyes had narrowed dangerously. In a savage undertone, he demanded, "Holloway?"

Sir Frederick nodded. He glanced warningly toward the two seated at the front of the box. "We shall confer later, my lord."

Lord Holybrooke hesitated, then reluctantly nodded. It was obvious that something of awful moment had occurred. Equally obvious, his sister had no desire to bring whatever it was to their mother's notice. It was apparent Sir Frederick knew what had happened, and he meant to preserve discretion until there were fewer ears. Lord Holybrooke was therefore also enjoined to trust in Sir Frederick's judgment. The young earl settled himself to watch the remainder of the play with a frustrated sense of impatience.

As soon as the curtain went down, Lord Holybrooke suggested to his mother that it would be best to return home. "I am persuaded that Guin has the headache. She will not be at all in her best looks on the morrow if she does not rest, and we are to go to Lady Beasely's *soirée*."

Mrs. Holland nodded. "Quite right, Percy. Guin, why did you not tell me that you were not feeling the thing? I would have sent you home hours ago with the coachman."

"I—I did not wish to spoil your pleasure, Mama," said Guin falteringly, glancing quickly at her brother and Sir Frederick.

"Well, you have in any event. It is so utterly boring to be obligated to bear with someone who feels unwell. No doubt that is why Lord Holloway and Miss Baker went off so precipitously," said Mrs. Holland. She smiled at her admirer. "I regret that we must part company this early in the evening, sir."

"If you do not object, Mrs. Holland, I would count it an honor to escort you and Miss Holland home," said General Layton gallantly.

Mrs. Holland bestowed another dazzling smile upon the general and accepted his kind offices.

"I had hoped that after you see Mrs. Holland and your sister safely home, Lord Holybrooke, that you might join me at White's," said Sir Frederick in a casual voice.

"Of course, sir. I shall be delighted to do so," said Lord Holybrooke promptly.

The party exited the theater. Sir Frederick took leave of Mrs. Holland and her daughter as their carriage was driven up. Miss Holland's fingers clung to his for an instant too long, and Sir Frederick smiled down into her anxious face. "I shall wait upon you tomorrow, Miss Holland, if I may?"

"Of course, Sir Frederick," she said in a somewhat subdued voice. She turned then and climbed up into the carriage. Mrs. Holland had already been handed inside by the general, and that gentleman then followed the ladies, at Lord Holybrooke's insistence.

Lord Holybrooke turned to Sir Frederick. With a meaningful look, he said, "I shall join you with all speed, sir."

Sir Frederick nodded. "I shall look for you, my lord."

Chapter Eighteen

Guin did not know precisely what Sir Frederick told Lord Holybrooke later that night. Whatever it was, her brother assured her that he had no immediate intention of calling out Lord Holloway. Guin was giddy with relief. "Thank God, Percy! I was so frightened on your behalf. Lord Holloway said he would kill you."

"Frightened for me! When it is you that—" Lord Holybrooke bit back his exclamation and in a tightly controlled voice said, "Guin, I have informed my uncle of Lord Holloway's dastardly conduct. Though he was at one with me in wishing to call Lord Holloway instantly to book, he agrees that we do not wish to be plunged into a scandal that would inevitably involve your fair name. Sir Frederick assures me that there is a better way to deal with his lordship."

"What way is that, Percy?" asked Guin curiously.

Lord Holybrooke's eyes were hard. "Never you mind. You are simply to put this ugly business out of your head. As for Mama's partiality toward Lord Holloway, *that* will shortly be a thing of the past, I assure you!"

Guin could not get another word out of him, and she quickly abandoned the attempt, recognizing that her brother was doing his best to protect her. She was inordinately glad that both Lord Holybrooke and Colonel Caldar knew about the horrible incident with Lord Holloway. She was no longer afraid to meet Lord Holloway, at least in company, and she was reassured that if his lordship ever attempted to be private with her again that she could rely upon Lord Holybrooke and Colonel Caldar to deliver her.

As for Sir Frederick, Guin told herself that she was truly fortunate. He had proven over and over what a steadfast friend he was to her. It was really too bad, she reflected on a sigh, that he did not feel the same toward her as she did toward him. At least he thought enough of her to take her driving often. The outings had become one of her chief pleasures.

Guin was waiting in the front parlor for Sir Frederick to arrive for one of their pleasant outings. A few minutes before, Mrs. Holland had been sitting with her, flipping through a ladies' magazine discontentedly, and roundly decrying the necessity of chaperonage.

Guin had had the happy thought of reminding her mother of a delivery from Mrs. Holland's modiste. "I don't wish to keep you here, Mama, when I know you would rather go upstairs to try on your new gown."

Mrs. Holland had brightened. "Indeed! Perhaps it would not be so very improper of me to leave you. After all, it is only Sir Frederick coming to take you driving! Pray say all that is proper for me, Guin."

"I shall do so, Mama," said Guin. Her mother exited, and she went over to the mirror, humming a little. The door opened and Lord Holloway was announced. Guin turned quickly from inspecting herself in the gilt mirror. "Oh!"

Advancing into the room, Lord Holloway saw at a glance that she was alone. He slowly looked her up and down. A smile touched his handsome face. "Vastly becoming, Miss Holland," he drawled.

Guin suddenly felt that her elegant carriage dress was too close cut to her figure. Her heart began to pound as she met Lord Holloway's knowing gaze. She took a steadying breath, telling herself that nothing could happen here in her own home. "You startled me, my lord. I shall ring to have a message sent up to my mother, for I am certain that she will be happy to see you." She quickly moved to the bell rope and took hold of it.

Lord Holloway was standing near enough to the bell rope that he was able to lay a restraining hand over hers. She snatched her hand away from his touch, taking a step backward. Lord Holloway was amused. "And you, dear Miss Holland? Are you not happy to see me?"

Guin shook her head. She looked up at the gentleman who was smiling at her so arrogantly. A little spurt of anger emboldened her. Taking her courage in her hands, she declared, "I am not nor ever shall be, Lord Holloway."

"What a pity! I had thought we had come to a good understanding. Once I apologize to Mrs. Holland for my . . . precipitate exit, I will be back in her good graces. And then, Miss Holland, we will pursue our acquaintance," said Lord Holloway, his lips widening in a smile.

Guin retreated strategically behind a chair, and her fingers tightened on its gilded edge. "Do not come near me."

Lord Holloway negligently waved his scented handkerchief. "It is an inopportune time, I fear. There is too much chance of interruption from a servant or—"

The door opened again, this time for Sir Frederick to enter. He stopped abruptly when his gaze fell on Lord Holloway. His eyes traveled to Guin's tense face. Without hurry he advanced farther into the room, leaving the door open wide behind him. "Lord Holloway, this is a surprise."

Lord Holloway had stiffened upon Sir Frederick's appearance. His habitual smile had vanished. "Sir Frederick. You seem to have acquired the habit of becoming de trop."

"Have I? How extraordinary. I had quite thought the boot was on the other foot." Sir Frederick flicked imaginary dust from his coat sleeve. He had his whip in his other hand, and now he tapped it gently against one shining boot.

Lord Holloway's eyes dropped to that suggestive movement. When he raised his eyes again, he said, breathing a little quickly, "I understand you, of course."

"I thought you would," said Sir Frederick quietly, his gaze and his voice very even.

Lord Holloway turned toward Guin. "There will be another time, Miss Holland."

"No, my lord, there will not," said Guin swiftly.

Lord Holloway whipped around on his heel and strode out of the front parlor.

Sir Frederick reached for the door and slammed it shut. Flinging aside his whip, he bounded across the room to catch Guin's hands in his. His eyes held concern. "My dear, you are all right?"

Guin nodded, pretty color rising in her face. "Yes, I was never more glad than when you walked in! He is an awful, awful man."

Sir Frederick impulsively folded her into his arms. "My dear girl," he murmured. She raised her face, a look of surprise in her eyes. She looked like a startled kitten. Sir Frederick laughed and bent his head to kiss her.

He meant it as nothing more than a fleeting touch. But she made a sound in her throat and melted against him. Her soft responsive lips pressed warmly against his. Sir Frederick's senses swam. His arms tightened about her.

Abruptly he realized what he was doing, and sprang back. He stared at her, appalled. "Miss Holland! I—I don't know what to say. I beg your pardon."

"Oh, pray don't! I didn't mind it in the least," exclaimed Guin, her deep blue eyes shining.

Sir Frederick shook his head. He was stunned alike by his actions and the feelings that had been roused inside him. "You don't understand. I have taken the worst advantage of you."

"Didn't you wish to kiss me?" asked Guin falteringly.

Sir Frederick hated the dejection he could see forming in her eyes and how it caused a perceptible wilting in her demeanor. "My dear girl! I should think that was obvious," he said quickly. "But that doesn't make it right! Why, I have behaved no better than Lord Holloway toward you! Worse, for I have taken advantage of our friendship."

Not looking at him, Guin began tracing a random pattern with her finger on the back of the chair. "Sir Frederick, I know that I am wholly ignorant about such things. But I assure you that you have not behaved badly toward me at all." She peeped up at him from under her lashes. She caught her underlip between her white teeth in an anxious moue.

Sir Frederick drew in his breath. He had never seen her appear more bewitching. It struck him blindingly that he had never really seen her at all. She had been a girl to be pitied, to be helped and guided. Now she had become someone precious to his existence. He felt protective, tender, passionate, all at once. Dazedly, he wondered where his head had been while his heart had been lost.

The door opened again. Colonel Caldar came in with a quick step. He was smiling. "Sir Frederick! I saw your phaeton outside. Have you come to take Guin driving?"

"Yes, I had meant to do so," said Sir Frederick. He bent down to retrieve his whip from the carpet.

Colonel Caldar watched with gathering surprise. "What has been going on here?"

"Lord Holloway was here, Uncle. He left when Sir Frederick came in," said Guin, feeling that some explanation needed to be made, since Sir Frederick stood unaccountably silent.

Colonel Caldar's face darkened. "That dastard! He dared to show his face here? I suppose your mother had everything to do with it! Did she leave you alone with him, Guin? Did she? I shall have something to say to her, believe me!"

"No, no, Uncle, you mistake! Mama went upstairs before Lord Holloway arrived. She did not know anyone but Sir Frederick was coming," said Guin quickly. "I suppose the servants did not realize that Mama had left me and so brought Lord Holloway up."

Colonel Caldar let out a sigh. He nodded to Sir Frederick. "Then we owe another debt of gratitude to you, Sir Frederick. I am glad you were close by. I don't like to think of that fellow pressing his unwelcome attentions on my niece."

Unaccountably, Sir Frederick flushed. "You owe me nothing, sir." He turned toward Guin. "Miss Holland, I hope that you will forgive me. I have recalled a rather urgent errand that I was commissioned to do by the Foreign Office. I trust that you will hold me excused from our drive today."

"Of—of course, Sir Frederick," said Guin, taken aback. She looked up into his face as he raised her hand to his lips. "Shall I see you again?"

He met her gaze. The shadow of a smile touched his mouth. "I suspect you will not be easily rid of me, Miss Holland."

"I am glad," said Guin, relieved by the rueful twinkle in his brown eyes. For an awful instant, she had feared that he meant to cut short their friendship, all because of a single kiss. It would have been a silly thing for him to have done, which she would have told him if her uncle had not been standing in the room. Instead, she smiled at him and watched him leave after saying good-bye to her uncle.

Once Sir Frederick was gone, Colonel Caldar turned with an anxious expression to his niece. He said gruffly, "You mustn't take it to heart, Guin. I am certain Sir Frederick would not have canceled if it had not been extremely important."

"Oh, I am not in the least upset, sir," said Guin, a small smile playing about her mouth. She hugged to herself the knowledge of Sir Frederick's kiss. Perhaps the gentleman had begun to care for her, just a little.

The date of Lady Beasely's *soirée* arrived, and Guin actually anticipated attending the function. Since her extraordinary conversation with Miss Beasely, curiosity had overcome some of her usual dread of going into company. Her trepidation was laid entirely to rest when Colonel Caldar persuaded Lord Holybrooke to accompany them and make it a full family party.

Since Lord Holybrooke had expressed not an iota of interest in Miss Beasely, or for that matter, in any lady, Guin entered the ballroom wanting to see just how Miss Beasely intended to captivate her brother.

Lady Beasely and her daughter stood at the head of the stairs to receive their guests as they arrived. Lady Beasely greeted Lord Holybrooke and the rest of the party graciously. She was all kindness, even going so far as to compliment Guin on her gown. "How delightfully you look this evening, my dear!"

"Thank you, my lady," said Guin, surprised and shyly pleased by her ladyship's condescension. She had little opportunity to say more before Mrs. Holland engaged Lady Beasely's attention. She was not put out, however, for then she was free to move on to Miss Beasely.

Miss Beasely greeted her as though they were fast friends. "Guin! I am so glad you came," she said warmly, holding out both hands and squeezing Guin's fingers. She tucked Guin's hand into her arm. "Mama released me from my duties just as you came up the stairs. Come, I wish to introduce you to my particular friends. Pray join us, Lord Holybrooke! We are to have dancing before supper, just an informal romp. It will be good fun, I promise you."

"I should like that, Margaret," said Guin.

She glanced over her shoulder at her brother, curious as to how he was perceiving Miss Beasely's animated style. Correctly interpreting Guin's look, Lord Holybrooke grimaced ever so slightly. As Miss Beasely also glanced back to share a friendly word, his expression in an instant changed to one of polite civility.

However, Lord Holybrooke's bland politeness was abandoned when he discovered that Lord Tucker and a couple of his other particular cronies were among the company. "I didn't expect you to be here, Chuffy," he exclaimed, clasping his friend's hand.

"Oh, I wouldn't miss one of Lady Beasely's functions. Her ladyship always provides an amusing evening," said Lord Tucker.

"Thank you, my lord!" said Miss Beasely, laughter on her face as she swept a teasing curtsy. Lord Tucker grinned in response as though at a good joke.

"Besides, her ladyship's cook is superb," put in one of the other gentlemen.

All of the young gentlemen laughed, and so did Miss Beasely and Guin. "For shame! One would think you were ruled by your stomach, Peter," said Miss Beasely with a mock frown, speaking with the familiarity of one who had known the gentleman from the cradle.

"Well, so I am," said Mr. Lychbold candidly. He was a very tall, very thin young man. "I am always hungry. Ask anyone."

There was another round of laughter. Miss Beasely seized the auspicious moment to introduce Guin and to suggest gently that Miss Holland was an elegant dancer, with the result that Guin had promises of partners for the evening. The unprecedented acceptance brought warmth to Guin's face and a sparkle to her eyes. More than one of the young gentlemen gave her a second look, and Lord Holybrooke had the pleasant experience of having his sister described as a "taking little thing."

The composition of Lady Beasely's guests tended toward the younger set, which, as her ladyship explained to Mrs. Holland and Colonel Caldar, was a deliberate move on her part. "I wish to foster friendly familiarity among the young people before the Season is well and truly begun," said Lady Beasely. "I am a firm believer that our younger set, our daughters especially, must benefit from trying their wings in comfortable surroundings. Do you not agree, Mrs. Holland?"

"Oh, of course," said Mrs. Holland with a nod and lovely smile.

When Lady Beasely remarked that she had several other duties to perform and graciously excused herself to them, Mrs. Holland said to her brother, "I am vastly disappointed, Arnold. This affair is not at all what I expected of Lady Beasely! It is such an undistinguished and small company. I was never more taken in."

"Were you not listening to her ladyship, Aurelia? This evening is for the younger set. Lady Beasely explained it all to us," said Colonel Caldar mildly.

"I know what she didn't say, and that was that she wished her daughter to have ample opportunity to sit in Percy's pocket," said Mrs. Holland.

"Really, Aurelia!" began Colonel Caldar, his brows snapping together. Then he saw Mrs. Roman crossing the floor and all desire to remonstrate with his sister died. "Excuse me, Aurelia. I have just seen someone I know."

Astonished and affronted at being so summarily abandoned, Mrs. Holland watched as her brother left her side. Colonel Caldar made his way purposefully across the ballroom to go sit down beside a tall, elegant woman whom Mrs. Holland had never seen before. "Well!" She gave a little toss of her head and turned away to find her own entertainment.

Chapter Nineteen

Guin enjoyed the dances promised her by Lord Holybrooke and the cadre of amiable young gentlemen, after which she unobtrusively went to sit down on a settee against the wall. She watched the rest of the company and thought herself fortunate to have had so much attention paid to her. She was grateful to Miss Beasely for having seen to her enjoyment of the dancing. If she did nothing else all evening, Guin thought, it was quite the nicest time she had ever had.

However, she quickly discovered she had not been abandoned by her new friend. Miss Beasely brought up to her another gentleman who had arrived late and performed the introductions. Mr. Howard Lloyd was a sober middle-aged gentleman with a grave smile, well dressed but sadly inclined already to portliness. Knitted pantaloons and pumps did not become him.

"Mr. Lloyd was most desirous to meet you, Guin. He will take the greatest care of you," said Miss Beasely, easing herself away with a smile.

"Your obedient servant, Miss Holland." Mr. Lloyd bowed. There was the unmistakable creak of corsets.

Guin stared up at the gentleman, disconcerted. For once in her life, all thought of her own awkwardness flew completely out of her head. She swallowed a gurgle of laughter and invited Mr. Lloyd to sit down beside her.

Mr. Lloyd was nothing loath. "You are too kind, Miss Holland." He shook out his handkerchief and absently flicked it across the surface of the beautifully upholstered settee, as though to dust it off before he sat down. As he lowered himself, there was again the disconcerting sound of a creaking corset.

Guin discovered that she was still staring at Mr. Lloyd. She had to tear her eyes away. Mr. Lloyd was the oddest creature of her small acquaintance, she decided. She wondered with real sympathy whether Mr. Lloyd suffered from much the same malady of shyness as she did herself and that was what made him behave with such eccentricity. In addition, the gentleman's sad dependence upon a corset must assure him of some ridicule, she thought compassionately.

Guin became quickly at her ease with Mr. Lloyd, in part due to her own sympathetic nature toward a fellow being, but in greater part to Mr. Lloyd's complete lack of self-consciousness. As Mr. Lloyd expounded on the worth of several scientific theories, it became slowly clear to Guin that he was not at all shy. Quite the opposite. Mr. Lloyd was totally absorbed by his intellectual pursuits and had not a particle of brain cell to spare for such mundane matters as social unease.

Guin very quickly became bored, so much so that she could scarcely hide her yawns. She glanced around several times, hoping that someone would come to her rescue, for Mr. Lloyd had dominated her company for an inordinate length of time. However, no one seemed inclined to break up their tête-à-tête and since Guin was herself too conversationally inept, she could not think of how to graciously extricate herself from Mr. Lloyd without wounding his sensibilities.

When dinner was announced, Lord Tucker sought her out to fulfill his obligation to squire her in, and Guin sprang up with relief. She held out her hand to Mr. Lloyd. "Th-thank you for your company, Mr. Lloyd."

Mr. Lloyd got ponderously to his feet and ceremoniously bowed over her fingers. "It has been delightful, Miss Holland. I shall see you again, if I may?"

Guin retrieved her hand hurriedly. "Yes, of course. I

am certain we shall meet again," she said brightly, while
unobtrusively pinching Lord Tucker's arm through his
coat.

"Here, I say!" exclaimed Lord Tucker, greatly astonished. He met her eyes and recognized the pleading expression in them. At once and with instant presence of
mind, his lordship took leave of Mr. Lloyd and swept
her away.

"Thank you, my lord! You cannot conceive how eagerly I looked forward to your company," said Guin in
all sincerity, with a backward glance. Mr. Lloyd was
watching her, met her astonished gaze, and bowed. Guin
hurriedly looked away again.

Lord Tucker cracked a laugh, his eyes dancing as he
looked at her. "I shall take that, not in the spirit it was
offered, but as a compliment, Miss Holland. Was Lloyd
too prosy?"

"Dreadfully so," said Guin, smiling. She realized, when
Lord Tucker laughed again, that she had actually managed an intelligible and amusing interchange. It was with
a light step that she allowed Lord Tucker to escort her
into the dining room. She didn't know why the evening
was going so well, but she intended to make the most of
it. She could not recall ever enjoying herself more, except
perhaps when she had danced and driven with Sir Frederick Hawkesworth.

Guin's happiness dimmed slightly. She had been disappointed to discover that Sir Frederick was not among
the guests. However, she had already realized that Lady
Beasely's party was not designed for the *haut ton*, and
so she was able to shake off the change of mood easily
enough. She would undoubtedly see Sir Frederick again
at some other function.

After an excellent two-course dinner, there was more
dancing. Guin stood up several times. There was no need
for Miss Beasely to again make certain that Guin's hand
was solicited. All of the gentlemen who had danced with
her earlier in the evening had discovered in her an unde-
manding and graceful partner.

Since the breaking of the ice between them before dinner, she and Lord Tucker had made excellent inroads into understanding one another, and his lordship danced with her twice. There were Lord Holybrooke's other cronies, Lord Holybrooke himself, and, of course, her dear uncle Colonel Caldar. Mr. Lloyd was not behind in his attentions, either, also standing up with Guin twice.

Guin did not know where to look when the creaking of Mr. Lloyd's corset made itself heard every time he bowed, and everyone around them turned to stare. However, since Mr. Lloyd seemed completely unconscious of the figure he was cutting, Guin pretended that she did not notice.

Seeing that Miss Holland was being steadily escorted onto the dance floor, a few other gentlemen also approached her. Guin was bewildered by the sudden wave of popularity.

"You've become quite the belle," commented Lord Holybrooke in passing.

Guin blushed and gave a quick smile to her brother. "It—it is all very strange to me, Percy."

He squeezed her fingers. "Didn't I tell you that all you needed was a little time? The fellows are all saying how pretty you are. You're going along famously, Guin!"

"I hope Mama will think so," said Guin. As always, her mother's approval was never far from her thoughts. "Where is she, Percy? I haven't seen her hardly at all, and she hasn't spoken to me above three or four times all evening."

"Lady Beasely set up a card room. Mama discovered an old rival, and they are playing loo for penny points," said Lord Holybrooke.

Guin looked at him, wide-eyed. "Mama is playing cards? At a party?"

Lord Holybrooke laughed, mischief dancing in his eyes. "It is a desperate contest, Guin. I wish you might see it. Mama and the other lady are determined to squash each other. I doubt we will be able to drag her away from the table until she has won."

"I am glad Mama is being entertained. I feared it was not just the sort of gathering she preferred," said Guin.

Lord Holybrooke grinned. "You're right, Guin. It may not be in Mama's style, but I am enjoying myself. I'm glad I came."

"Are you, Percy? Even if Lady Beasely thinks you are a marital prize?" asked Guin with a quizzing look.

Lord Holybrooke shrugged and said philosophically, "Oh, well, I suppose one can't escape that sort of thing. At least I was wrong about Miss Beasely. She hasn't dogged me at all when I half expected her to."

"Yes, Margaret has been very busy," said Guin, nodding. She looked across the room toward her friend, who was standing amid a small group of guests and laughing. "She has been very good to me, even making certain that I had a partner for dinner. Lord Tucker and I got along famously."

Lord Holybrooke's eyes followed his sister's, and there was a warm look of approval on his face as he watched Miss Beasely. "Yes, I must thank her for that. She is quite nice, really. I am glad you have become friends with her, Guin."

Guin glanced swiftly at her brother in surprise, then thoughtfully returned her attention to Miss Beasely as Lord Holybrooke sauntered away from her and toward the group that surrounded the vivacious lady.

Throughout the evening Guin had watched how Miss Beasely helped Lady Beasely by acting the hostess, pairing couples for dinner, finding partners for those who were not dancing, and mingling with the guests. Guin did not see that Miss Beasely had spent an inordinate amount of time with her brother. In fact, Miss Beasely seemed to treat Lord Holybrooke with the same impartial friendliness as she did the rest of the guests.

Guin had wondered whether Miss Beasely had changed her mind about Lord Holybrooke. However, now observing how her brother was making himself attentive toward Miss Beasely, Guin began to perceive that Miss Beasely was going about her business in a very subtle way. She was not chasing Lord Holybrooke, but was causing the earl to chase her. Guin could not help chuckling over her brother's naïveté and, indeed, her own.

When they left the Beasely town house, it was well on midnight. Lord Holybrooke pronounced it to have been a jolly party. Guin agreed. "I have never spent a more pleasant evening," she added on a happy sigh. Not once had she disgraced herself, and she had been able to hold sensible conversations with scarcely a stammer with all manner of persons.

"For my part, I thought it insipid," said Mrs. Holland flatly. "I was forced to spend the entire evening with Maria Clyborne playing at loo for penny points. I have scarcely spent a more boring time in all my life."

Guin and Lord Holybrooke looked at one another. Guin's expression was questioning, and Lord Holybrooke mouthed silently that their mother had lost. Guin gave a small understanding nod. That would go far in explaining her mother's petulant mood.

"I must disagree with you, Aurelia. It was just the sort of entertainment I like best, being somewhat informal and intimate," said Colonel Caldar. He covered a contented yawn with a large square hand. "In any event, I for one would not think twice about accepting another invitation from Lady Beasely."

"Nor I," said Lord Holybrooke quickly. A reminiscent smile touched his face.

"Well! It seems I am outvoted," said Mrs. Holland with a pettish shrug. She turned her face to the window, where the passing lights cast her discontented expression into relief.

"I noticed that Mr. Lloyd seemed rather taken with you, Guin," remarked Colonel Caldar casually. "He certainly monopolized you for some little time."

"Indeed, Uncle," said Guin with a small grimace and shake of her head. "I was glad when Lord Tucker claimed me for dinner."

Mrs. Holland turned back, her interest instantly engaged. "What is this? Mr. Lloyd, did you say? I knew that I should not have remained in the card room! Tell me everything, Guin."

"Why, Mr. Lloyd is very pleasant, Mama," said Guin hesitantly. "But I found him to be rather—rather—"

"The gentleman is a dead bore, Mama," said Lord Holybrooke roundly. "When I met him, he began giving me his opinion of some theory in which I had not a particle of interest. Is that what he did with you, Guin?"

Guin smiled gratefully at her brother. "Well, yes, he did. I assure you, I know more now than I have ever wanted to about all sorts of scientific questions."

"A poor figure of a man, too. He'll run completely to fat before many more years, and he can't be a day above forty," said Colonel Caldar. He shook his head. "One can only pity the gentleman."

"Nonsense! I am certain that he is a very sensible gentleman. I met him very briefly, and I was instantly struck by his stable demeanor," said Mrs. Holland. "Lady Beasely told me something of his circumstances. Mr. Lloyd possesses a handsome fortune, and he is additionally the Marquis of Ford's heir! Mr. Lloyd is quite a feather in your cap, Guin."

Mrs. Holland's congratulatory tone was obvious. Guin and her brother exchanged quick, dismayed glances.

"That sobersides on cat-stick legs? All he could find to talk about to a pretty girl was scientific theory! Percy is right. He is a dead bore, poor fellow," said Colonel Caldar.

Lord Holybrooke cracked a laugh, while Guin giggled. "He was rather tedious," she agreed. "And he wears a corset, besides."

"No!" exclaimed Lord Holybrooke, revolted.

"Nonetheless, Guin, you must be certain to encourage Mr. Lloyd. He is just the sort of gentleman to suit you," said Mrs. Holland.

Guin's mouth dropped open, and she regarded her mother in complete consternation. Surely her mother could not be serious. Why, Mr. Lloyd was nothing near her embodiment of the perfect gentleman. He was far too old, and he creaked, besides. "But, Mama—!"

Lord Holybrooke at once took up the cudgels on her behalf. "Mama, Guin would be bored to tears within a week of Mr. Lloyd's company," he said with a touch of impatience.

"I have yet to observe any marked degree of liveliness in your sister, Percy," said Mrs. Holland with a reproving glance at her son. "When Guin becomes better acquainted with Mr. Lloyd, I am persuaded that she will come to appreciate all of his excellent qualities. They shall deal excessively well together."

Lord Holybrooke looked ready to argue the point, when Colonel Caldar intervened, saying hurriedly, "We needn't decide the future tonight." He greeted with relief the stopping of the carriage. He thrust open the door. "Here we are! Aurelia, allow me to give you an arm. Have I told you how vastly becoming that gown is to you?"

"Why, Arnold!" exclaimed Mrs. Holland in accents of surprise. "What a pretty thing to say!" She was never impervious to flattery, and her attention was diverted as she allowed her brother to help her out of the carriage.

"I assure you," said Colonel Caldar. "It is grown quite chilly. You must not stand about in the night air, Aurelia. Let us go inside directly." With a backward glance for his niece and nephew, who were just descending from the carriage, he hurried his sister up the town house steps.

Standing on the walkway, in the pool of light cast from a flambeau, Guin and Lord Holybrooke looked at each other. They shared a rueful smile. "Thank God for our uncle," said Lord Holybrooke, offering his arm to his sister. "I very nearly said something quite sharp to Mama."

"I could see that you were, and I was in dread of it," said Guin. "I am glad our uncle stepped in to such good purpose. I would not like you to quarrel with Mama, Percy, especially on my behalf."

Lord Holybrooke ushered her through the door that

the porter was holding open for them. "There's nothing in that, Guin. I am coming to the point where I can scarce keep my tongue between my teeth. Some of the things Mama says and does!"

Guin pinched him warningly. "Sh, Percy! The servants shall hear you."

"I don't care whether they do or not," said Lord Holybrooke, though he did lower his voice as they went up the stairs to the upper landing. "I tell you, Guin, Mama and I shall have it out one day."

"I hope not, Percy. I truly do," said Guin, a pucker of anxiety forming between her brows.

Lord Holybrooke chuckled. "Now, don't worry about it, Guin! You know that I shall always come about with Mama."

Her expression cleared. "Of course, how silly I am being."

"Well, you are." Lord Holybrooke yawned. "In any event, it was a jolly party. Miss Beasely is an unaffected girl, isn't she? I like her better than I thought I did."

"Do you, Percy? I like her, too. She surprises me into laughing," said Guin eagerly.

Pausing with her outside her bedroom door, Lord Holybrooke tweaked one of her dusky curls. "Capital, for you don't laugh enough, Guin. I'm off to bed." He walked off down the hallway, humming tunelessly.

Guin murmured good night and went into her own bedroom. Her maid, Morgan, was waiting up for her and helped her to change for bed. Before Guin fell asleep, she reviewed everything that had happened that evening. With a smile, she snuggled beneath her covers. Even her mother's disturbing approval of Mr. Lloyd could not dim her contentment.

Chapter Twenty

After the Beasely *soirée,* there was a spate of visits from several young gentlemen. Mrs. Holland was surprised that they were not all calling for Lord Holybrooke, but rather to further their acquaintance with Guin. Among their lively number was to be counted Mr. Lloyd's more sober figure.

It became quickly apparent that Mr. Lloyd had entered his suit in earnest. Mrs. Holland was delighted, especially since Mr. Lloyd met all of her criteria of birth and fortune and had firm expectations of a title. She began to weave plans for a brilliant society wedding, and only the groom's face was in doubt, for Mrs. Holland could not decide whether it would be Lord Holloway or Mr. Lloyd. However, one afternoon the odds became shortened in Mr. Lloyd's favor.

"Well! It seems that you are finally beginning to come into your own, Guin," said Mrs. Holland with a rare note of approval as she came into the back sitting room and found her daughter. "I have just come from talking with Percy. He wishes to see you in the library, Guin."

"Does he, Mama? Whatever for?" asked Guin, surprised, looking up from her embroidery.

Mrs. Holland laughed, her eyes sparkling. "Run along, child. I shall allow Percy to give you the good news."

Guin obeyed, wondering what news could have persuaded her mother to be so kind toward her. She knocked and entered the library. "Percy?"

Lord Holybrooke turned from contemplating the fire on the hearth. He wore a slight frown. "Guin, please sit down. I thought it best to break the news to you myself."

Guin sank down into a wing chair, her gaze fixed on her twin brother's face. She eyed him with foreboding. "Why, what is it, Percy?"

Lord Holybrooke said baldly, "Mr. Lloyd left me less than an hour ago. He has applied to me, as head of the family, to make a formal request for permission to address his suit to you."

"Oh, my!" exclaimed Guin faintly. "Mr. Lloyd! How—how odd, to be sure!"

"That is a rare understatement, my dear," said Lord Holybrooke with a lopsided grin. "My feelings were rather stronger, though I managed to maintain a polite front. Guin, do you wish to wed Mr. Lloyd?"

"Of course I don't! Why should you think that?" asked Guin, astonished.

"Mr. Lloyd assured me that he already knows he has Mama's support and only applied to me out of courtesy. He told me that Mama has implied you would not look with disfavor upon him," said Lord Holybrooke.

Guin bounced up from her chair. In greatest agitation she exclaimed, "That is not true! Oh, Percy, she is determined to thrust me willy-nilly into marriage. If it is not Mr. Lloyd, it will be Lord Holloway! What am I going to do?"

Lord Holybrooke took hold of her shoulders and looked down at her with a grimness about his mouth that Guin had never seen before. "Listen to me! You cannot let it just happen, Guin. You must have the fortitude to refuse Mr. Lloyd when he offers, if you don't want him."

"Yes, of course I must," said Guin doubtfully. "But it would have made it so much easier if you had simply refused him, Percy!"

"I couldn't very well do so when I know nothing disreputable about Mr. Lloyd," retorted Lord Holybrooke. "Be reasonable, Guin! You must stand up for yourself sometime, you know."

Guin pulled herself free. She stared at her brother with

open hurt. "You promised, Percy. You promised to help me!"

"And so I shall! Stay here, Guin. I wish you to be here when I talk to Mama," said Lord Holybrooke. He yanked open the door of the library and exited, to return a bare minute later with Mrs. Holland.

"Really, Percy, I don't know what all the heat is about," said Mrs. Holland. She glanced toward her daughter. "Pray do not tell me that Guin is being difficult!"

"No, Mama, she is not," said Lord Holybrooke evenly. He shut the door with a snap. "However, I felt it timely to bring to your attention a certain matter since we have been speaking of eligible *partis*. Pray be seated, Mama. And you, Guin."

When the ladies were seated, Lord Holybrooke leaned against the front of the mahogany desk. "Mama, you agreed that I should inquire into the circumstances of any gentleman who seemed interested in my sister. Some time ago, I did so with Lord Holloway."

"Lord Holloway! Why, Percy, I am certain that was not at all necessary. His lordship is quite an eligible *parti*, as we already know," said Mrs. Holland with a little laugh.

"On the contrary, Mama." Lord Holybrooke told his mother and sister that from everything he could discover, Lord Holloway's estates were mortgaged to the hilt, while his personal fortune was rumored to be in danger of evaporation through his gaming excesses.

"I am told that Lord Holloway faces immediate fore-closures on all of the mortgages. It appears certain his lordship will lose those fine northern estates of his," said Lord Holybrooke. He glanced toward his sister. "There is more that does not rebound to the gentleman's credit, but I shan't sully your ears with it."

Guin knew instantly what sort of thing her brother was referring to and flushed. Fortunately, her mother was too concerned with what Lord Holybrooke had imparted to wonder at her daughter's obvious discomfiture.

"But, Percy, are you certain?" asked Mrs. Holland in

acute dismay. "How came you by this information? Surely it is mere conjecture!"

"It is indeed true, Mama. Sir Frederick brought the information to me. You know how well connected he is. There can be no question," said Lord Holybrooke firmly.

Guin's eyes flew to her brother's face. "Sir Frederick! But why—" She stopped, warned by the quick frown that her brother threw her. She gave a tiny shrug. The why was not so important, she supposed. Warmth coursed through her, and a quiet smile lit her face. It was enough to know that once more Sir Frederick had come to her rescue.

However, Mrs. Holland was quick to grasp her daughter's point. "Yes, why would Sir Frederick come to you with this, Percy?"

"Sir Frederick considers himself to be a friend of our family, Mama. He took steps—that is, Sir Frederick knew something about the mortgages held on Lord Holloway's estates. I am more than satisfied," said Lord Holybrooke. He spoke quietly, with a peculiar smile, and there was a hardness in his eyes. Once more he glanced at his sister.

Of a sudden, Guin recalled what her brother had said about there being a better way to settle accounts with Lord Holloway. She had it in her to feel an instant compassion for his lordship.

"I suppose the news of Lord Holloway's ruin will be all over London before the week is out," said Mrs. Holland thoughtfully.

The earl gravely nodded. "I don't know how you may feel about it, Mama, but it is my opinion that our stature would not be enhanced if my sister were to form an alliance with Lord Holloway."

"No, indeed! I am profoundly shocked, Percy," exclaimed Mrs. Holland. She shook her head, her lips firming to a straight line of determination. "We shall no longer receive his lordship here. Guin, you will be guided by me in this. On no account are you to encourage Lord Holloway, though you may accord him a civil bow in company. Do you understand me, Guin?"

"Yes, Mama," said Guin obediently, even as a rush of relief ran through her. Guin did not know why her brother had set inquiries afoot concerning Lord Holloway, but the upshot was gratifying, at least to her. She had disliked Lord Holloway at first meeting, and she had never had cause to revise her initial reaction. There had been something about his lordship's mincing manners and the way he had of looking her over. Then had come that disgraceful interlude at the theater, when she had been so ignobly discovered in Lord Holloway's arms by Sir Frederick. The memory of it still had the power to fill her with shame. She was tremendously relieved when Mrs. Holland announced her intention to drop Lord Holloway from her guest list.

"For it is of no use pretending that his lordship is anything but a liability to us now," said Mrs. Holland, rising to her feet. "Thank you, Percy. It is good of you to look out for our interests so closely."

Guin looked at her brother, tears forming in her eyes. She felt wretched at treating him so badly. "Yes, thank you, Percy."

Lord Holybrooke flashed a quick grin. He made a graceful bow. "I live to serve."

A few days later, Guin was walking in the park with Miss Beasely and confiding to her friend the misgivings she felt about Mr. Lloyd's suit. "The gentleman is perfectly amiable, but I simply don't wish to marry him."

"Of course you do not," said Miss Beasely emphatically. "How nonsensical of Percy to give his permission. I am certain there are any number of gentlemen whom you would find more attractive."

Guin did not say so, but she could have told Miss Beasely there was only one gentleman who held any portion of her heart. Instead, she asked, "Has my uncle been to call on Mrs. Roman again today?"

Miss Beasely laughed. "Oh, yes! It is the dearest thing, too! Colonel Caldar has quite swept my cousin off of her feet. I feel it must be a match between them."

"I think you are right. My uncle actually blushed when I teased him just a little about Mrs. Roman," said Guin with a smile.

The young ladies heard themselves hailed and looked around. Mrs. Richardson pulled up her phaeton beside them and smiled down at them. "I perceive you are enjoying this fine weather!"

They exchanged pleasantries for a few minutes, before Miss Beasely complimented Mrs. Richardson on the stylish carriage and team she was driving. Mrs. Richardson laughed. "Thank you, Miss Beasely! I plume myself having achieved just the right effect. May I offer you and Miss Holland a ride home?"

With real regret, Miss Beasely said, "My mother's carriage is waiting for me at the gate, ma'am. But since Miss Holland came with me, there is no reason that she cannot take you up on your very flattering offer!"

Mrs. Richardson nodded at Guin, her eyes twinkling. "Will you trust yourself to my handling of the ribbons, Miss Holland? I shall endeavor to bear you safely home."

"I should like that very much, ma'am!" said Guin with alacrity. She told her friend good-bye, parting from Miss Beasely with assurances that they would meet again on the morrow, and climbed nimbly up onto the seat beside Mrs. Richardson.

Guin closely watched Mrs. Richardson's driving skills, and she was much impressed. "I should like very much to learn to drive as well as you, ma'am."

"Well, perhaps one day you shall. I am positive there must be some gentleman of your acquaintance who would be more than willing to give you lessons," said Mrs. Richardson with a quick smile.

Guin colored slightly and smiled, nodding her head. "Oh, I am persuaded that Sir Frederick would do so if I asked him. He is so very kind to me, ma'am, that there is no explaining it."

Mrs. Richardson turned an interested glance on her. "Indeed? Sir Frederick has been a friend of mine for a number of years. He is utterly charming and affable, of course."

Guin turned to her with enthusiasm. Her eyes glowed. "Exactly so! I don't think I shall ever meet anyone half as nice. Sir Frederick is truly a gentleman. He tells me just how to go on, and he is never cross or betrays the least impatience with me."

Mrs. Richardson was slightly taken aback. "Do you see much of Sir Frederick, then?"

"Oh, yes! He is quite one of our closest acquaintances," said Guin with the flash of a smile. "Sir Frederick often takes me driving, and I may be certain of having a dance partner whenever we attend the same function. I am so very grateful to him."

"I see! Well, that is something, indeed." Mrs. Richardson attended to her driving for a few minutes, her fine brows drawn together as she negotiated a corner, shooting between a dray wagon and a coach.

"Bravo, ma'am! I don't think even Sir Frederick could have done better," said Guin.

Mrs. Richardson glanced at her. "This is flattery, indeed," she said dryly.

Guin looked swiftly around. When she saw Mrs. Richardson's somewhat ironic gaze, she colored. "Forgive me, Mrs. Richardson! I did not intend to go boring on in such a fashion. It is just that Sir Frederick is such a particular friend of mine."

"You have no need to apologize, my dear. I am too well acquainted with Sir Frederick's charm to doubt the impression he could make on a susceptible heart," said Mrs. Richardson, smiling.

"You misunderstand!" said Guin quickly. "Sir Frederick does not fl-flirt with me. He is always a gentleman. It is only that I am so grateful to him. You see, I—I have always been awkward in company. Sir Frederick has been at pains to teach me how to go on so that I shall be more comfortable."

"You have made a hero of him, my dear. That is a dangerous thing for a young lady to do," said Mrs. Richardson, her smile fading. "You are likely to lose your heart to him if you are not careful."

Guin dropped her gaze. "Will—will I, ma'am?" She looked up again, to meet Mrs. Richardson's eyes. "Would it be such a bad thing? I know that I am beneath Sir Frederick's touch, but I am confident I shall not take hurt at his hand. And—and when I do wed, I shall know better how to go on just because I have known him."

Mrs. Richardson felt she had learned more than she had ever anticipated. "My dear!" She was silent a few moments, at last throwing her young friend a measuring glance. "Miss Holland—Guineveve! Pray do not be offended that I offer you a word of advice. More than anyone, I believe making a good match is essential to one's future happiness. It is not fortune or a handsome face or any other worldly consideration that will count in the end, as much as it will be whether one loves and is loved in return. Those other things are important, of course, but they will be as ashes where there is also indifference or perhaps even hatred."

"Mrs. Richardson, are you warning me against Sir Frederick?" asked Guin falteringly.

"No, I am not! What I am telling you, my dear, is to be very sure of your own heart. And when you are, bestow it where it will be received with gladness and tenderness. It would be a grave mistake to wed where there is not love," said Mrs. Richardson.

"I see." Guin drew a long breath. She smiled at Mrs. Richardson, who continued to look at her with a grave, even anxious, expression. "You have given me something to think about, ma'am. I do thank you."

"I trust that my advice will prove useful to you, Guineveve," said Mrs. Richardson. She pulled on the reins to bring the phaeton to a stop beside the curb. "Here we are! Just as I promised you, I have brought you safely home, Miss Holland."

"Thank you, ma'am," said Guin, climbing down from the phaeton. She looked up at Mrs. Richardson. "I shall remember what you have said."

Mrs. Richardson smiled, nodded, and then started her team up. Guin watched her drive away and then turned to walk up the steps of the town house. She had been sincere in her promise. She knew that she would not forget what Mrs. Richardson had told her.

Mrs. Richardson had given her the benefit of a totally different perspective. It ran counter to everything Guin had ever heard from her mother. Mrs. Holland had never addressed the question of love and where it fit into the equation when seeking a good match. On the contrary, all that seemed to matter to Mrs. Holland was the prestige and worldly goods that a gentleman could bestow on his chosen bride.

Guin felt confused, but also cautiously hopeful. Mrs. Richardson was a savvy, fashionable lady. Surely she could not be wrong when she advised Guin to seek love in marriage. Surely Guin could find some benefit from such sage advice.

Having virtually resigned herself to the inevitability of accepting whatever offer Mrs. Holland deemed most advantageous, Guin began to entertain the radical notion of accepting the suit of a gentleman for love. Guin had not realized, until Mrs. Richardson had taken it upon herself to speak to the point, that considerations besides worldly position and fortune could be measured as equal in importance. Now it came to her as a blazing revelation, and one that was underscored by a touch of fear. Dared she obey the dictates of her heart? She had been taught all of her life that social position and fortune were the epitome. She had no foundation upon which to build any other belief. She had suppressed her feelings and her emotions for so many years. Dared she even trust her heart?

Chapter Twenty-one

Guin entered the town house with her mind whirling with conjecture, alternating between hope and fear. There was no question that she loved Sir Frederick Hawkesworth, and she knew that he cared for her if only a little. How wonderful it would be if Sir Frederick was to offer for her! Of course, there would be Mrs. Holland's objections to overcome, for Guin knew that her mother thought less of Sir Frederick than she did of Mr. Lloyd. If only her mother could be brought to recognize Sir Frederick's superior qualities!

Guin was met with the intelligence that Mrs. Holland and Lady Smythe were closeted in the upstairs sitting room, and that she was wanted as soon as she came in.

All thought of the problem of her future flew out of her head as Guin ran upstairs to her bedroom to put off her hat and gloves and to make herself presentable. Within a few short minutes, during which her maid drew a brush ruthlessly through her hair and helped her to change into a day gown, Guin was able to knock on the door of her mother's private sitting room. Upon being bidden to enter, she opened the door. "Mama? You wished to see me?"

"Come in, Guin. Here is Lady Smythe, waiting for you this age," said Mrs. Holland waspishly.

Guin flushed, but pretended not to notice her mother's displeasure. She advanced, holding out her hand toward her ladyship. "My apologies for keeping you waiting, my lady. I have just come in from an airing in the park."

"You had no way of knowing that I would call, my dear," said Lady Smythe with a smile and handshake. Her graciousness was in direct contrast to Mrs. Holland's censorious attitude. "Were you out with friends?"

"Miss Beasely, ma'am, but I returned with Mrs. Richardson, who was kind enough to offer to drive me home," said Guin, sitting down beside her mother on the sofa.

"Mrs. Richardson! Well! I am surprised that she bothered with you, Guin, when I have heard any number of times that the lady is most assiduous in matching up eligible *parties*," said Mrs. Holland with a tinkling laugh.

"Mrs. Richardson has a certain talent in that direction, certainly," said Lady Smythe suavely. "Perhaps her friendship will prove advantageous for Miss Holland."

"As to that, I am certain that no one could have my daughter's best interests more to heart than myself, my lady," said Mrs. Holland defensively.

"There can be no argument with that, Mrs. Holland," said Lady Smythe.

Mrs. Holland smiled and agreed. It was left to Guin to stiffen at what she discerned to be a contemptuous expression in her ladyship's eyes. Much as her mother succeeded in embarrassing her or throwing her out of countenance, Guin could not stand it when Mrs. Holland was herself perceived with anything less than respect.

"We are naturally flattered by your visit, my lady. How may we be of service to you?" asked Guin coolly.

Lady Smythe raised her thin brows. Her shrewd eyes thoughtfully regarded Guin's flushed face. "Why, the shoe is quite on the other foot, Miss Holland. In point of fact, your mother has graciously granted her permission to allow me to throw you a ball."

"Isn't it wonderful, Guin! You are to go stay with her ladyship the entire fortnight beforehand so that she may instruct you in just how all the details for such a function are handled. It is her ladyship's exquisite consideration which impels her to such an unprecedented step, for I am certain that my own nerves could never stand up to the planning," said Mrs. Holland with her lovely smile.

The glitter of satisfaction in her eyes was obvious. "Of course, I shall not neglect my duty in chaperonage so that you may rest perfectly easy. I shall be there to be certain all goes just as it ought."

Guin understood perfectly that her mother was delighted with the arrangement. No doubt being freed of the expense and the organization of a ball exactly suited Mrs. Holland's taste. She therefore bit back the instinctive protest that rose to her lips, for it would not do the least bit of good to voice it. Indeed, Guin knew well enough that she would fall under her mother's severe displeasure if she were to even hint that the arrangement was not entirely welcome. She summoned up a smile. "Why, then, I must assuredly thank her ladyship for her condescension, and humbly hope that we do not trespass too hardily on her good nature."

Mrs. Holland threw a glance at her daughter, but since Lady Smythe greeted this speech with an amused disclaimer, she laughed. "Such a nonsensical girl! As if we could, when Lady Smythe has assured me quite otherwise! You will be glad to know, Guin, that I have already given instructions for your trunks to be brought up so that your things may be packed."

Guin stared in consternation. "But, Mama," she stammered, "you have surely forgotten! We are to go to Lady Conrad's musical *soirée* this evening and afterward to Vauxhall with Sir Frederick and his party."

"I certainly have not forgotten, Guin," said Mrs. Holland, shaking her head, smiling, but with a dagger glance. "Of course we shall fulfill our obligations; however, instead of returning here tonight, you will return home with Lady Smythe."

"I, too, am attending Vauxhall this evening, Miss Holland," said Lady Smythe. "Nothing could be simpler than for you to go home with me afterward."

"I—I know that I am being very stupid," said Guin. In point of fact, she was reeling from the abruptness with which things were happening.

"Yes, you are!" agreed Mrs. Holland. "You are insulting, besides."

Guin's face flamed. Her hands twisted in her lap. She turned an anxious gaze on Lady Smythe. "It is just that I have not had time to adjust myself to the notion, ma'am. I did not mean to offend you. I do hope you understand, my lady."

"Of course I do," said Lady Smythe. She rose to take her leave. "I know that you have a great many things to do yet this afternoon, Mrs. Holland, and so I shall leave you now. I shall see you both again this evening."

Mrs. Holland assured her of it and walked with her ladyship out of the room, ostensibly to show Lady Smythe to the door.

Guin knew that she could not flee to her bedroom, as she very much wanted to do, because her mother would certainly follow her. She had seen the look in her mother's eyes, just as Mrs. Holland had walked past her, and with a sinking feeling in the pit of her stomach had known that she was in for a thundering scold.

She did not have to wait very many minutes for Mrs. Holland's return. However, her mother was not alone. Lord Holybrooke came into the sitting room with her. Guin's eyes met her brother's, a single pregnant moment during which she realized that Percy knew there had been trouble and had come to help her. She sent him a slight smile of gratitude.

"How can you smile, Guin? I was never more put out with you in my life!" exclaimed Mrs. Holland.

"What has Guin done now, Mama?" asked Lord Holybrooke, casually strolling over to the sofa and flinging himself down. He caught Guin's hand and pulled her down so that she sat beside him.

Mrs. Holland gave an annoyed titter. "Why, she insulted Lady Smythe by daring to question her ladyship's arrangements to have her to stay. When I think of the advantage you have been handed, Guin, I could shake you for your idiocy!"

Lord Holybrooke had stiffened beside Guin. His expression was still, only his eyes showing emotion. "What is this, Mama? Guin is going to stay with Lady Smythe?"

"Lady Smythe wishes me to stay with her for a fort-

night, beginning this evening," said Guin in a subdued
voice. She glanced into her brother's astonished eyes and
smiled. "It is all right, Percy. I—I was merely surprised,
that is all."

"I should say so!" exclaimed Lord Holybrooke, rising
to his feet. "Mama, how can you countenance this?"

"Why, Percy! Whatever is the matter with you? Lady
Smythe is giving a ball in Guin's honor a fortnight hence.
She merely wishes to afford your ungrateful sister the
opportunity to learn what must go into the planning of
such a function. I find nothing in that to set up your
hackles!" said Mrs. Holland, surprised by her son's reaction. "Indeed, I am thankful that Lady Smythe is taking
such a close interest in Guin. It will undoubtedly be the
making of her, if she will but acknowledge it!"

"I grant you that Lady Smythe's friendship is advantageous to Guin—to us! What I don't understand is her
ladyship's willingness to be so helpful. Why, Guin is a
stranger to her. What possible motivation is there for
Lady Smythe to concern herself so nearly in Guin's affairs?" exclaimed Lord Holybrooke.

"You are making a piece of work over nothing, Percy.
It is very plain to me that Lady Smythe has been influ-
enced by the fact that you are the Earl of Holybrooke.
That is the reason her ladyship is being so obliging," said
Mrs. Holland, much in the tone reserved for reasoning
with a child.

"I have never entirely believed that, Mama," said Guin
quietly. As she expected, her mother took exception to
her voicing of an opinion that ran counter to Mrs. Holland's own.

Mrs. Holland gave an angry exclamation, before saying, "Then you are a great zany, Guin! Let me tell you
that being the Earl of Holybrooke is counted as something in this world and—"

"Have done, Mama," said Lord Holybrooke wearily,
throwing up his hand. "I have heard you on this subject
until I am sick to death of it. I agree with my sister.
Lady Smythe is herself too up in the world to care one

way or the other what I am called. That alone does not suffice to explain this patent interest in Guin's affairs."

"I shall not argue with you, dearest," said Mrs. Holland with a determined effort toward a smile. Her eyes still snapped with anger, and she avoided glancing at her daughter. "I am going upstairs to rest before I change for dinner. You will congratulate your sister on her good fortune!" Mrs. Holland swept out of the sitting room, slamming the door behind her.

"Lord, Guin, what's to be done? You can't go stay with Lady Smythe! It's the queerest turnout I've ever heard of," said Lord Holybrooke, taking a turn about the room.

"Actually, I think that I *should* do so," said Guin thoughtfully. When her brother swung around to stare at her, she chuckled. "No, don't look at me like that, dear Percy! I haven't run mad, I assure you. And I am not knuckling under, as you would say! I am just remembering something our uncle said to me not too long ago. When Lady Smythe made her first overtures, he told me that he had the feeling that it might be the very thing for me."

"I don't see how," said Lord Holybrooke. His eyes were hard, and there was a mulish look about his mouth.

Guin rose to her feet and smoothed her skirt. "Nor do I, Percy. However, I am very willing to find out if our uncle is right. Oh, don't look so tragic, Percy! I shall be back in a fortnight, after all. And it is not worth fighting Mama over. I should prefer you to keep your worst outburst for if she decides on someone perfectly repulsive for me."

Lord Holybrooke laughed. He shook his head. "I still don't like it. But I shan't stand in your way if you truly don't mind."

"Well, I do *mind,* but only because I shall miss you and our uncle," said Guin. "However, it is not for very long, and you will come see me every day."

"Yes, of course I will!" said Lord Holybrooke quickly, sliding an arm around her shoulders for a quick hug. He opened the sitting room door for her. "You know, I was engaged with a party of friends, but I think I shall go along with you and Mama to this music *soirée*. Just to keep an eye on you, you know."

"Thank you, Percy. I know that I may always count on you," said Guin, smiling up at him as she passed through the door.

Sir Frederick proved himself the perfect host. He had spared no detail or expense. He had secured one of the best situated boxes, where the activity in Vauxhall Gardens could be observed like a show and, later, would prove to be an excellent vantage point to watch the fireworks display. The supper that he had ordered for his guests was superlative, the champagne excellent. The mix of guests was skillfully done, providing even Mrs. Holland a compatible companion in her elderly admirer, General Layton.

It proved to be a successful gathering, and Sir Frederick was complimented more than once by his various guests for his efforts. When the fireworks began, there was a general move toward the front of the box. Most of the ladies chose to have their chairs resituated, but Guin stood at the rail, watching as the fireworks exploded high overhead across the soft night sky. It was a glorious sight, as the appreciative murmurs and laughter proved.

The evening air had grown cool, and Guin pulled her shawl closer. A warm hand drew the edge of the shawl gently over her shoulder, and she turned a surprised face.

Sir Frederick smiled down at her. His face was half in shadow, lit flickeringly by the glare from the fireworks. "Is that better?" he asked quietly.

Guin nodded. "Thank you, Sir Frederick. You always see to my comfort."

"I should like to have the right to do so, certainly," he said softly.

Guin's pulse leaped. She found that she could not breathe properly. She stared up into his face, attempting to read his expression in the uncertain light. "Yes, Sir Frederick?"

"Would you object if I were to call on you, in a formal way, Miss Holland?" asked Sir Frederick in a low voice. There was an undercurrent of meaning in the polite phrase.

Guin scarcely dared to hope that he meant what she thought he did. Her fingers tightened on the rail. "Oh, I would have not the least objection, Sir Frederick."

Sir Frederick sought her hand and carried it to his lips. His salute was pressed lightly on her tingling fingers. "I am honored, Miss Holland."

Guin blushed and was glad for the darkness. She was anxious that he knew what was happening in her life. "I—I shall not be at home for the coming fortnight, Sir Frederick." In a particularly bright explosion, she saw that his brows had quirked upward. She rushed into explanation. "I am to go to Lady Smythe's this evening. Her ladyship is giving a ball in my honor, and she wishes me to be involved in the planning of it."

"I see," said Sir Frederick, a slight frown coming into his face. He glanced down at her, a rueful smile touching his mouth. "My timing is obviously off by a fraction. Perhaps it will be best to wait on what I wished to say to you until you have returned home."

"If—if you think it best, Sir Frederick," said Guin civilly, even as she felt her heart plunge into acute disappointment.

He covered her hand, just for a moment, where it lay again on the rail. "Believe me, I would not for worlds interfere with Lady Smythe's plans for you. Her ladyship is a great lady, and a good friend to those whom she likes."

"Then you do not think that her ladyship is being kind to me because Percy became an earl?" asked Guin.

His astonishment was plain, even in the half-light. "My dear! Of course not. Lady Smythe has chosen to befriend you because it pleases her to do so. That is the full sum of it."

"I had wondered, you see," said Guin.

There was no further opportunity for private conversation, since Sir Frederick's attention was claimed by one of his other guests. He moved away and Guin felt his absence. Yet, as she drew her fingers along the edges of her shawl, she was happy. She tipped back her head and lost herself again in the wonder of the magnificent fireworks.

Chapter Twenty-two

When Lady Smythe disembarked from her carriage, followed by Guin, her ladyship did not linger in the spacious entry hall of her large town house, but ordered her guest to follow her into the sitting room. Refreshments were brought while the ladies made themselves comfortable. Lady Smythe told her servants to go away. They did so, noiselessly closing the ornately carved door.

Lady Smythe did not allow Guin to reflect on the awkwardness of her situation. Quite dispassionately, her ladyship said, "You are probably a sensible girl, so I shall not waste time in pretty phrases. I have persuaded your mother to allow you to come stay with me for precisely three reasons. When I decided to see whether or not I could bring you into fashion, it was an object with me to separate you from your mother. You do not shine in Mrs. Holland's presence. In addition, while it is quite true that I shall instruct you in how to put together a successful ball, I am also determined to see that you acquire a bit of town bronze before you stand at the top of my stairs and greet my guests. You have very little countenance, and I will not have my ball pronounced a failure because you shrink into the woodwork."

Guin scarcely knew whether she should be crushed or indignant at her ladyship's plain speaking. She decided that indignation gave her the greater dignity. "All of what you say about me may be true, my lady. However, I never asked you to sponsor me, and so I fail to understand why you should put yourself to such trouble at all!"

"No, quite true," said Lady Smythe unperturbedly. "I am glad that I was not mistaken when I thought I detected a bit of spirit in you on a couple of occasions. It will make things all the easier. You would be a beauty if you showed your teeth more often, my dear."

"Thank you, I am sure, ma'am," said Guin, obeying this injunctive in a literal spirit by lifting her lips in what looked suspiciously like a ladylike snarl.

Lady Smythe chuckled. "No, no, my dear! Such ferocity won't do. You must be more subtle and allow the flash in your eyes to convey your displeasure. The barest smile will suffice for those who are to be accorded cold civility. As for those you wish to encourage, lower your lashes and glance upward through them. Any man worth his salt will respond to such an invitation!"

Guin spluttered on a laugh. "Ma'am, you are absurd!"

"That's good," said Lady Smythe approvingly. "You must cultivate that delicious chortle."

Guin shook her head, smiling at her hostess. "I understand at least that you mean me no harm."

"Of course I don't! Oh, you are still puzzling over my motives, are you? Well, they are not at all pure, for I am no philanthropist! Simply put, my dear, you are in the way of being an experiment and a challenge," said Lady Smythe.

Guin blinked. "I don't follow you, my lady."

Lady Smythe sighed. "Really, it is so fatiguing to be forced to explain oneself. I am bored, Miss Holland. You can have no notion how boring society can be when one sees the same faces and goes to the same sort of functions Season after Season. The only relief is to be found in scandal, but I am far too old to become the center of one. Failing that diversion, I decided that taking a nonentity, yourself in fact, and turning her into the toast of the Season could afford me several weeks of amusement."

Guin turned red. She could not recall ever being so angry in her life. "I am not at all enamored of your scheme, ma'am!"

"Who asked you to be?" asked Lady Smythe with a

wicked smile playing about her thin lips. There was an understanding gleam in her eyes. "Oh, I've insulted you finely, haven't I? But perhaps you should look at it in a different way. I am making use of you for my own ends, of course, but I offer you the chance to learn to shine when otherwise you would go your insignificant way. You would undoubtedly end the Season the despair of your mother without a single suitor to your credit."

Her ladyship's neat summation gave Guin pause for reflection. She was forced to acknowledge the legitimacy of Lady Smythe's supposition. It had been abundantly demonstrated that she lacked the background to handle herself well in the social milieu into which she had been thrust. By herself, she did not have the confidence to overcome this crippling drawback. When she thought about Miss Beasely and Lady Beasely, Mrs. Richardson and Lady Smythe, as well as others she had met, Guin knew quite suddenly that she wanted to become just as assured and poised. She didn't care very much about acquiring a number of suitors, of course, but it would be nice to see a flicker of admiration in a gentleman's eyes, such as Sir Frederick's.

"Very well, my lady. I accept the situation as you have outlined it," said Guin quietly. "What must I do?"

Lady Smythe regarded her for a long moment. "So you have made up your mind?"

"Oh, yes. My uncle told me that your interest in me would prove to be to my advantage, and I quite see that he is right," said Guin in an even voice.

"The devil he did! I must further my acquaintance with Colonel Caldar. He is obviously a gentleman of perception," said Lady Smythe. The glimmer of a smile lit her rather cold blue eyes as she looked at her houseguest. "I intend for you to work very hard, Miss Holland. You will not find me an easy taskmistress this fortnight."

"I am ready, Lady Smythe," said Guin, drawing in a determined breath.

Guin was to wonder in the next several days if she

would have made such a declaration if she had known what she would be subjected to. Morning to evening, there were lessons. Lady Smythe engaged the services of experts she thought essential. A dancing master honed Guin's twirls and lightness of foot on the dance floor; a refined lady of uncertain origin drilled Guin in all the social graces at table and in the drawing room until she could pour tea or faultlessly place personages in the proper order at a dinner party; a teacher in elocution taught her to project her voice and enunciate clearly so that her naturally soft tones would not be drowned out or sound incoherent. She tumbled into bed every night exhausted by her exertions.

In addition, Lady Smythe directed her personal secretary to guide Miss Holland in the work of addressing invitations and making up lists for decorations and wine and refreshments and engaging an orchestra. In short, Guin found herself taking a pivotal role in organizing the ball that Lady Smythe was sponsoring. It frightened her, but it was all very exciting at the same time.

Lady Smythe was given reports of Miss Holland's progress by all of the personages who were working so diligently to transform her. Her ladyship was pleased and even a little surprised, for Miss Holland seemed to be driving herself as hard as did any of her teachers.

Colonel Caldar and Lord Holybrooke frequently came to call at Lady Smythe's town house. Her ladyship said that she knew that they did not come to see her, and after several visits she declared herself on too familiar terms with the two gentlemen to stand on ceremony with them any longer. As often as not Lady Smythe simply began sending down her compliments and allowed her protégée to meet with her family in private. Guin was grateful. There was always news to be exchanged of one another's doings, and she thought it awkward to do so when Lady Smythe was present, for her ladyship surely could have little interest in what most nearly concerned Guin's relations.

However, during one visit, Colonel Caldar particularly

requested her ladyship's presence and his news aroused even Lady Smythe's jaded palate when her ladyship heard it.

Colonel Caldar announced that he was wedding Mrs. Roman by special license. "It is to be a small wedding with just family and a few friends. I wish you to come, Guin. It would make me very happy."

"Of course I shall come!" exclaimed Guin, leaping up to hug her uncle. "I am not at all surprised, for you and Mrs. Roman have been smelling of nosegays for weeks."

Colonel Caldar flushed and laughed. He diffidently extended the invitation to Lady Smythe, who promptly declared her intention of being the first to congratulate Mrs. Roman on her good fortune.

"You are a sensible man, Colonel Caldar. There are not many such around," said Lady Smythe astringently.

Colonel Caldar was made speechless. With great presence of mind, he made a formal bow in acknowledgment. This further endeared him to Lady Smythe, who observed after the colonel had left that she never had liked men who talked in flowing periods.

Since Guin knew that this was a direct reference to Mr. Lloyd, who had also called several times, she giggled. "Yes, dear ma'am! You prefer someone like Sir Frederick, who flirts with you so outrageously!"

Lady Smythe darted a shrewd look at her. "And do you not also prefer Sir Frederick, my dear?"

Guin blushed furiously and replied, with dignity, that she thought there must be some further help she could give to her ladyship's overworked secretary. Lady Smythe chuckled as her protégée left the room.

It was not Lady Smythe's intention to keep Guin locked away from society while she was being groomed. Naturally Guin joined her mother's party whenever that lady wished for her company.

However, since Mrs. Holland's desire for her daughter's presence was at most lukewarm, that lady was content enough with the arrangement as it was. Mrs. Holland was enjoying the Season far more than she had coming out as a young miss. Old scandals had in a fair way been forgotten, and the gentlemen were pleasantly inclined to flirtation. Mr. Lloyd, apparently feeling that it was advantageous to his cause, called as often on his prospective mother-in-law as on the lady he had solemnly decided to make his wife.

It was gradually borne in on Guin that she felt happier and more content than she had ever been in her life. Lady Smythe, and those her ladyship had under her, were exacting, but Guin was never made to feel stupid. She began to gain more confidence, and it showed in her manner and in the way she carried herself.

In fact, on one of his visits to her, Lord Holybrooke said, "I don't know what it is, Guin, but you're changing. And I like what I see." He swooped over and kissed her on the forehead.

Guin laughed and pushed him away. She was actually very pleased by her twin's observation. "Thank you, dear brother! Now, unless you wish to drive out with Lady Smythe and me, you must go away so that I can go upstairs and put on my hat."

"I'm away, then," said Lord Holybrooke promptly. "Give my regards to her ladyship and tell her that I approve."

Lady Smythe often drove out in her carriage, with Guin accompanying her, to call on friends. Guin's manners grew to be very pretty as she spent time with Lady Smythe and her particular cronies. On several occasions Lady Smythe was gratified to be told that her protégée behaved just as she ought. It was not long before vouchers for Almack's were extended to Miss Holland, and she had made her debut at that august club. In short order, Miss Holland was granted permission by the patronesses to participate in the waltz.

Lady Smythe was too shrewd to neglect Guin's interaction with the younger set. She was allowed to go for frequent walks with her bosom-bow Miss Beasely or riding with her brother and whatever others could be made up into a party.

Sir Frederick was a frequent caller at Lady Smythe's town house. At first Guin was somewhat surprised but hesitantly pleased that Sir Frederick was apparently such a close friend of her new mentor. Lady Smythe commented acidly that he was constantly underfoot. However, Guin could not but be glad for it. She could be assured of practicing her latest dance step with Sir Frederick or play off the company manners that Lady Smythe was instilling in her and not feel the least discomfiture. Sir Frederick had always a ready word of encouragement or humorous quip for her. Guin was becoming more and more convinced that she would never meet another gentleman quite like him.

On the eve of the ball, Guin received not one but several posies with silver-gilt cards tucked into them. All were from gentlemen whom she had met since coming to London. She was astonished. "Why, my lady, whatever am I to do?"

"Do? Listen to yourself, child! You must choose one of these pretty offerings and pin it to your gown," said Lady Smythe, rather amused by her young companion's amazed consternation.

"But which one?" said Guin helplessly, surveying the row of beautiful tiny bouquets tied with ribbons.

Lady Smythe rose with a rustle of silk. "I shall wash my hands of you in a moment, Guineveve! Which one, indeed! Why, the one from the gentleman who most nearly possesses your heart, of course. It is a subtle way to encourage the male of the species in his pursuit." Her ladyship's brows rose in pointed query.

Guin's color rose, yet she laughed across at her ladyship. "I see! Very well, ma'am! I shall do just as you say."

"And I suppose you will not reveal to me the gentleman's name?" asked Lady Smythe.

Guin shook her head, still smiling. "He—he has not declared himself, you see."

"Then most assuredly you must encourage him, whomever he is," said Lady Smythe with a wicked, knowing glance. She exited the bedroom well satisfied. The girl was coming along nicely, better than she had ever expected when she had first discussed Miss Holland with Sir Frederick. Lady Smythe's smile widened as her thoughts dwelled a little longer on Sir Frederick Hawkesworth. "I really ought to speak again to Mrs. Richardson," she murmured to herself.

When Guin went downstairs to join Lady Smythe in greeting the guests, and later, when she had been released to mingle with the company, she felt herself to be moving on a gilded cloud. For the first time in her life, she knew herself to be beautiful. It had taken long, unhappy weeks and the inexplicable kindness of several individuals to bring Guin to the realization, but she was at last convinced of her own worth. All that she had endured, and had learned, became supremely worthwhile when Sir Frederick's gaze fell on the posy pinned at her breast.

Guin saw the leap of light in his eyes, and she knew Lady Smythe had been right. Everything faded somewhere into the background, until there existed just herself and Sir Frederick. He held out his hand to her, and without a word she placed her own in it. His fingers closed over hers, and he swept her into the waltz.

Guin laughed breathlessly. "How did you know that I had been given permission to waltz?"

"I am a consummate diplomat, Miss Holland. I have many, many connections," said Sir Frederick with mock pomposity. When she giggled, he flashed his quick smile. "Actually, Lady Smythe let it drop when I called to leave flowers for you. You are wearing them."

"Yes." The charm of his smile took her breath away. She shook her head and sighed regretfully, but a tiny smile touched her lips. "It—it was such a difficult decision. I had so many to choose from."

Sir Frederick's dark brows rose. His arm tightened about her waist. "I trust it was not *too* difficult?" he asked softly, looking down at her with a possessive light in his brown eyes.

Guin blushed and dropped her gaze. "Oh, no, it was not," she acknowledged, unable to continue her flirtatious teasing when he looked at her in just that way.

"I am glad, Guin," said Sir Frederick quietly.

Guin swiftly looked up, surprised by his familiar use of her Christian name. What she saw reflected in his eyes caused her heart to pound. Guin was whirled away into a night to be forever remembered.

Chapter Twenty-three

Lady Smythe's ball was pronounced a sad crush and a smashing success. Miss Holland was touted as a ravishingly lovely, very prettily behaved young lady. The invitations swelled in number, and Lady Smythe's ball proved to be but the beginning of a long crest breaking toward the end of the Season.

Mrs. Holland was in high alt. Though there were titled gentlemen who called on her daughter and paid Guin court, Mrs. Holland was shrewd enough to realize that most were simply drawn by her daughter's inexplicable social success. Mrs. Holland decided that Guin's future, and her own social consequence, would be best served in the person of Mr. Lloyd.

A few offers were actually made for Miss Holland's hand, which Mrs. Holland had no hesitation in declining. She did not deem it necessary to inform her daughter of these passages, since none of the gentlemen in question came up to her expectations. It would be time enough to inform Guin of the name of her future husband when the gentleman presented himself.

Guin had thought long and hard about what Mrs. Richardson had said to her that day in the park. She had come to know her own heart very well, and had for a little while denied it because of all the difficulties she had foreseen, but at last she acknowledged to herself that she was in love with Sir Frederick. It had seemed to her, especially recently, that Sir Frederick was not entirely indifferent to her and that gave her hope when she had before been utterly convinced of her own unworthiness. However, that did not mean the primary obstacle in the thorny path she was weaving toward happiness had been overcome.

Guin had grown in confidence, but it took all the courage she could muster to broach the subject of Sir Frederick's attentions toward her to her mother. She chose a particularly auspicious moment, when her mother had just finished addressing an acceptance to a particularly flattering social invitation from a well-placed hostess.

"Mama, Percy is quite impressed with Sir Frederick Hawkesworth. He—he feels that Sir Frederick is just the sort of gentleman who would make a good husband for me," said Guin hopefully. Her cheeks were tinged with color at actually voicing such a possibility, for though her heart was firmly attached, she thought she knew better than to trust in the dream that Sir Frederick might return her affection in such full measure. After all, Sir Frederick had yet to approach either her mother or her brother as he had hinted he would that evening at Vauxhall Gardens. However, if her mother's ambitions could be swayed in favor of Sir Frederick, then Guin felt she would not altogether despair.

"Sir Frederick Hawkesworth! Why, he is a mere baronet! I look higher than that for you, Guineveve. You are the sister of the Earl of Holybrooke, after all," said Mrs. Holland complacently, sanding the sheet and folding it.

Guin knew at once, and with a sinking heart, exactly what her mother had in mind. Though none of her serious admirers was a peer, there was one who would one day step into a title. It would be just like her mother to latch onto a future expectation for her, for Mrs. Holland had done that very thing when she married Guin's father. Of course, it had not turned out just as Mrs. Holland had hoped; instead, Percy had inherited the title, which was almost as good in Mrs. Holland's estimation.

"Mr. Lloyd is not a peer, Mama," ventured Guin.

"He is not now, but he is Lord Rockham's heir! My dear, only think of it! You could one day become a marchioness." Mrs. Holland cut off her raptures to study her daughter's pensive expression. "Why, never tell me that you have taken Mr. Lloyd in dislike!"

Guin made haste to reassure her mother. "Oh, no! Of course I haven't. Mr. Lloyd is all consideration and—and I like him very well! But—"

"I knew that I could count on your good sense, Guin," said Mrs. Holland, bestowing a rare smile on her daughter. In congratulatory accents, she continued, "You have grown amazingly longheaded this Season, which I never thought to be possible, as stupid as you behaved when we first came to town. But I shall not scold you, for you have improved amazingly since then." She moved away with a swish of skirts to the gilded mirror, where she inspected her reflection with a critical but not unappreciative eye. She fluffed the laces at her bodice, tilting her head to study the effect.

"But, Mama, about Mr. Lloyd—" said Guin, somewhat desperately, tensely clasping her hands together.

"Yes, Mr. Lloyd! I am very well content, Guin, for I hourly expect him to make an offer to you. You would be a great fool to refuse such a well-bred, distinguished, and well-connected gentleman! His fortune is merely respectable, but we shan't refine too much upon that, since he has large expectations!" said Mrs. Holland, smiling contentedly at her reflection.

"Oh, dear!" exclaimed Guin, half under her breath. Dismayed, she perceived that her mother would never countenance the thought that she might not wish to wed Mr. Lloyd.

"What did you say, Guin?" asked Mrs. Holland, turning to her daughter. There was a hardening glint in her eyes. Something of her daughter's daunted attitude had begun to penetrate through her thick complacency, and she had begun to suspect that not all was as settled as she would like it to be.

Guin sighed, defeated, and shook her head. "Nothing,

Mama! I was merely reflecting upon my—my good fortune! I have made many friends this Season and—and acquired almost a score of suitors. It has me in a puzzle how it all came about!"

Mrs. Holland laughed, at once completely in charity with her again. "Indeed! I did not expect you to go off so well, certainly! However, between Lady Smythe and myself, we have made a success of you and I hope you are properly grateful!"

"Of course I am, Mama," said Guin with a quick, lopsided smile. "How could it be otherwise? I shall never forget Lady Smythe's kindness, nor that of Mrs. Richardson."

A faint frown flitted across Mrs. Holland's face. She did not care for Caroline Richardson, though that lady had never been uncivil or backward in any attention. "Well! I should hope that your uncle and your brother and I might expect an expression of thanks."

"Oh, of course!" said Guin hastily, not at all backward at perceiving her mother's displeasure. She was aware of her mother's dislike for Caroline Richardson, and she had known instantly she had made a mistake in bringing the lady's name up. "And then there is Sir Frederick Hawkesworth, who has been so unfailingly kind and obliging from the very beginning."

"Yes, indeed! We must not forget what we owe to Sir Frederick. He was the one who uncovered Lord Holloway's unpalatable circumstances to us, after all! Why, we might not have otherwise found out until you were well and truly wed to Lord Holloway! What a mistake *that* would have been," said Mrs. Holland, at once forgetting her irritation. "I shall be particularly gracious to Sir Frederick when next I see him."

However, when Sir Frederick sent his card up the following afternoon and was received by Mrs. Holland, it was not graciousness that was her uttermost feeling upon learning his errand to her.

Sir Frederick was civility itself, and nothing could have exceeded his affability, though it was tinged with a slight diffidence that sat ill on one usually so easy in company. The reason was shortly forthcoming. Sir Frederick cleared his throat and plunged into the business at hand. "Mrs. Holland, you cannot have overlooked the attentions which I have shown to your daughter, Miss Holland."

"No, indeed! As Guin and I were saying just yesterday, you have been extremely kind and obliging toward her this Season. Will you not have a biscuit, Sir Frederick? I assure you that they are quite good," said Mrs. Holland, offering the plate.

Sir Frederick politely declined. He was a little at a loss, for Mrs. Holland had spoken in quite a normal tone and without seeming to have a hint what he was getting at. "I am happy that I have won such accolades, ma'am. However, I hope I may persuade you that my regard for Miss Holland is more than that of friendship. Indeed, Mrs. Holland, I have come here today in hopes that you will grant me permission to pay suit to your daughter. That is, if Miss Holland would find my suit agreeable, of course!"

Mrs. Holland regarded him with astonishment, her expression swiftly undergoing transformation as she absorbed his meaning. Her smile firmly in place, but with a less friendly light in her eyes, she said, "Sir Frederick! You have caught me quite by surprise. If I had known—! However, I suppose it is not too late to tell you! I am sorry, Sir Frederick, but I fear that I cannot countenance your suit!"

Sir Frederick was utterly taken aback. "Ma'am! Am I to understand that you deem me unsuitable? I can assure you of the sincerity of my sentiments. I—I am most attached to Miss Holland, and I have thought that she regarded me with some degree of warmth. I can assure you, too, of my ability to support a wife. In fact, I will be most happy to lay before you and Lord Holybrooke, as well as your man of business, all facts concerning my estate."

Mrs. Holland shook her head, still smiling. "I do not

doubt the truth of everything you have said, Sir Frederick. But alas! I fear it is not in my power to encourage you! You see, and I know you will not put it about, since nothing has been announced just yet, but my daughter is contemplating an offer from Mr. Howard Lloyd."

Sir Frederick's mind reeled. He felt like he had been kicked in the chest by a horse. "I—I see." He could scarcely draw breath. When he focused on Mrs. Holland's face, he saw that she was regarding him with something like pity. With an effort he managed to pull himself together. With what dignity he could muster, he said, "I am severely disappointed, naturally. Pray convey my felicitations to Miss Holland. You—you will forgive me if I do not stay, Mrs. Holland. I have an engagement to keep."

"Of course, Sir Frederick." Mrs. Holland rose at once and held out her hand. There was a peculiar satisfaction in her eyes. "I shall not stand on ceremony and show you out, Sir Frederick, for I am certain you know the way. Why, I have counted you as our friend for some months! I hope that we may continue to do so?"

Sir Frederick shook his hostess's hand. Her words underscored the disastrous outcome of an interview upon which he had pinned every expectation of a happy future. A friend! That was all he was to Miss Holland! His years of diplomatic training were all that kept his emotions under rigid control. Only the telltale tick at one corner of his mouth betrayed him. He knew that he smiled and said something civil, but ever afterward he could not remember what it was, or indeed, recall how he got out of the town house.

He looked around him in a dazed fashion, recognizing at last that he was standing on the flagged walkway. Sir Frederick squared his shoulders and began to make his way down the street. A short rain shower had started, but he scarcely noticed it. The only thing that stood out in his thoughts was that once again he had fallen in love with a woman who had preferred someone else.

A voice penetrated his consciousness. "Sir Frederick!

I say, Sir Frederick!" From a great distance, he summoned his thoughts and brought them to focus on the gentleman who was regarding him with an increasingly concerned expression. Mechanically, he inquired, "Colonel Caldar. How do you do, sir?"

"I am very well, thank you. But you, sir!"

Sir Frederick drew himself together. He managed a smile. "Forgive me, Colonel. I was deep in abstraction. I have much on my mind at present. I—I have accepted a post in Paris, and I shall be leaving London shortly."

"Oh!" Colonel Caldar stared at him with obvious surprise. "Well, that is news indeed."

"Yes, if you will excuse me, sir?" Sir Frederick scarcely waited for the gentleman's hurried acquiescence, but walked swiftly away.

Colonel Caldar stood frowning after Sir Frederick for only a minute or two, before he strode swiftly toward the town house. There was no reason that he knew of for Sir Frederick to be in this street except if he had come from calling at the town house. After seeing the stricken look in Sir Frederick's eyes, Colonel Caldar could leap to only one conclusion. He hoped very much that he was wrong.

However, when he reached the town house and demanded a private interview with his sister and taxed her about Sir Frederick's visit, he was appalled to realize the truth of his unwanted conclusion. "How could you have done such a thing, Aurelia?" he gasped. "How could you reject Sir Frederick's offer out of hand in such a crude fashion?"

Mrs. Holland twitched her shawl straight with some annoyance. "Really, Arnold! You are being incredibly obtuse. Why shouldn't I reject Sir Frederick's suit? Guin is going to marry Mr. Lloyd or someone like him. My daughter is not to be thrown away on a mere baronet, as I have told you before!"

"Doesn't Guin's happiness count with you at all, Aurelia?" demanded Colonel Caldar in growing anger.

Mrs. Holland stared, then laughed. "My dear brother,

Guin shall be quite happy when she becomes a titled lady."

"You cannot have considered! Aurelia, unless I miss my guess, your daughter is half in love with Sir Frederick," said Colonel Caldar baldly.

"My daughter," said Mrs. Holland with emphasis, her brown eyes very hard, "will not disoblige me by marrying someone of whom I do not approve. And let me remind you, Arnold, that I am Guin's mother and neither you, nor my new sister-in-law, have any rights where she is concerned. I shall do precisely what I think best, and you cannot say a word against it!"

Colonel Caldar bit back an exclamation. After a short struggle, he said stiffly, "I am aware of it! And I bitterly regret it. However, you are wrong in at least this respect, Aurelia! I care deeply about Guin, and you may be certain that I shall continue to air my opinion on this subject."

Mrs. Holland dissolved into tears. She looked reproachfully at her brother. "Arnold! How can you abuse me in such a fashion? I am only doing my poor best!"

"It is very poor, indeed!" exclaimed Colonel Caldar hotly, before slamming out of the sitting room.

That evening Colonel Caldar and his wife came to dinner. Guin observed there seemed to be some tension between her mother and her uncle. They were meticulously polite toward one another. Mrs. Caldar regarded all with a thoughtful gaze, her usual serene composure unruffled.

Afterward, when Colonel Caldar had followed the ladies to the sitting room for after-dinner coffee, he remained unusually silent. Guin knew that her mother still very much disliked it when Lord Holybrooke was engaged elsewhere when she and her mother dined at home. No doubt Mrs. Holland had complained to Colonel Caldar about it, and he, not wishing to enter into fruitless argument, had simply become uncommunicative.

Her supposition seemed substantiated when Mrs. Holland expressed her pride in her son's achievement yet also voiced pique that he was drawing away from her. "I don't understand, brother, why Percival must be out every evening. I have greater need of him than ever before as my escort. It seems strange to me that he is not here," said Mrs. Holland plaintively.

Guin looked up from her embroidery, entirely sympathizing with her mother's feelings. "I, too, miss Percy terribly. He is gone so much with his new friends."

Colonel Caldar smiled at his niece even as he addressed his sister. "While I am here, I shall be pleased to squire you and Guin anywhere you wish. And Clara is perfectly willing to help chaperon Guin, as you know."

Mrs. Holland ignored both the colonel's reference to his wife and his quick, smiling glance in Mrs. Caldar's direction. "I do appreciate your company, Arnold. However, it is not quite the same, is it? After all, Percival is my son and an earl besides."

Colonel Caldar contemplated his sister for a long silent moment, until she asked sharply what ailed him. Colonel Caldar shook his head on a sigh. "Nothing ails me, Aurelia, except this notion you have that Percy should be tied firmly to your apron strings. He's a man grown by any standard."

"He's just a boy! He needs me to guide him and to tell him how best to go on," said Mrs. Holland, looking with surprise at the colonel.

"Leave well enough alone, Aurelia. The boy is having his first taste of liberty, and I think it is a good thing," said Colonel Caldar shortly.

"Arnold, I think perhaps it is getting rather late," interpolated Mrs. Caldar in her cool well-bred voice.

The lady's interjection might well have been left unsaid, for all the heed it was paid. Brother and sister had come to dagger point at last.

Mrs. Holland smiled sweetly, but there was the flash of steel in her brown eyes. "We must disagree on that point, Arnold. I did not scheme and pinch every penny after my husband died, only to see my sacrifice scorned!

My children shall reap the fruits of my labor, I promise you!"

"We have never seen eye-to-eye on any number of things, have we, Aurelia?" asked Colonel Caldar with a grim little smile. "It is all the result of ambition. Scandal and dishonor never signified to you when they stood in the way of your rapacious ambition."

Mrs. Holland whisked out a lacy handkerchief and dabbed at her suddenly swimming eyes. Throwing out her other hand in a dramatic gesture of appeal, she exclaimed, "Brother! How can you be so unfeeling? Love prompted me to my life's course! You know how affected I was when my dear husband died and—"

Colonel Caldar cracked a laugh. "That is a prime piece of nonsense! You never shed a tear, except to mourn the death of his possible inheritance!"

Mrs. Holland gave an outraged cry and allowed the tears to roll down her cheeks. "How utterly beastly you are!"

Instantly Guin jumped up from where she was to sit down beside her mother. Placing a slim arm around her mother's shoulders, she said reprovingly, "Uncle, you must not! You wound Mama's sensibilities."

His expression stiff, Colonel Caldar bowed. He became aware of his wife standing beside him, her hand on his sleeve. He squeezed Mrs. Caldar's fingers. "In order to spare you a painful scene, Guin, I shall not pursue some home truths as I should like! Come, Clara, let us go home to our lodgings." He walked quickly from the parlor, accompanied by his wife.

Mrs. Holland, who had wilted in a vulnerable posture against her daughter, straightened as soon as the door closed with a snap behind the Caldars. She dried her eyes matter-of-factly. "Well! Your uncle is the oddest man, Guin. Pray, have you finished with that piece? I should like my laces mended on my green gauze. You may go up and get it."

"Yes, Mama," said Guin, slowly withdrawing her supporting arm from her mother. She felt a pang at being so summarily dismissed, though perhaps not as strongly as she might once have.

As she sped upstairs to her mother's dressing room, she wondered what could possibly have sparked the conflict between her mother and her uncle.

Chapter Twenty-four

Guin knew before Mr. Lloyd touched his whip to his horses that the drive was to be no commonplace event. First had been her mother's archly worded goodbye and the coy smile that had accompanied it. Then there had been Mr. Lloyd's overly solicitous queries concerning her comfort. Generally the gentleman was so wrapped up in his scientific theories that very little else penetrated the mists of his mind.

Guin decided that Mr. Lloyd must have come to a momentous decision, one which involved herself. She hoped that she was equal to the task of speaking to her future.

She was proven right in her assumption. Mr. Lloyd, all correctness when it came to driving with his groom up behind, never paid heed to servants. He introduced the subject that Guin suspected he might with a portentious cough.

"Miss Holland, I have come to a momentous decision," he announced.

Guin nearly laughed, his opening gambit being almost word for word to how she imagined it might be. She took a moment to steady her sadly lacking self-control. She affected a cool, rather indifferent tone, much as she had heard Lady Smythe use when depressing pretensions. She had no desire to give Mr. Lloyd the least sign of encouragement. If she could spare herself and the gentleman the embarrassment of a suit, she would do it. "Indeed, sir?"

Mr. Lloyd did not consider himself to be unencouraged. "Miss Holland, for some time I have been aware that my uncle is in ill health. I—"

"Your uncle, sir? Which uncle would that be?" asked Guin swiftly.

Mr. Lloyd's mouth opened, but nothing came out of it. His face bore a disconcerted expression. There was a blankness in his eyes. "Which uncle?"

"Yes," said Guin, nodding, looking at him with a slight smile expressive of her interest.

"That would be my uncle, Lord Rockham, the Marquis of Ford," said Mr. Lloyd.

"The Marquis of Ford? Have I had the pleasure of his lordship's acquaintance? I cannot recall offhand, but I daresay I should if you jogged my memory, Mr. Lloyd," said Guin artlessly.

Mr. Lloyd's mouth opened again with nothing issuing forth. Then he shook his head. "Miss Holland, I have just told you that my uncle is in ill health. You cannot have met his lordship, for he is bedridden and is in residence on his estates."

Guin nodded, as though satisfied. "I knew that I could not have met the Marquis of Ford, and that quite explains it. Thank you, Mr. Lloyd. You have quite relieved my mind of anxiety. Have you another uncle?"

There was a snigger from the groom, who was seated up behind. Guin ignored the soft sound, and she hoped Mr. Lloyd would not be angered by his servant's break in impassivity.

However, she had reckoned without Mr. Lloyd's imperviousness. Mr. Lloyd never noticed servants unless it was a question of his own comfort. "Miss Holland, I have not got another uncle," he replied with precision. "What I wished to say to you—"

"Have you not, sir? I do truly care for my uncle, Colonel Caldar. You are acquainted with him, of course," said Guin.

"I have met Colonel Caldar on any number of occasions, yes," said Mr. Lloyd. "Miss Holland, pray allow me to lay open to you what is on my mind. It is for this purpose that I have asked you to drive out with me today and—"

With desperation Guin cast about in her mind for something else she could say to delay Mr. Lloyd's declaration. With relief, she recognized the occupants of a carriage that was coming toward them.

"Oh, there is Lady Beasely and her daughter. Pray do stop, Mr. Lloyd! Miss Beasely is such a good friend of mine," said Guin, waving to the occupants of the passing carriage.

Obediently Mr. Lloyd slowed his carriage until it had stopped abreast of the Beaselys' equipage. He endured the exchange of pleasantries between the ladies, nodding politely to Lady Beasely and Miss Beasely. However, his absolute silence was felt, and soon, too soon for Guin's taste, Lady Beasely gracefully excused herself and her daughter.

Miss Beasely, eyeing Mr. Lloyd's set countenance and having already received signals from Guin, said with a bright look, "I shall be certain to call on you, Guin, so that I can get all of the news!"

Guin grimaced ever so slightly. "Yes, pray do so, Margaret!" she retorted.

Miss Beasely laughed and waved gaily as the carriages parted.

Guin sat back with a sigh, feeling somewhat drained by all of the subterfuge that she had been forced to put to use. If she had hoped that Mr. Lloyd would be permanently put off by such evasive tactics, she swiftly learned that it was not so.

"Miss Holland, I beg of you to give me audience," said Mr. Lloyd. The expression in his eyes was grave and very direct.

Guin did not have the heart to gainsay the gentleman in the face of such dignity. She sighed. She folded her hands in her lap. "Very well, Mr. Lloyd. I shall listen to you," she said quietly.

Mr. Lloyd made a slight bow from the waist, his obeisance accompanied by the usual unmistakable creak. He did not appear discomfited by it, however, but proceeded in his ponderous fashion to lay out the advantages of his suit.

As Guin listened to him as she had promised to do, it came to her that he had given much reflection to his offer for her hand. She was a little touched, for she knew how the gentleman's scientific papers and journals absorbed him almost to the exclusion of all else.

Guin's interest began to wane, and she hid a yawn behind her glove. Indeed, she thought, it appeared that the question of his marriage to her had exercised so much of the gentleman's intellect that he was in danger of boring on forever. When Mr. Lloyd began to expound about such minuscule details as the shade and pattern of the new upholstery for the chairs in the dining room he meant to order in honor of their betrothal, Guin decided it was time to interrupt.

She threw up her hand. "Sir! Mr. Lloyd, I must insist that you stop now. I fear you are on the verge of embarrassing me by these descriptions of your largesse."

Mr. Lloyd frowned as though he found her statement unfathomable. "That was indeed not my intent, Miss Holland. My intent was to illustrate to you how happy it would make me to have you as my bride."

Guin smiled kindly at him. "I am fully aware of the honor you have bestowed upon me in making me this offer, Mr. Lloyd. But I must tell you in all sincerity that my heart is already engaged by another. I am very sorry that I must disappoint you in such a fashion."

Mr. Lloyd looked at her blankly for several moments. "Are you saying you have accepted another offer, Miss Holland? For I quite understood from Mrs. Holland and from Lord Holybrooke that my addresses would be acceptable to you."

"Indeed they are, Mr. Lloyd," said Guin warmly. "But

you see, I am quite certain that my heart lies elsewhere. And—and so I must refuse your very flattering offer. I am sorry to cause you pain, sir."

"Pain? Why, as to that, there is none since my affections are not engaged," said Mr. Lloyd matter-of-factly.

Guin gaped at him. "Really? I was quite certain that Mama said—" She abruptly abandoned what she was going to say. "Mr. Lloyd, why ever did you offer for me?"

"As I explained to you, my uncle is not expected to live much longer. As a peer, I shall be obligated to take my place in Parliament and to entertain. I shall need a wife who will act as my hostess," said Mr. Lloyd on a depressed sigh. "I shall no doubt have far less time to devote to my studies."

"Then you do not need to marry for the sake of an heir?" asked Guin, surprised.

Mr. Lloyd palpably shuddered. "I do not care for children, Miss Holland. I have a cousin who possesses a fair number of the little brutes. I do not lack for heirs, thank God."

Revelation dawned on Guin. She had just been handed the perfect instrument to forever persuade Mr. Lloyd that she was not the bride for him. "I understand you perfectly, dear sir. I am more happy than ever before that we have had this talk, Mr. Lloyd. You see, I wish to have children," she said firmly. As a rider, she added, "Quite a lot of them, actually."

"I am glad that you have been so open with me, Miss Holland," said Mr. Lloyd with some emotion in his voice. "In fact, I am overcome that your scruples will not allow you to accept the position which I offered to you. I humbly withdraw my suit."

That wasn't quite what she had said, but Guin was willing to let Mr. Lloyd put whatever concept on her refusal that he wished. "I trust that we may remain friends, Mr. Lloyd. And I hope that you will continue to call upon myself and my mother?"

"Be assured that I shall do so. Mrs. Holland will discover in me a good friend," said Mr. Lloyd, bowing and creaking.

There was silence for a few minutes, while Guin turned over in her mind what Mr. Lloyd had said and not said. Somewhat hesitantly, but with more boldness than she would ever have thought possible of herself only weeks ago, she asked, "Mr. Lloyd, I don't quite understand one thing. If you were not enamored of me, why did you decide that I would make a suitable bride for you? I have very little fortune, as I believe."

Mr. Lloyd gave her his grave smile. "Of course I did not base my decision on fortune, Miss Holland. When one has expectations such as I have, fortune means little. I hope I do not offend when I tell you that it was your face which initially attracted my notice. I thought you quite lovely."

"Oh!" Guin blushed. She looked at Mr. Lloyd in a considering way. Mr. Lloyd was perhaps twenty years older than she was; he was a dead bore when he became absorbed with his scientific theories; he wore a corset. Yet Guin thought he was a very kind gentleman to pay her such a compliment. She impulsively laid her fingers on his sleeve. "I believe that is one of the nicest things anyone has ever said to me and meant it, Mr. Lloyd."

He looked astonished, and a dull red traveled up from under his cravat into his face. "Well, ahem, you are very welcome, Miss Holland. Perhaps I should take you back to the town house now."

"Yes, I think that will be best," agreed Guin.

Apparently feeling that the subject of matrimony was closed, Mr. Lloyd began expounding upon one of the latest articles in one of the scientific journals to which he subscribed. Guin listened more closely than she would have done an hour before and even put a pertinent question to Mr. Lloyd that pleased him very much. He waxed eloquent for several minutes, and when he had driven up to the curb in front of the town house, he expressed regret that their outing had ended so quickly.

Mr. Lloyd wrapped the reins and ponderously climbed down out of the carriage to go around and give a hand to Guin. She lightly descended and accepted his escort to the front door. The porter had opened the door, but Guin paused before entering. "Will you not come in and greet my mother, Mr. Lloyd?" she asked.

"Perhaps I should not. The circumstances, you know. However, rest assured that I shall call upon you and Mrs. Holland again," he promised.

"We shall look forward to it, sir," said Guin. She was surprised that she meant it. She waved good-bye to the gentleman before going inside.

When Guin walked into the entry hall and greeted the butler, he informed her that Lord Holybrooke was awaiting her return in the library. Guin was surprised and wondered what her brother could possibly want. Without going upstairs to put off her hat or gloves, she crossed to the library door. Opening it, she said, "Percy? Did you wish to see me?"

Her brother had been standing at the mantel, staring into the fire, but at her appearance he at once strode over to her. Lord Holybrooke grasped her wrist and drew her forward. "Come in here, Guin. I have something to say to you."

"Of course, Percy. But may I not put off my hat first?" asked Guin gaily.

He gave scarcely a glance at her headgear. "I would rather you didn't."

It struck Guin that her brother was looking unusually somber. At once she entered the library and turned toward Lord Holybrooke, rather worriedly studying his abstracted expression. "Why, Percy, whatever has happened? You appear upset."

Lord Holybrooke laughed shortly. "Do I? It is all on your behalf, sister." He shut the door with a snap and looked across at her. There was a rather grim expression in his eyes, and his lips were held tight. "I have learned something from my uncle that I think you should know. Two days ago, Sir Frederick made an offer for your hand."

Guin's color fluctuated as she stared up at her brother. Her heart pounding, she said shakily, "Pray don't tease me, Percy! Has Sir Frederick really offered for me?"

"Yes, I tell you! But Mama rejected his suit." Lord Holybrooke had not meant to be so brutally frank and regretted it instantly. He stepped forward quickly to catch his sister under an elbow as she seemed about to crumple. "Guin! Are you all right?"

"Of—of course. How—how very silly of me, to be sure," said Guin faintly. She groped blindly with her hand for a convenient chair and sank down upon it. Her gaze was fixed painfully on her brother's concerned face. "Mama rejected Sir Frederick? But why, Percy? When she must know how much I care for him, why would she do such a thing?"

Lord Holybrooke took a hasty turn around the room, flinging over his shoulder, "Surely you must know why, Guin! You are aware of Mama's inordinate ambition for me—for you!"

"Yes, yes, of course I do," said Guin in a tight, shaking voice. "But I did not know—did not realize! I knew that Mama looked higher for me. Of course I did, for she told me so. And recently she has taken an unaccountable dislike to Sir Frederick, besides. But if he offered for me, that would explain it!" She threw out her hands in distress. "Oh, Percy, what am I to do?"

"I don't know! My uncle and I have both talked to Mama. She is adamant and refuses to listen to reason. She insists that you are to wed Howard Lloyd," said Lord Holybrooke in a sharp, clipped manner.

He smashed his fist down on the mantel, making his sister jump. "I have never quarreled with Mama more bitterly. She is like to ruin your life with her stratagems and lofty ambitions. Lloyd! My God, I would laugh if it were not so pathetic."

"I am not going to wed Mr. Lloyd. I turned down his most obliging offer not an hour past," said Guin mechanically.

Lord Holybrooke turned around to stare at her. "You don't say so! Lord, won't Mama be thrown into a rage when she hears! I don't envy you, Guin."

Chapter Twenty-five

Guin was scarcely aware of what her brother had said. Her head seemed to be whirling with what had been told to her, and she felt quite sick. She had wondered why she had not seen anything of Sir Frederick for the past two days, and now she knew. She swallowed past the tightness in her throat. "If—if Sir Frederick does indeed wish to wed me, I must do something. I cannot allow Mama to have her way this time, Percy. I cannot! I must tell Sir Frederick of my true feelings."

Lord Holybrooke continued to stare at her, the deep frown gathering on his face again. There was surprise in his eyes. "Why, Guin! I have never heard you talk in such a fashion before."

"Do be quiet, Percy! I must think," said Guin, pressing her fingers against her temples.

Obediently Lord Holybrooke subsided. He watched her with mingled curiosity and continued surprise for several minutes, while her mind was obviously bent upon the problem.

When Guin looked up again, there was such a look of determination in her eyes and a never-before-seen mulish set about her mouth that Lord Holybrooke was startled. "Percy. I shall need your help."

"Whatever I can do, Guin, I assure you! If you want me to speak to Mama again—"

"That won't do a bit of good. I've come to realize it," said Guin, shaking her head. "Instead, Percy, I wish you to carry a note to Sir Frederick at once. I shall pen it directly. I shall not be here when you return. I am going to Lady Smythe. She will stand my friend, I am persuaded. And I am sending a note round to our uncle. I wish him to procure a special license for me and Sir Frederick."

Lord Holybrooke's mouth dropped open. "Have you gone quite mad, Guin?"

She gave a shaky laugh. "I think I have, indeed. I am going to wed Sir Frederick out of hand, if he will have me."

"But, Guin—! You cannot have thought! You are not of age," said Lord Holybrooke, pointing out the most obvious flaw in her declared plan of action.

Guin's eyes danced as a mischievous smile hovered on her lips. "But you are head of the family, Percy! If I have *your* approval, and that of my uncle, I may scrape through without Mama's consent."

Lord Holybrooke's eyes kindled. "Yes, by Jove! I had forgotten that! I do have something to say to the point, haven't I?" He straightened his shoulders. "Very well, Guin! Pen your notes. I shall engage to carry the one to Sir Frederick and persuade him to meet you at Lady Smythe's."

Guin was already at the desk, dipping a pen into the inkwell. Hurriedly writing what she needed to, she dusted the sheet and folded it. "Yes, if you please! Now I must write to my uncle, too, and have it delivered at once by a footman. Pray pull the bell, Percy. I wish my maid sent to me."

Lord Holybrooke did as she requested, completely mystified but trusting that she knew what she was doing. He dropped a kiss on the top of her bent head. When she looked up, he put one hand on her shoulder and squeezed it slightly. "I'm off then, my dear. I hope this all goes just as you have planned."

"Yes, so do I, Percy, for I am fighting for my life," said Guin with quiet intensity.

The door opened and a footman entered, having answered the summons of the bell. Guin put the second hurriedly scrawled note into his hand, requesting also that word be sent to her maid to meet her upstairs in her bedroom. Then Guin went quickly upstairs.

When Morgan entered, she discovered her mistress pulling clothing and personal items out of drawers and from the wardrobe and throwing them onto the bed. In some astonishment the maid asked, "Why, miss, what is this?"

"I need you to pack for me, Morgan. Also for yourself. We are going back to Lady Smythe's," said Guin. She paused in her feverish activities to say, with a smile trembling on her lips, "The worm has turned, Morgan. I am leaving my mother's protection."

"Indeed, miss!" The light of approval entered the maid's eyes. "Very good, Miss Guin! I shall pack your trunks."

"No, only a portmanteau or two for now, Morgan. I shall send for the rest," said Guin quickly. "I wish to be gone before Mrs. Holland returns from her drive in the park."

"Of course, miss," said the maid, a wealth of understanding in her glance. She began expertly to fold and set apart certain garments. "How long shall we be staying with her ladyship, miss?"

"I hope not above a day or two," said Guin. Clasping and unclasping her hands in a nervous fashion, she added, "I hope to wed Sir Frederick Hawkesworth from Lady Smythe's residence, Morgan. I shall need you to go with me when I leave there."

The maid blinked, her hands faltering in their task. Then her mouth upturned in a smile. "I am sure I wish you happy, miss. And I shall be glad to serve you in any capacity you should choose."

Guin gave a laugh that sounded a little uncertain. The enormity of the course she had embarked upon was beginning to make itself felt to her. "I trust that you may, Morgan. Indeed, I hope that you may!"

Guin was beset by reservations and doubts and trepilation of mind when she and her maid set out in the carriage for Lady Smythe's town house. She had given some consideration to, and finally discarded, the idea of leaving a note for her mother. Mrs. Holland would learn later of her marriage, if it indeed took place.

All sorts of objections jostled together in Guin's mind, primary among them the fear that Sir Frederick did not really wish to marry her, that Percy would not be able to deliver her note, or that Sir Frederick would refuse to honor her plea and come to meet her at Lady Smythe's, that Colonel Caldar would not be able to get the special license in time, that the clergyman would refuse to perform the ceremony, that—

Guin sat bolt upright on the carriage seat with a dismayed cry. "Morgan! I have forgot to engage the services of a clergyman. I don't even know one! What am I to do? That is, if Sir Frederick does wish to wed me and in such a hole-in-the-wall fashion! Oh, what am I doing? I must be mad, indeed!"

"Never you fret, Miss Guin," said Morgan stoutly, ignoring most of this impassioned speech. "Her ladyship is a knowing one. She'll know what to do about the clergy."

"Yes, but what about Sir Frederick?" asked Guin, the anguished question swiftly taking possession of her mind.

The maid could not offer any advice and could only shake her head in a somewhat helpless fashion.

When Guin reached her destination, she and her maid were ushered into a small sitting room to await her ladyship's pleasure. The butler went away to apprise Lady Smythe of their arrival.

Lady Smythe had just come in from visiting with friends. She was mildly astonished to hear that Miss Holland, who appeared to be in some agitation, wished to see her. She was given considerable food for thought when the butler added, with a slight cough, that Miss Holland's maid had accompanied her and brought two portmanteaus.

"Well, send her in," said Lady Smythe, pulling off her

gloves and setting them aside on an occasional table before seating herself.

In a few short minutes, Guin was ushered into the sitting room where Lady Smythe awaited her. She looked doubtfully across at her mentor, not at all certain now that the moment had come of her reception.

Lady Smythe smiled. "Well, child? What have you done that you must bring your maid and your belongings with you?"

Her ladyship's kindness and affability were all that was needed to overset Guin's overwrought nerves. She burst into tears and ran to Lady Smythe, falling to her knees beside her ladyship's chair and burying her face in her hands.

Greatly taken aback, Lady Smythe could not at first decide what was to be done. Rather helplessly, she patted Guin's shoulder and uttered sympathetic noises while the girl wept. However, as disjointed sentences tumbled from Guin's quivering lips, containing references to Sir Frederick and a declared determination not to submit tamely to what was certain to lead to lifelong unhappiness, Lady Smythe's interest was aroused to no small degree. She begged her guest to subdue her emotional outburst and to be more coherent. "For I am unable to make head or tail of it, my dear. Here is my handkerchief. Now stop wailing and give me a round tale, if you please!"

Lady Smythe's astringency was just what was needed. Guin gave a gurgling laugh and sat up. She accepted Lady Smythe's handkerchief, mopped her eyes, and blew her nose. "I beg pardon, my lady."

"That's much better. No, no, keep it, my dear. I have any number of handkerchiefs, I am sure. Now, tell me, what has pitched you into such a lachrymose state?" demanded Lady Smythe.

"You will think me a perfect zany, ma'am," said Guin, getting up and sitting down opposite her ladyship in a well-padded chair. "I have run away from home."

"My word!" exclaimed Lady Smythe. All sorts of thoughts flitted through her mind, as well as dismay, for it seemed obvious that the girl had come to her for sanctuary, and she did not know how she could offer it when she was in no way related to her.

Unaware of Lady Smythe's dilemma, Guin was determined to make a clean breast of the shocking whole. "Moreover, I have sent word to Sir Frederick to wait on me here. I intend to wed him if he will still have me."

Lady Smythe stared. Shaking herself, as though rousing from a dreaming state, she vigorously tugged the bellpull hanging within convenient reach of her chair. "What we need is a glass of wine. Then you will tell me the whole from the beginning," she said firmly.

The wine was brought, and once Lady Smythe had fortified herself, she commanded Guin to tell her everything. Her ladyship listened closely and almost unblinkingly, the wineglass held between her fingers forgotten as the tale unfolded.

At the end of Guin's recital, Lady Smythe set her glass down with a decisive click. "You did very well to come to me, my dear. I shall certainly stand by you in this, for even though we are not blood kin, I have come to regard you in the light of a granddaughter, and I wish you to be happy."

"Oh, my lady!" exclaimed Guin, fresh tears starting to her eyes.

"You mustn't start crying again, my dear! If you do, only think how red your eyes will be when Sir Frederick arrives," said Lady Smythe hastily.

Guin gave a watery chuckle, wiping her eyes. "Quite true, my lady. I shall not cry, I promise."

"Very good," said Lady Smythe, relieved. The case was not nearly as bad as she had originally thought. Though her ladyship had shrunk from the possibility of sheltering her young protégée from the girl's rightful guardian, she had far fewer scruples regarding helping the girl to a respectable marriage. It was wonderful, indeed, that the girl had ever shown such spirit. Lady Smythe regarded Guin with some interest. "I never thought you would exhibit such courage or, indeed, act with such fortitude and forethought. Have you really sent Colonel Caldar scurrying off for a special license, child?''

Guin laughed at the tinge of amazement in Lady Smythe's voice. It had relieved some of her anxiety when Lady Smythe had accepted her story and had actually expressed willingness to help her. "Indeed I did, ma'am. But I gave no thought to a clergyman.''

"What would you know about clergymen? I daresay you are not even acquainted with one here in London. I, however, am!'' said Lady Smythe. "One of my oldest friends is a bishop. I shall invite his excellency to dine here with me, and while I am about, I shall drop a hint that his ecclesiastical services may be required. That shall pique his curiosity.''

As Lady Smythe finished speaking, the butler entered with word that Lord Holybrooke and Colonel and Mrs. Caldar had sent in their cards in hopes that her ladyship would receive them.

"My aunt!'' exclaimed Guin. "I never expected this!''

"Send them in, Porton. And let my cook know that I shall probably be entertaining these guests for dinner, as well as Bishop Turner,'' said Lady Smythe.

"Very good, my lady,'' said the butler, effacing himself.

Lord Holybrooke, followed by his uncle and Mrs. Caldar, were ushered directly in. Mrs. Caldar calmly greeted Lady Smythe and then turned to reach out both her hands to Guin, who caught them in her own. Squeezing Guin'a hands, Mrs. Caldar gave her niece an encouraging smile.

The gentlemen also proffered polite greetings, which Lady Smythe unceremoniously cut off short. She waved her hand in Guin's direction. "Well, gentlemen? What have you to say to this extraordinary business?''

"Extraordinary, indeed!'' exclaimed Colonel Caldar. "I was never more floored in my life. I still do not know what to think.''

"We agreed, did we not, that we must do just as Guin wished?'' said Mrs. Caldar quietly, standing close beside her niece.

"Did you bring the special license, then?" demanded Lady Smythe.

"Aye, reluctantly and only at my wife's and my nephew's strenuous and oft-repeated insistence, my lady," said Colonel Caldar. He turned to his niece, surveying her anxiously. "My dear, I am not quite sure you know what you are about."

"But I do, dear sir," said Guin quietly. "You made me realize how likely I would be to acquiesce to whatever match Mama proposed for me. I have learned quite a number of things over the past several weeks, including my own heart. Mama will not listen to anything I might say. But I am still determined to stick to my ground, as you would say, uncle."

"Bravo, Guin!" exclaimed Lord Holybrooke, wrapping one arm about her shoulders in a quick supportive hug.

"Indeed, I am very proud of you, my dear," said Mrs. Caldar.

The butler came in again, this time with the intelligence that Sir Frederick was asking to see her ladyship and Miss Holland.

"Ah! Now we shall see whether this little drama shall have a happy ending or not," said Lady Smythe. "Lord Holybrooke, Colonel and Mrs. Caldar, pray step upstairs to my private sitting room, where we shall comfortably await events. I must send a note round to my bishop, in any event."

"Bishop?" repeated Colonel Caldar in bewildered accents.

"All in good time, my dear," said Mrs. Caldar calmly. "I feel certain that her ladyship will explain everything to us."

"I shall indeed explain it to you, sir, but upstairs," said Lady Smythe firmly. She looked over at Guin. "My dear, I trust you are ready to meet with Sir Frederick?"

Guin clasped her hands tightly together. There was a nervous fluttering in her stomach. "I think so, my lady."

"Guin?" asked Lord Holybrooke softly, inquiry in his eyes.

Guin smiled at her brother, understanding what he had left unsaid. "I must do this on my own, Percy."

Lord Holybrooke nodded and went swiftly from the sitting room. Colonel Caldar and his wife left, as well.

"Very well! I shall have Sir Frederick sent up," said Lady Smythe. She followed Lord Holybrooke and the Caldars from the room, and quietly closed the door.

Chapter Twenty-six

So it was that when Sir Frederick entered the sitting room, thanking the butler civilly for showing him in, that he discovered only Miss Holland awaiting him.

He stopped short, then slowly came forward a few steps. He looked across at her in some puzzlement and concern. "Miss Holland? I came as soon as I had your note. I felt anxious when I read it. What is amiss? How may I be of service?"

"Sir Frederick!" Guin clasped and unclasped her hands. It was harder than she had imagined it would be to broach what burned in her heart. Again, upon seeing the kindness in his handsome face and hearing his politely worded query, the trepidation rose up inside her. Surely he could really have no overwhelming desire to wed her. He could not really love someone like her.

She started again. "Sir Frederick, I—I—" She turned away, her hands coming up to cover her burning cheeks. "Oh, how I wish I wasn't such a timorous mouse!"

She heard Sir Frederick chuckle. Then he was close behind her, and his hands dropped comfortably onto her shoulders.

"Come, Guin! We have become too good of friends to find ourselves unable to reveal our thoughts to one another," he said.

Guin took courage from the humorous quality in his voice, even though there was nothing in his words to encourage her. She turned under his hands so that she could look up into his face. In a breathless voice she asked, "Did you indeed offer for me, Freddy?"

Sir Frederick's smile was wiped from his face. He stepped back from her, his hands dropping to his sides. "I thought you would have been told."

Guin nodded. "I was, but not by my mother. It was Percy who told me. He quarreled bitterly with Mama over it, for he knew what would be my feelings when I learned of it."

Sir Frederick grasped the salient point. "Your feelings?" His closed expression became suddenly intent. "What do you mean, Miss Holland? You are going to wed Mr. Lloyd."

"That is Mama's notion of a good match, but it is not mine. I have refused Mr. Lloyd's offer," said Guin baldly.

Her breath felt suddenly constricted in her throat as she saw a strange light kindling in his brown eyes. She hurried to finish all that she wanted to say. "Sir Frederick, I am not a great beauty or terribly sophisticated or even a well-trained hostess, such as you must require in a suitable wife, but—oh, Freddy! I do most sincerely love you, and if you will still have me—"

"Have you? My dearest darling!" Sir Frederick gathered her swiftly into his arms, smothering her with hard kisses, nearly crushing her with his impassioned embrace.

Guin made an inarticulate protest, and instantly he loosened his hold, though he kept his arms close about her.

Sir Frederick looked down into her face, his blazing gaze devouring her.

Guin blushed rosily under the warmth of his scrutiny. "Oh! You mustn't look at me just so. It—it makes my heart pound."

"I am glad," said Sir Frederick simply. He kissed her again, then regretfully set her a little away from him. "I love you profoundly, Guin. But we cannot be wed. We have not your mother's consent, and you are underage."

"But Percy, who is head of the family, gives his approval, and my uncle has brought a special license, and

Lady Smythe is sending for a bishop," said Guin with triumph. She laughed breathlessly at the bewilderment crossing his face.

Sir Frederick threw up his hand, shaking his head. "A moment! You go too fast for me, Guin. What is all of this?"

Guin moved apart to pull on the bell rope. She looked at him, her eyes gleaming with laughter. "I see that I must have Lady Smythe and the others help me to explain it to you. I think it only fair to warn you that I have every intention of wedding you out of hand, sir!"

When Lady Smythe and her guests came into the sitting room, it was to be greeted with the sight of Guin sitting quite close beside Sir Frederick on the sofa, her head on his shoulder and her hand clasped in his.

Lord Holybrooke whooped and stepped forward. As Sir Frederick rose, he enthusiastically grasped his hand and shook it. "Sir Frederick, I wish you and my sister very happy."

"Thank you, but—" began Sir Frederick.

"Well, my dears, it turns out very well indeed," said Lady Smythe approvingly, stooping to kiss a laughing Guin on one blushing cheek.

"As to that—" said Sir Frederick.

"I've got the special license right here," said Colonel Caldar, patting his pocket. At his shoulder, Mrs. Caldar nodded and smiled.

"But, sir, I cannot wed your niece out of hand," said Sir Frederick, finally able to get out a full sentence.

"Pooh! Nonsense!" said Colonel Caldar. "No such thing. Nothing more respectable than having myself and my wife and her brother in attendance."

"I am head of the family, and besides, I will talk my mother round to accepting it afterward," said Lord Holybrooke breezily.

"Nothing could be more respectable than a private ceremony, performed by a bishop of the church, with family and friends in attendance. Lord Holybrooke shall send a notice to that effect to the *Gazette*," said Lady

Smythe. "It is already widely known you have accepted a post in Paris, Sir Frederick. If you and your bride choose to honeymoon in the French capital, I am certain none shall wonder at it."

Sir Frederick burst out laughing. He drew Guin up to stand beside him. With his charming smile, he said, "It appears that we are to be wed willy-nilly, my dear. Shall you dislike it?"

"Oh, no! I am quite, quite ready," said Guin with a blazing smile. "But I must tell you that I do not wish Mama to reside with us once we are returned to England. I do not think that would be at all comfortable."

"No, by God!" exclaimed Sir Frederick, struck forcibly.

"I shall take care of Mama," said Lord Holybrooke, squaring his shoulders manfully.

"Thank you, Percy," said Guin, bestowing a luminous smile on her twin. "I knew that I could count on you."

The butler entered for the last time, to convey a whispered intelligence to Lady Smythe. Her ladyship turned once more to the assembled company. "The bishop has arrived!"

With great presence of mind, Lord Holybrooke plucked a bouquet of roses and baby's breath out of a vase and handed them to his sister. Colonel Caldar straightened his coat and took his wife's hand. Lady Smythe ushered in the bishop.

Sir Frederick clasped his bride's hands, and together they faced the future.

A month later, in Paris, Guin received a letter from her brother. As she perused it, a smile on her face, her eyes widened in astonishment. She looked up, seeking her husband's face across the breakfast table. "Freddy! You will never guess! Mama is to be married!"

Sir Frederick paused in buttering his toast. He looked his interest. "Indeed? Who is the unfor—I mean *fortunate* fellow?"

Guin started laughing, tears actually starting to her eyes. Through her mirth, she exclaimed, "Why, none other than Mr. Howard Lloyd! Freddy, Mama will one day be a marchioness!"

"Will she, by Jove! And she will have any number of residences of her own, I expect! I always liked that fellow Lloyd!" exclaimed Sir Frederick.

Signet Regency Romances from Allison Lane

"A FORMIDABLE TALENT... MS. LANE NEVER FAILS TO DELIVER THE GOODS." —*ROMANTIC TIMES*

THE NOTORIOUS WIDOW
0-451-20166-3

When a scoundrel tries to tarnish a young widow's reputation, a valiant Earl tries to repair the damage—and mend her broken heart as well...

BIRDS OF A FEATHER
0-451-19825-5

When a plain, bespectacled young woman keeps meeting the handsome Lord Wylie, she feels she is not up to his caliber. A great arbiter of fashion for London society, Lord Wylie was reputed to be more interseted in the cut of his clothes than the feelings of others, as the young woman bore witness to. Degraded by him in public, she could nevertheless forget his dashing demeanor. It will take a public scandal, and a private passion, to bring them together...

To order call: 1-800-788-6262